A CURSE
FOR
TRUE
LOVE

Also by Stephanie Garber

Once Upon a Broken Heart
The Ballad of Never After

Caraval
Legendary
Finale

A CURSE FOR TRUE LOVE

STEPHANIE GARBER

HODDER &
STOUGHTON

First published in Great Britain in 2023 by Hodder & Stoughton
An Hachette UK company

4

Copyright © Stephanie Garber 2023

The right of Stephanie Garber to be identified as the Author of the Work has been asserted by her in accordance with the Copyright, Designs and Patents Act 1988.

Map illustration by Virginia Allyn

A CIP catalogue record for this title is available from the British Library

Hardback ISBN 978 1 529 39928 8
Trade Paperback ISBN 978 1 529 39929 5
ebook ISBN 978 1 529 39930 1

Printed and bound in Great Britain by Clays Ltd, Elcograf S.p.A.

Hodder & Stoughton policy is to use papers that are natural, renewable and recyclable products and made from wood grown in sustainable forests. The logging and manufacturing processes are expected to conform to the environmental regulations of the country of origin.

Hodder & Stoughton Ltd
Carmelite House
50 Victoria Embankment
London EC4Y 0DZ

www.hodder.co.uk

*For anyone
who's ever hoped
for a second chance*

Tree of
Souls

Cursed Forest

The Hunt

Wolf Hall

Merrywood Forest

The Phoenix Tree

in the Magical North

PART IV

*Happily
Ever After*

Evangeline

Evangeline Fox always believed she'd find herself inside of a fairytale one day. As a young girl, whenever a new shipment of curiosities would come into her father's shop, Evangeline would immediately rush to the crates. She would examine each item inside and ask herself, *Could this be it? Could this be the object that would thrust her into a fantasy?*

Once there had been an enormous crate with only a doorknob inside. The knob was an exquisite jeweled green and sparkled in the light like magic. Evangeline was convinced that if she attached it to the right door, it would open up to another world and her fairytale would begin.

The doorknob, sadly, never opened up to anything out of

the ordinary. But Evangeline never gave up hope that someday she'd find herself *elsewhere*.

Hoping and imagining and believing in magic had always been like breathing to Evangeline. And yet it was suddenly very difficult to breathe as she finally found herself *elsewhere*, wrapped in the arms of a handsome young man who said he was her husband.

Husband. The word made her head spin. *How? How? How?* She was too overwhelmed to ask more than that one word. In fact, she couldn't even manage to speak it aloud.

If she wasn't being held, Evangeline might have crumpled back onto the floor. It was too much to take in and too much to lose all at once.

One of the last things she remembered was sitting with her father as he died at home. But even that memory was ragged around the edges. As if his death were part of a faded portrait, only it wasn't just faded—pieces of it had also been ruthlessly ripped away. She couldn't clearly remember the months before her father's death or anything that had happened afterward. She didn't even recall how he'd caught the fever that had killed him.

All she knew was that, like her mother, her father was gone—and he had been for some time.

"I know this must be frightening. I imagine you feel alone, but you're not, Evangeline." The stranger who'd said he was her husband held her tighter.

He was tall, the sort of tall that made Evangeline feel small as he held her close enough for her to feel that he was shaking, too. She didn't imagine he was as terrified as she was, but clearly he didn't feel as confident as he looked. "You have me—and there is nothing I wouldn't do for you."

"But I don't remember you," she said. She was a little reluctant to pull away. But it was all so overwhelming. *He* was overwhelming.

A deep line formed between the stranger's brows as she pulled back. But he replied patiently, his voice low and soothing as he said, "My name is Apollo Acadian."

Evangeline waited again for a flare of recognition, or even just a tiny spark. She needed something familiar, something to hold on to that would keep her from collapsing back onto the ground, and Apollo looked at her as if he wanted to be that. No one had ever looked at her with so much intensity.

He made her think of a hero from a fairytale. Broad shouldered with a strong jaw, dark smoldering eyes, and clothing that spoke of the sort of wealth that conjured images of treasure chests and castles. He wore a high-collared dark red coat with rich gold embroidery covering the cuffs and the shoulders. Beneath it was some sort of doublet—at least she thought that was what it was called. The men at home in Valenda dressed quite differently.

But clearly, she wasn't there anymore. The thought brought a new wave of panic that made her words come out in a rush.

"How did I come to be here? How did we meet? Why don't I remember you?" she asked.

"Your memories were stolen by someone who's been trying

to tear us apart." Something flickered in Apollo's brown eyes, although if it was anger or pain, she couldn't tell.

Evangeline wished she could remember him. But the harder she tried, the worse she felt. Her head hurt and her chest felt hollowed out, as if she'd lost more than just her memories. For a second the agony was so deep and so brutal, she clutched her heart, half expecting to find a jagged hole. But there was no wound. Her heart was still there; she could feel it beating. Yet for a devastating moment, Evangeline imagined that it shouldn't have been, that her heart was supposed to be as broken as she felt.

Then it hit her, not a feeling but a thought—a sharp, fragmented one.

She had something important to tell someone.

Evangeline couldn't remember what it was, but she felt as if her entire world depended on this one thing she needed to share. Just thinking about it made her blood rush. She tried to remember what this *something* was that she needed to say and who it was she needed to tell—could it be this Apollo person?

Could this be why her memories had been stolen?

"Why is someone trying to tear us apart?" Evangeline asked.

She might have thrown out even more questions. She might have asked once more how they'd met and how long they'd been married, but Apollo suddenly looked nervous.

He shot a furtive glance over Evangeline's shoulder before quietly saying, "It's complicated."

She followed his gaze to the strange wooden door she'd been

curled up against. On either side of the door were two warrior angels made of stone, although they looked more lifelike than stone carvings were supposed to. Their wings were outstretched and spattered in dried blood. The sight of it brought another pang in her chest, as if her body still remembered even though her mind had forgotten.

"Do you know what happened here?" she asked.

For a split second something crossed Apollo's face that almost looked like guilt, but it might have just been sadness. "I promise, I'll answer every question you have. But now we need to get out of here. We need to leave before he comes back."

"Who is *he*?"

"The villain who erased all of your memories." Apollo took Evangeline's hand, holding her firmly as he quickly led her from the room with the door and the warrior angels.

Grainy late-morning light lit shelves of manuscripts tied up with ribbons and tassels. It appeared they were in an ancient library, although the books looked newer the farther they ventured.

Floors changed from dusty stone to gleaming marble, ceilings grew taller, the light became sharper, manuscripts turned into leather-bound volumes. Evangeline once again tried to search for something familiar in the late-morning glow. Something that might make her remember. Her head was clearer now, but nothing was familiar.

She was truly elsewhere, and it seemed she had been for long enough to meet heroes and villains, and to find herself in a battle between them.

"Who was he?" she pressed. "The one who stole my memories?"

Apollo's steps faltered. Then they picked up faster than be-fore. "I promise I will tell you everything, but we should get out of here—"

"Oh my!" someone exclaimed.

Evangeline turned to see a woman in white robes standing between the shelves of books. The woman—some kind of a librarian, Evangeline supposed—brought a hand to her mouth as she stared. Her expression was one of awe, eyes wide and unwavering as they latched on to Apollo.

Another librarian strode into the hall. This one gasped, then promptly fainted, dropping a stack of books as the first librarian yelled, "It's a miracle!"

More librarians and scholars came forward, all crying out similar exclamations.

Evangeline curled toward Apollo as they were quickly sur-rounded. First by the librarians, then by servants and courtiers. Finally, by wide-chested guards in shining armor who rushed in, no doubt drawn by all of the clamor.

The room they were in was at least four stories tall, but sud-denly it felt small and suffocating as more and more unfamiliar people closed in on them.

"He's back . . ."

"He's alive . . ."

"It's a miracle!" they all repeated, voices turning reverent as tears began to glisten down cheeks.

Evangeline didn't know what was happening. She felt as if

she were witnessing the sort of thing that usually took place in a church. Was it possible she had married a saint?

Looking up at Apollo, she tried to remember his surname. *Acadian,* that was what he'd told her. She couldn't recall a single story about an Apollo Acadian, but clearly there were stories. Upon meeting him, she'd imagined he was some kind of hero, but the crowd looked at him as if he was even more.

"Who are you?" Evangeline whispered.

Apollo brought her hand to his lips and pressed a kiss to her knuckles that made her shiver. "I am the one who will never let anyone harm you again."

A few nearby people sighed as they overheard the words.

Then Apollo raised his free hand toward the rumbling crowd in a gesture that universally meant *quiet.*

Those gathered immediately fell into a hush. Some even dropped to their knees.

It was uncanny to see so many people fall quiet so quickly— they didn't even seem to breathe as Apollo's voice rang out over their heads.

"I can see that some of you are having a difficult time believing your eyes. But what you're seeing is real. I'm alive. When you leave this room, tell everyone you see that Prince Apollo died and then went through hell to get back here."

Prince. Evangeline barely had time to process the word and everything that came with it—for almost as soon as Apollo spoke, he released Evangeline's hand and swiftly took off his velvet doublet, followed by his linen shirt.

Several of those gathered gasped, including Evangeline.

Apollo's chest was flawless, smooth and carved in muscles, and over his heart was a vibrant tattoo of two swords in the shape of a heart with a name in the center: *Evangeline.*

Until that moment, everything had felt a bit like a fever dream she might have woken up from. But her name on his chest felt permanent in a way that Apollo's words had not. He wasn't a stranger. He knew her intimately enough to mark her name across his heart.

He turned around then, showing off another sight that stunned not only her, but the entire crowd. Apollo's beautiful, proud, straight back was covered in a web of violent scars.

"These marks are the price I paid to return!" he cried. "When I say I went through hell, I mean it. But I had to come back. I had to right the wrongs done in my absence. I know many believe that it was my brother, Tiberius, who killed me, but it was not."

Shocked whispers moved through the crowd.

"I was poisoned by a man I thought to be a friend," Apollo roared. "Lord Jacks is the man who killed me. Then he stole the memories of my bride, Evangeline. I will not rest until Jacks is found and he pays for his crimes with his life!"

2

Evangeline

Voices echoed against the walls of stretching book-shelves as the library erupted with noise. Guards in armor vowed to find the criminal Lord Jacks, while polished courtiers and robed scholars shot out questions like showers of arrows.

"How long have you been alive, Your Highness?"

"How did you return from hell, Lord Prince?"

"Why did Lord Jacks steal your memories?" This inquiry, from an older courtier, was directed at Evangeline and punctuated by a narrow-eyed glare.

"Enough," Apollo cut in. "I did not tell you about the horror my wife has gone through so that she could be attacked with questions she has no idea how to answer. I shared this information because I want Lord Jacks found, dead or alive. Although right now, I would prefer him dead."

"We won't fail you!" shouted the guards.

More declarations involving justice and Jacks rattled the ancient library shelves and pounded against Evangeline's head, and suddenly it was all too much. The noise, the questions, the flood of unfamiliar faces, Apollo's tale of going through hell.

More was said, but the words turned to ringing in her ears.

Evangeline wanted to cling to Apollo—he was all she had in this new reality. But he was also a powerful prince, which made him feel less like hers and more like everyone else's. She was afraid to bother him with more questions, though she had so many. She still didn't even know where she *was*.

From where she stood, Evangeline could see an oval window seat tucked under an arch of bookshelves. The window was a soft pale blue glass, and outside were full green needle trees as tall as towers covered in a picturesque layer of snow. It rarely snowed in Valenda, and never as thick as this, as if the world were a cake and the snow was dollops of thick white frosting.

As she had noticed before, the fashion here was different as well. The guards looked like knights from old tales, and the courtiers wore formal clothing similar to Apollo's. Men were dressed in doublets, while women wore elaborate velvet gowns with off-the-shoulder necklines and dropped waists decorated with brocade belts or strings of pearls.

Evangeline had never seen people dressed like this. But she'd heard stories.

Her mother had been born in the Magnificent North, and she'd told Evangeline countless tales about this land, fairytales that made it sound as if it were the most enchanted place in all the world.

Unfortunately, Evangeline felt far from enchanted at this moment.

Apollo met her gaze then and turned away from the shrinking crowd surrounding them. It seemed people had already left to spread word that Prince Apollo was back from the dead. And why wouldn't they? Evangeline never heard of someone coming back from the dead. A thought that made her feel quite small as she stood next to him.

Only a few people remained, but Apollo ignored them all as he gazed into Evangeline's eyes. "There's nothing for you to be afraid of."

"I'm not afraid," she lied.

"You're looking at me differently." He smiled at her then, a smile so charming she wondered how she hadn't immediately known what he was.

"You're a prince," she squeaked.

Apollo grinned wider. "Is that a problem?"

"No, I . . . just—" Evangeline almost said she'd never imagined herself married to a prince.

But of course she had. Only her imaginings weren't as elaborate as this. This was beyond every pastel dream she had ever had of royalty and castles and faraway places. But she would have traded it all to remember just how she'd gotten here, how she'd fallen in love and married this man and lost what felt like part of her heart.

It hit her then. In fairytales, there was always a price for magic. Nothing came without a cost; peasants who turned into princesses always had to pay. And suddenly Evangeline wondered if her lost memories were the price she had paid for all of this.

Had she traded her memories, along with part of her heart, to be with Apollo? Could she have been that foolish?

Apollo's smile softened, turning from teasing to reassuring. When he spoke, his words were gentler as well, as if he sensed part of what she was feeling. Or maybe it was just that he knew her well, even though she did not know him. He did have her name tattooed over his heart.

"It will all be all right," he said quietly, firmly. "I know it's a lot to take in. I hate to leave you, but there are a few things I need to take care of and, while I do that, my guards are ready to escort you to your suite. But I'll try not to leave you alone for long. I promise, there is nothing more important to me than you."

Apollo pressed another kiss to her hand and gave her one last look before he marched off, followed by his personal guards.

Evangeline stood there feeling suddenly alone and bursting with more questions than she had answers for. If Apollo had just come back from the dead, how did he already know what had happened to her? Maybe he was wrong about this Lord Jacks stealing her memories, and Evangeline was right about having foolishly traded them—which left her wondering if she could trade them back.

This question haunted her as she followed the guards that Apollo had assigned her through the castle. They didn't say much, but they did tell Evangeline that Apollo's castle was called Wolf Hall. It had been built by the first king of the Magnificent North, the famed Wolfric Valor, making her think of all her mother's Northern stories.

Compared to where Evangeline had grown up, the North felt incredibly old, as if every stone beneath her feet held a secret of a bygone era.

One hallway was lined with doors that all had the most elaborate handles. One was shaped like a little dragon, another looked like fairy wings, and then there was a wolf's head wearing a pretty flower crown. These were the types of handles that tempted her to pull them and made her suspect they might be a little alive, like the bell that had hung outside the door to her father's curiosity shop.

Evangeline felt an arrow of grief at the thought of it—not just the bell, but the shop and her parents and everything that she had lost. It was a dizzying torrent that hit her so suddenly she wasn't aware she'd stopped moving until a guard with a thick red mustache leaned close and said, "Are you all right, Your Highness? Do you need one of us to carry you?"

"Oh no," Evangeline said, instantly mortified. "My feet work just fine. It's just so much to take in. What is this hall?"

"This is the Valors' wing. Most people think these were the

rooms of the Valor children, although no one knows for sure. These doors have stayed locked ever since they died."

But you could open us.

The strange voice sounded as if it came from one of the doors. Evangeline looked at each of her guards, but none of them appeared to have heard it. So she pretended she hadn't heard it, either. Evangeline was in a difficult situation as it was. She didn't need to make things worse for herself by saying she heard voices coming from inanimate objects.

Thankfully it didn't happen again. When the guards finally stopped in front of a pair of ornate double doors, the jeweled doorknobs sparkled but didn't say a word. There was only a gentle whoosh as they opened up to the most opulent suite of rooms that Evangeline had ever seen.

It was all so lovely that she felt as if harps should be playing and birds should be singing. Everything was glittering and golden and covered in flowers. There were boughs of harlequin lilies framing the two-story fireplace and vines of white starmires curling around the bedposts. Even the great copper tub Evangeline spied in the bathing room beyond was full of flowers—the steaming water inside was violet and covered in soft white and pink petals.

Evangeline walked to the bath and dipped her fingers in the water. Everything was *perfect.*

Even the maids who entered to help her bathe and dress were all perfectly lovely. There were also a surprising number of them, nearly a dozen. They had sweet voices and gentle hands that helped her into a gown as delicate as a whisper.

The dress was an off-the-shoulder confection of blush tulle with sheer sleeves adorned with dark pink ribbons. The same ribbons lined the low neckline of the gown before twirling into little rosebuds that covered the bust of the fitted bodice. The skirt flowed and fluttered down to Evangeline's toes. A maid completed the look by braiding Evangeline's rose-gold hair into a crown and then decorating it with a circlet of gilded flowers.

"If I do say so myself, you look lovely, Your Highness."

"Thank you—"

"Martine," the maid supplied before Evangeline had to fumble around to try to find the name. "I'm also from the Meridian Empire originally. His Highness the prince thought having me here might help you adjust a bit more."

"It sounds as if the prince is very thoughtful."

"I think, when it comes to you . . . he tries to think of everything."

Martine smiled, but the bit of hesitation in her words gave Evangeline a second of pause, a flutter of a feeling that said Apollo was too good to be true. That all of this was.

When Evangeline was alone and looked in the mirror, she saw the reflection of a princess. This was everything she could have wanted.

Yet she didn't feel like a princess.

She felt like the idea of a princess, with the dress and the prince and the castle, and yet she also felt *without*. She felt as if she were simply wearing a costume, that she'd stepped into a role that she could simply step out of, only there wasn't anywhere else to step to. Because she also didn't feel like the girl she'd been before, the eternally hopeful girl who believed in fairytales, love at first sight, and happily ever afters.

If she had been that girl, it might have been easier to accept all of this, to not want to ask so many questions.

But something had happened to that girl—to *her*. And Evangeline couldn't help but think it went beyond her missing memories.

Her heart still hurt, as if it had been broken and only jagged bits remained. She put a hand on it, as if to keep more pieces from breaking off. And once again, she was struck with the inescapable feeling that among everything she'd forgotten was one thing more important than all the rest, more important than anything.

There was something absolutely vital she needed to tell someone. But no matter how hard she tried, she could not remember what it was or who it was she needed to tell.

3

Evangeline

Evangeline was only vaguely aware of the setting sun and the slow darkening of her rooms as she paced across the carpets, fighting desperately to remember anything at all. She hoped that when Apollo returned, he'd be able to give her more answers. But when the door to her rooms finally opened, instead of the prince, she was greeted by an aged physician and a couple of his younger apprentices.

"My name is Dr. Irvis Stillgrass," said the senior physician, a bearded man with spectacles perched on the tip of his pointed nose. "Telma and Yrell are my apprentices." He motioned to the others. "His Highness wanted us to ask you a few questions to see just how many of your memories were taken."

"Do you have any way to bring them back?" Evangeline asked.

Dr. Stillgrass, Telma, and Yrell all pursed their lips at once. A response that Evangeline took to mean *no*. She wasn't surprised, which was almost as disturbing. Evangeline almost always felt hopeful, yet she couldn't summon that hope today. Again, she wondered what had happened to her.

"Why don't you take a seat, Princess." Dr. Stillgrass motioned toward a tufted chair near the fire, which Evangeline dutifully took.

The physicians remained standing, towering over her as Dr. Stillgrass asked his questions.

"How old are you?"

"I'm ..." Evangeline had to pause to think about it. One of her last clear memories was from when she was sixteen. Her father was still alive, and she could faintly remember him smiling as he opened up a new crate of curiosities. But that was all she could recall.

The rest of the memory was blurry around the edges, like a dirty pane of glass that gave the impression of an image without actually showing what it was. Evangeline was sure her father had died some months after this weak memory, but she couldn't recall any of the particulars. She just knew in her heart that he was gone and more time had passed since then. "I believe I'm seventeen."

Telma and Yrell appeared to jot down notes about her answer, while Dr. Stillgrass asked another question. "When is your first memory of meeting Prince Apollo?"

"Today." Evangeline paused. "Do you know when we actually met?"

"I am here to ask, not to answer," Dr. Stillgrass said briskly before continuing with his questions: Did she recall her engagement to Apollo, her wedding, the night he died?

"No."

"No."

"No."

It was the only answer Evangeline had, and whenever she tried to turn the questions around, Dr. Stillgrass refused to answer.

At some point during the interview, a new gentleman entered the room. Evangeline hadn't even seen him slip inside, but suddenly he was there, standing just behind Telma and Yrell. He was dressed much like them, in a long brown leather tunic worn atop fitted black pants and belted with two straps of leather that secured a series of knives and vials to one hip and a harness for a book to the other. The book appeared to be in his hands now, but something about the way he jotted things down in his notebook was different from the other apprentices.

This young man wrote with a flourish, swishing his feathered pen in a way that kept drawing Evangeline's eyes. When he caught her staring, he winked and brought a finger to his lips, gesturing for her not to tell.

And for some reason, she didn't.

Evangeline had a feeling this man wasn't supposed to be here, despite his similar manner of dress. But he was the only one of this group who seemed to feel anything for her as she struggled for answers. He nodded encouragingly, smiled at her sympathetically, and whenever Dr. Stillgrass said something particularly unkind, he rolled his eyes.

"I can confirm that your memories of the last year are entirely gone," Dr. Stillgrass said self-importantly and quite callously. "We'll report this to His Highness, and one of us will return each day to see if any memories come back."

The trio of physicians turned to leave. Dr. Stillgrass swept past the young man without a glance, but Yrell and Telma finally noticed him then.

"Doctor—" Telma started.

But Yrell, who looked slightly dazzled by the interloper, yanked the sleeve of her robe, stopping her from saying more as the trio exited.

Only the nameless young man lingered.

He sauntered toward Evangeline and pulled a rectangular red card from his pocket.

"I would not have believed it if I had not seen it with my own eyes," he said softly. "I am sorry for the loss of your memories. If you'd ever like to talk and perhaps answer some questions, I might be able to fill in a few blanks for you."

He handed her the card.

Kristof Knightlinger
Southern Morningwatch Tower
The Spires

"What kind of questions . . . ?" Evangeline started to ask as she finished reading the curious card.

But the gentleman was already gone.

The fire crackled.

Evangeline felt herself startle awake, although she hadn't meant to fall asleep. She was curled up in the fireside chair where she'd puzzled over the little red card from Kristof Knightlinger. She could still feel it in her hand.

She could also feel something else. A man's arms sliding under her, carefully picking her up and holding her close to a chest that smelled of balsam and something woodsy.

Apollo.

Her stomach dipped.

She couldn't be entirely sure it was Apollo picking her up. Her eyes were still closed and she was tempted to keep it that way. She didn't know why she had this urge to pretend or why her heart beat faster as he carried her. Apollo had to have answers to at least some of her questions. Yet she felt unexpectedly afraid to ask them.

She wasn't sure if it was because he was a prince or because he was still a stranger.

His arms tightened around her. Evangeline tensed. But then suddenly she felt as if she was starting to remember something. There wasn't much there, just a vague recollection of being held and carried, followed by a thought.

He would carry her through more than just freezing waters. He would pull her through fire if he had to, haul her from the clutches of war, from falling cities and breaking worlds . . .

The thought made something unclench inside her and, for a second, Evangeline felt safe. More than safe, actually. But she didn't quite have words for the exact feeling. She only knew it wasn't something she'd experienced before—this deep level of protectiveness.

Slowly, she cracked open her eyes. Outside it was now full night, and inside there was only firelight, leaving most of the room cloaked in shadows, save for the prince who held her. The light clung to him, gilding the edges of his dark hair and his strong jaw as he carried her toward the bed.

"I'm sorry," Apollo murmured. "I didn't want to wake you, but you looked uncomfortable on the chair."

Gently he laid Evangeline on a downy quilt. Then he brushed a quick kiss to her cheek. It was so soft she might not have felt it if she weren't so acutely aware of his every move, of the slow slide of his warm hands releasing her body. "Sweet dreams, Evangeline."

"Wait." She grabbed his hand.

Surprise briefly colored his features. "Did you want me to stay?"

Yes probably should have been her answer.

They were married.

He was a prince.

A commanding prince.

A very attractive prince.

A prince she might have sacrificed quite a lot to be with.

He stroked her hand with this thumb, waiting patiently for her reply.

"I'm sorry that I don't remember you—I'm trying," she whispered.

"Evangeline." Apollo lightly squeezed her hand. "The last thing I want is for you to be in pain, and I can see how much it hurts you to have forgotten so much. But if you never remember, it will be all right. We'll make new memories together."

"But I want to remember." And more than that, she felt as if she *needed* to remember. She could still feel the pressing need to tell someone something critically important, but she couldn't remember what this crucial something was or who she needed to tell it to. "What if there's a way to get my memories back?" she asked. "Maybe we can make some sort of bargain with the man who took them."

"*No.*" Apollo shook his head vehemently. "Even if that were possible, it wouldn't be worth the risk. Lord Jacks is a *monster,*" he added roughly. "He poisoned me on our wedding night and framed you for the murder. While I was dead, you were almost executed. Jacks has no conscience, no remorse. If I thought for a second that he could help you, I'd do whatever necessary to bring him to you. But if he ever finds you, I fear I'll never see you again—"

Apollo took a deep breath, and when he spoke once more, his voice was softer. "I can only imagine how hard it is to let this go, but it really might be for the best, Evangeline. Jacks has done atrocious, unforgivable things to you, and I truly believe you might be happier if those things stay forgotten."

4

Apollo

The late King Roland Titus Acadian had always disdained the word *nice*. Nice was for servants, peasants, and other people who lacked personality. A prince should be clever, formidable, wise, shrewd, even cruel if he had to be—but never nice.

King Roland often told his son Apollo, "If you are nice, it means you are not enough of anything else. People are nice because they must be, but as a prince you must be *more*."

As a boy, Apollo had taken this advice as a license to be careless with life and with others. He was not cruel, but neither did he embody any of the other virtues his father extolled. Apollo had always imagined he had time to become clever, formidable, wise, or shrewd. It never occurred to him that, in the meantime, he was becoming something else.

Apollo realized this alarming truth upon first waking up from the suspended state of sleep that his former friend, Lord Jacks, had placed him in. Upon discovering that the entire Magnificent North believed him to be dead, Apollo had expected to find monuments of flowers and bastions of stubborn mourners who continued to weep for him, even though the official period of grieving had ended.

Instead, he'd found the kingdom had already moved on. Within the span of a fortnight, he'd become a footnote, remembered as a single unremarkable word in a scandal sheet.

While he'd been under the Archer's curse, he'd come across this particular scandal sheet from the day after he'd been supposedly killed. The paper had mentioned only that he'd died. Just one word, *beloved,* had been used to describe him, but that was it. The paper had said nothing of his great deeds or his acts of bravery. And how could it have, when the bulk of what he'd done was sit for portraits?

Apollo could barely stand the sight of the pictures now, as he strode through Wolf Hall on his way to meet with Mr. Kristof Knightlinger of *The Daily Rumor.*

This was his second chance to finally make himself *more,* as his father had urged. After his shocking return from the dead yesterday, Apollo noticed the different way people regarded him. Voices were more hushed, heads were quicker to bow, and eyes were full of wonder, as if he were more than a mere mortal.

And yet he'd never felt more human, more vulnerable, or more miserable.

It was all a lie. He'd never returned from the dead. He'd merely been cursed, and cursed, and cursed again. Now, for the first time in nearly three months, he was no longer under any spell, and yet he felt cursed by what he had done to Evangeline.

Apollo had thought that once he was free of the Archer's curse, he'd think about her less. The curse had forced him to hunt her. Under its influence, he'd thought about her every second. At every moment, he'd wondered where she was and what she was doing. There'd been a constant picture of her angelic face in his mind. All he'd wanted was *her*—and when he'd found her, all he'd wanted was to eviscerate her.

Now he still wanted her, but in a different way. When he saw her, he didn't want to kill her. He wanted to protect her. To keep her safe.

This was why he'd erased her memories.

He knew it was for the best. Jacks had tricked her, just as he'd fooled Apollo into being his friend. If Evangeline fell under Jacks's thrall again, he would only destroy her. But Apollo would make her happy. He would make her a queen who would be loved and adored. He would more than make up for what he'd done to her in the past, as long as she never found out.

If she ever found out he'd taken her memories, it would all come crumbling down.

Only one other person knew that Apollo had taken her memories. After today, if all went well, he wouldn't have to worry about that person. And as far as finding Jacks, Apollo hoped this morning's interview would assist with that.

Finally he reached the small tower room where he'd arranged for this meeting to take place. Normally he preferred grander settings: large rooms with lots of light and windows and ornamentation that made it impossible to forget that Apollo was royalty. But today he had chosen an unadorned tower room to make sure no one overheard the conversation that he would be having.

Kristof Knightlinger stood and bowed as soon as the prince stepped into the room. "It's good to see you alive and looking so excellent, Your Highness."

"I'm sure my return is also quite helpful for the sale of papers," replied the prince. He might have still been somewhat bitter over the small amount of fanfare that he'd been given after his death.

Of course the journalist didn't appear to notice.

Kristof smiled enthusiastically. He always seemed to be in good humor. His teeth were as white as the lacy jabot at his throat. "This interview will help as well. Thank you for taking the time to meet with me this morning. I know my readers have so many questions about how you returned from the dead, what it was like to be dead, if you were able to watch any of us who were still alive."

"I won't be answering any of those questions today," Apollo said brusquely.

The journalist's smile faded.

"I would like your article to focus on the dishonorable deeds of Lord Jacks and how important it is that he be captured immediately."

"Your Highness, I'm not sure if you're aware, but I already mentioned his misdeeds in this morning's paper."

"Then mention them again and make them uglier this time. Until this criminal is apprehended, I want his crimes printed every day. I want his name to become synonymous with vile. This isn't just for me, this is for Princess Evangeline and all of the Magnificent North. Once he's caught, you can have your interview and I'll answer whatever questions you want. But until then, I'm going to ask that you print what I need you to say."

"Of course, Your Highness," Kristof said with a pleasant smile.

But it wasn't the same smile as before. This wasn't his natural good humor. This was a *nice* smile that was there only because Apollo was a prince and there was nothing Kristof could do but smile.

Apollo felt something like guilt twist inside of him at the sight of it. For a second, he considered softening his demands. Then he reminded himself of what his father had said about never being nice.

After his meeting with Kristof, Apollo wanted to check on Evangeline. There were servants, of course, who provided him with updates on her. Thus far he'd been told she was healthy and well, and still without any memories.

Apollo hoped that after his warning from last night, she'd give up any ideas of pursuing her memories. But the Evangeline he knew was not one to give up. She'd found a way to cure him of the Archer's curse, and he imagined that, if given a chance, she'd also find her missing memories. Therefore, Apollo did not plan to give her a chance.

He'd already made provisions to make sure she'd be fully occupied this morning. He would have preferred to be the one occupying her time, but there would be opportunities for that later.

First, there was one more matter to take care of.

The Council of Great Houses.

Yesterday he'd met with a few of the members to prove he wasn't an impostor and that he'd truly returned from the dead. After that there'd been a lengthy discussion about what to do with the actual impostor heir who'd tried to steal his throne. That, however, had proved entirely unnecessary, as the whelp seemed to have fled sometime during the discussion.

It seemed the impostor heir had been warned by a couple of servants who were enamored with him.

Apollo had sent a number of guards after him, but the impostor wasn't his priority for now.

The prince slowed his steps as he reached the door that led to the chamber where the council met. The room on the other side always reminded Apollo of a giant pewter goblet. The walls were slightly rounded and the air was subtly silver, giving everything a sharp, swordlike quality. In the center of the room was an aged white oak table that was said to have been there since the days of the first king of the Magnificent North, Wolfric Valor, a rugged man from another era who now sat at the far end of the table.

All conversation stopped as soon as Apollo entered the room. But it was clear from the tableau that until this moment, the conversation had centered entirely around the newest member of the council—the famed Wolfric Valor. Although, only Apollo knew who Wolfric really was. No one else on the council knew that Wolfric, along with the entire Valor family, had been locked away in the Valory until the previous day.

Wolfric now went by the name Lord Vale. And yet every man and woman at the council table still leaned or angled his way. Which was good—it made what Apollo needed to do so much easier. But it was also a little unnerving to see the way the council responded to the legendary first king of the North without even knowing who he really was.

"Here he is, returned from the dead!" bellowed Wolfric, followed by a clap that spread like wildfire until every council member was standing and applauding as Prince Apollo strode toward the white oak table.

Wolfric winked. *We are allies,* said the gesture. *We are in this together. Friends.*

But Apollo could only too freshly remember how his last friend had betrayed him. If Wolfric chose to do the same,

Apollo would be no match for him and his famed family. All Apollo could do now was keep his word and hope that Wolfric would, too.

"I see that many of you have already met our newest council member," said Apollo, intentionally phrasing it like a statement rather than a question.

Although Apollo had yet to be officially crowned king, he still had more power than the council. In the Magnificent North, a prince could not become king until he wed. But that law, like his upcoming coronation, was mostly for show. Royal events like coronations and Nocte Neverending endeared princes to their people and filled kingdoms with hope and love.

That said, the Council of Great Houses was not entirely powerless. They couldn't stop Apollo from naming a new Great House, but they could fight him over it and, in the process, dig up dangerous truths that Apollo didn't want to risk anyone discovering.

The last thing he needed was the kingdom to learn that the legendary Valors had returned from the dead and were now posing as House Vale.

He'd been dead only a few weeks, but the world believed the Valors had been dead for hundreds of years.

Apollo was still struggling to wrap his mind around the fact that the tales of the Valory had been true and that the Valors had been locked away inside it. He hated to imagine what kind of fuss the kingdom would make if they found out. And he didn't even want to think about the questions Evangeline would ask if she discovered that she had been the one to unlock the Valory Arch.

It seemed his brother, Tiberius, had been right about what she would do all along.

Apollo only hoped that Tiberius was wrong about what would happen after the arch was opened.

"Lord Vale and his family were there when I returned from the dead," Apollo explained smoothly, as this was actually partially the truth. Honora Valor, Wolfric's wife, had cured him from the Archer's curse and the mirror curse. He truly felt indebted to her, making it easy to say earnestly, "Without this family, I might not be here today. As a reward, I've decided to make them a Great House and gift them lands where they might care for others in the same manner they cared for me."

For a moment the entire council was quiet. Apollo could see that even though the members had been drawn toward Wolfric earlier, they were uncertain about this bear of a man, and even more nervous about Apollo's proclamation.

Apollo had never bestowed the honor of Great House upon a family, nor had his father before him or his father's father before him. It was fairly simple to do but once it was done, it was very difficult to undo. To give power was a far easier thing than to take it away.

Although Apollo could sense that each council member feared this declaration had taken power away from them.

He could almost see the questions on the tips of their tongues: *You've only just come back from the dead. Are you certain this is wise? Are you planning to make other Great Houses? How do you know this house is truly deserving to be Great—to be one of us?*

"My family is grateful for your generosity, Your Highness. It is truly an honor to be on this council among so many fine men and women." Wolfric's voice was mild, but his gaze was firm and unwavering as he looked around the council. One by one, he met the eyes of each member, and more than a few appeared to hold their breath.

As a boy, Apollo had been told countless stories of this man. It was said that Wolfric Valor could fell entire armies with one battle cry and rip off the heads of enemies with his bare hands. He'd united the fighting Northern clans to form a kingdom and built Wolf Hall as a wedding gift for his wife after stealing her away from another.

On the surface the man before him didn't appear as forbidding as the stories claimed. Apollo was taller and dressed in clothes far finer. Yet Wolfric possessed that indefinable *more* his father had always spoken of. Wolfric embodied everything that Apollo had never attempted to be.

The council didn't speak a word until finally Wolfric released them from his gaze.

It was Lord Byron Belleflower who spoke up then. "Welcome to the council, Lord Vale. I hope you've already been apprised of all recent kingdom matters. There are a few other important issues that must be discussed today."

Belleflower turned toward Apollo. Unlike nearly everyone else in the castle who had looked upon the prince since he'd made his dramatic return from the dead, Byron Belleflower did not gaze upon Apollo with wonder or awe.

He and Apollo had not gotten along for years, and it appeared from the young man's derisive gaze that Byron had become even more disagreeable during the time Apollo had been away from his throne. There were rumors Belleflower's paramour had died, though Apollo wouldn't have been surprised to learn she'd faked her death to get away from him.

"Now," Belleflower droned loudly, before pausing dramatically to make sure that everyone else at the large table was looking his way.

Most of the other council members were older, but Lord Belleflower was around Apollo's age. The two had been friends as boys, until young Belleflower grew old enough to understand that Apollo was to inherit an entire kingdom while he was set to inherit only a castle on a cold dreary mountain. Apollo would have removed Byron from the council years ago, but unfortunately Belleflower's castle came with a sizable private army that the prince didn't want to risk being on the wrong side of.

It was like that with most of the council members. If any were removed, it would cause a degree of fallout that Apollo was better off avoiding.

"I know you spoke with a couple of other council members yesterday about a quick and speedy coronation," Belleflower continued. "But there are some of us who feel it imprudent to move forward when there are still questions about your wife."

Apollo stiffened. "What kind of questions about my wife?"

Belleflower smiled suddenly, as if Apollo had just said exactly what he wanted to hear. "There are some of us that can't help but wonder: Why did Lord Jacks erase Evangeline's memories? What does she know that could harm him? Unless . . . she had worked with him to poison you?"

"That's a treasonous statement," Apollo interrupted.

"Then prove it," Belleflower pressed.

"I don't need to prove it," Apollo said.

"But it might be helpful," chimed Lady Casstel. She was one of the oldest and wisest council members, and as such, she often led the way for the majority of the others. "I do not believe your bride to be a murderess. But the rumors that swirled around Evangeline after your death were nasty, and she is a foreigner. It could only work in her favor to find a way to show the people that she is now truly part of this kingdom and is fully loyal to you."

"How do you propose I do that?"

"Get her pregnant with an heir," said Lady Casstel without pause. "It's not just for the sake of the kingdom, but to protect you. With your brother stripped of his title and currently missing . . ."

Apollo flinched at the mention of his brother, Tiberius, and for a second the scars on his back stung afresh. A few council members seemed to notice.

Fortunately, reacting to mentions of his brother was nothing new. No one would assume Tiberius was the true reason Apollo's back was covered in scars. Only Havelock and a few of the un-dead were aware of the truth. Havelock would take the secret to the grave, and Apollo tried not to think about vampires. There were already enough unpleasant matters to deal with, like the council's sudden request that he produce an heir.

Although from the way Lady Casstel spoke on the matter, it was clear this subject had been discussed prior to the council meeting.

"There is no one else in direct line for the throne," she continued. "It would be far too easy for another impostor to take the crown in the event something else happens to you."

"Nothing is going to happen to me again," Apollo said. "I've already bested death. It won't be coming back for me anytime soon."

"But it will eventually return for you." These words came from Wolfric Valor. "Death comes for us all, Your Highness. Having an heir will do more than protect the kingdom—it might scare death away for a little longer."

Wolfric looked across the table solemnly. If Wolfric had wanted to, this could have been the moment where he told the entire council that Apollo had never actually come back from the dead, but he didn't.

And although Apollo didn't like it, he had to concede that Wolfric was correct. People were less likely to make plays for the throne when there was a clear successor in place. Having an heir would also protect his relationship with Evangeline. Once she had his child, there was no way she would leave him. But he didn't want to force her into staying this way.

"Evangeline still doesn't remember me," Apollo said.

"Does that really matter? You're a prince," Belleflower inserted. "The girl should feel lucky to be married to you. Without you, she would be no one."

Apollo shot him a dirty look, and he wondered briefly if there was more to his disdain than the suspicion that Evangeline had worked with Jacks to kill him. "Evangeline isn't *no one.* She's my wife. I'll work on an heir after she feels more comfortable."

"And how long will that take?" Belleflower raised his voice, clearly trying to rally the others to his cause. "I was there yesterday. Your wife looked like a frightened ghost beside you, all pale and quivering! If you cared about this kingdom, you'd rid yourself of her and find a new one."

"I am *not* replacing my wife." Apollo shoved up from his chair hard enough to rock the pitchers of wine and make a number of grapes spill from their platters on the table. This conversation was moving too far out of bounds.

It was also veering too far from what really needed to be discussed.

"Evangeline is no longer a topic of conversation. The next person who disparages her will not say another word at this table. If anyone in this room really cares about the kingdom, they'll stop worrying about Evangeline's loyalty and start looking for Lord Jacks. Until he's dead, no one is safe."

5

Evangeline

In the light of a fresh day, everything felt less like a blurred fever dream and more like a picture-perfect stained-glass window. Evangeline's room smelled of lavender tea, buttery pastries, and some unidentifiable grassy sweetness that made her think of exquisitely manicured gardens.

For one beautiful moment, she found herself thinking: *This is what perfect feels like.*

Or it should have felt that way.

The broken bits inside of her warred with this elegant scene. A small but firm voice in her head said, *This isn't perfect, this isn't right.* But before the voice could say much more, it was drowned out by a host of other perkier sounds.

They started out softly on the other side of Evangeline's

door. Then, like a pop of soft flowery fireworks, the owners of the voices entered her suite.

Seamstresses, three of them, all smiling as they greeted her:

"Good morning, Your Highness!"

"You look so refreshed, Your Highness!"

"We hope you slept soundly, for your day will be busy, Your Highness!"

The women were trailed by a parade of servants carrying bolts of fabric, spools of ribbons, baskets of baubles and feathers, strings of pearls, and silken flowers.

"What's all this?" Evangeline asked.

"For your royal wardrobe," all three women said at once.

"But I have a wardrobe." Evangeline looked questioningly toward the little alcove full of clothes that was situated between her bedroom and the bathing room.

"You have an everyday wardrobe, yes," replied the head seamstress, or perhaps she was just the most vocal. "We're here to fit you for special occasions. You'll need something spectacular for your coronation. Then there will be your coronation ball, and the Hunt could happen *any* day."

"Then of course you'll be putting together your own council," the tallest of the seamstresses chimed in. "You'll need to be smartly dressed for each of those meetings."

"And you'll want some frothy gowns for all the upcoming spring festivals, and formal dinners," said the third seamstress.

Then they all started chattering about how perfect her coloring was for spring, and wouldn't it be lovely to make sure every gown she wore had at least a hint of pink to match her lovely hair?

In the midst of it all, more servants appeared. They wheeled in golden carts covered in snacks and treats as pretty as treasure in a chest. There were cookies shaped like castles, tarts topped in glistening pastel fruit, poached pears in a swirling golden sauce, candied dates wearing miniature crowns, and oysters on ice with pink pearls that glistened under the light.

"We hope this is all to your liking," said one of the servants. "If there's anything else you need, just ask. His Highness the prince wanted you to know that you can have whatever you wish."

"And if you ever need a break, merely let us know," said the tall seamstress before reaching into her little apron and pulling out a measuring tape.

It was shortly after this, when Evangeline's arms were being measured for gloves, that she noticed the scar. It was on the underside of her right wrist, thin and white, shaped like a broken heart. And it had definitely not been there before.

As soon as the measuring was done, Evangeline lifted her wrist to examine the strange broken heart. She ran a finger over it carefully. Her skin prickled as she touched it.

In that instant, it was as if the precious bubble she was inside of burst. *Pop. Pop. Pop.*

The wonder of all the treats and sweets and beautiful fabrics faded as Evangeline stared at the little broken heart. She couldn't remember it at all, but she did remember the little voice in her head from earlier, warning her that everything wasn't perfect.

Evangeline continued to study the scar, trying hard to remember how she'd received it, until she caught the tall seamstress staring at her oddly. Evangeline quickly covered the scar with her hand.

The seamstress didn't say anything about the heart. But something about the way she had stared at it made Evangeline feel inexplicably nervous. Then she noticed the woman covertly slipping away from the suite as the other seamstresses continued working.

Evangeline didn't know if the scar was truly something to worry about, or if maybe she was just imagining the woman's reaction. Evangeline had no reason to feel alarmed other than the voice in her head telling her that something wasn't right. But maybe what was really wrong was that she was hearing a voice in her head.

Maybe she could have trusted it if she'd been tossed in a dungeon. But she was in a castle straight out of one of her mother's stories and married to a dashing prince who'd come back from the dead *and* who was desperately in love with her. This new life was not just a fairytale—it was more like something from a legend.

While fabrics and feelings continued to swirl around her, another visitor arrived—one of the physician's apprentices from yesterday. Evangeline remembered her name was Telma.

Evangeline didn't know how long it was she'd been standing

there. The current fitting was for a hooded raspberry cape made of deep velvet fabric that had been covering her eyes until a moment ago.

"I've just come for a quick checkup, Your Highness," said Telma. "Is this a bad time?"

"Oh no, I'm just practicing being a pincushion," said Evangeline, hoping to sound more cheerful than she felt.

"How are your missing memories?" Telma asked. "Have any returned?"

"I'm afraid not," Evangeline said. She wondered then if maybe she should mention the voice in her head.

But Telma's reply gave her pause. "I'm sorry you still can't remember," she said.

And it could have just been Evangeline's overeager imagination, but she could have sworn this assistant didn't look sorry at all. If anything, she appeared relieved. The reaction brought to mind what Apollo had told Evangeline last night: *Jacks has done atrocious, unforgivable things to you, and I truly believe you might be happier if those things stay forgotten.*

Until then, Evangeline had tried not to think about it. Thinking about her missing memories too much made her feel overwrought, overwhelmed, and in too far over her head. She so wanted to believe that if she could just find a way to get the memories back, it would all be better.

But what if Apollo was right? What if remembering only made everything worse? He'd seemed truly concerned at the prospect of her getting them back. And now this assistant looked as if she felt the same way, as if Evangeline was genuinely better off forgetting.

And yet it was difficult to completely dismiss her unease. Perhaps it was because thus far, she really had nothing but Apollo's word.

"Telma, I heard something last night, and I'm just wondering if it's true. I heard Apollo was murdered on our wedding night and I was framed for the crime."

Telma paled at the question. "I never believed you did it."

"But it's true that others believed I did?"

Telma nodded grimly. "It was a terrible time for everyone. But now that Apollo is back, hopefully all of that's come to an end."

Telma slowly exhaled and something dreamy filled her eyes. "It's amazing, isn't it, that the prince came back from the dead for you?" The look she gave Evangeline was so earnest, so sweet and pure and awed, Evangeline couldn't help but feel a little foolish for thinking about trusting a little paranoid voice in her head.

When the seamstresses, the physician, and the servants finally left, it was night, and Evangeline's suite turned from a hive of activity to a quiet sanctuary only enlivened by the crackling fire and the distant chime of a tower clock. It was the first time Evangeline had been alone all day.

But the quiet did not last. Shortly after she found herself alone, a knock sounded on her door.

"May I enter?" asked Apollo.

Evangeline quickly looked in the closest mirror to check her reflection and smooth her hair, unexpectedly flustered, before she replied, "Come in."

The door opened quietly and Apollo strode confidently inside.

He was still handsome, and he was still a prince.

Not that Evangeline had expected him to stop being handsome or a prince. She was just overcome by the truth of it once again. By his standing in her suite, all tall and regal. And she imagined he knew how good he looked and exactly what effect he was having on her.

He smiled wider as her cheeks grew warmer. She hoped it wouldn't always be this way. It had been only a day and a half since she had met him, at least that she remembered.

"I heard you've been indoors all day. Join me for a walk?" He said the word *walk* with a twist of his mouth that made Evangeline think they'd be doing more than just walking.

Her stomach did a giddy little tumble.

She didn't know if it was perhaps her memories coming back, or if maybe she was simply attracted to him.

"Yes, I'd love to join you."

"I'm glad to hear that."

Apollo brought Evangeline a fluffy white cloak lined in snow-white fur. He helped her with her cloak, warm fingers lingering at the nape of her neck as he moved her hair. It felt more intentional than accidental. In fact, Evangeline was beginning to suspect that everything Apollo did was by design.

After leaving her rooms, he nodded at the waiting guards. It was an almost imperceptible tilt of his chin, but it seemed to hold the power of a barked command.

The guards dipped their heads in unison and stepped back so the pair could pass. Then they followed the two from behind, mindful to keep a respectable distance.

Evangeline and Apollo walked the first few castle halls in silence, flanked by the warm light of all the sconces on the ancient walls. She still had so many questions for Apollo, but now all she felt were nerves buzzing inside her.

Perhaps it was the cadre of guards in their shining bronze armor that stopped her from speaking. They were about a half a hall behind, but Evangeline could hear the fall of their boots against the stone floor, so she imagined that were she to speak, they would hear her as well.

Apollo took her hand.

Evangeline felt a shock.

"So that you'll stop thinking about the guards and you'll think of this instead." Apollo gave her fingers a gentle squeeze.

Evangeline had never held hands with a young man before, at least not that she could remember. Yesterday Apollo had taken her hand, but it had been more to tug her through the castle.

This was . . . *nice.* The soft pressure of Apollo's fingers, the way her hand felt small and sheltered inside of his. Of course, it didn't help the problem of being too nervous to speak. If anything, she felt more anxious than before. This was all so new that she wasn't quite sure what to do. Apollo wasn't a mere boy who worked in a stable or in his father's bakery. He was the ruler of a kingdom. He had the power to hold lives in the palm of his hand. But right now, he was only holding her hand.

She was about to finally ask him once again how the two of them had originally met when she saw the poster nailed to one of the castle's rounded doors.

LORD JACKS

WANTED

DEAD or ALIVE

for **Murder** *and*
More Heinous Crimes
Against *the* **Crown**

Evangeline's blood went cold.

Underneath the list of Lord Jacks's crimes was a portrait—if it could be called that. The image was more shadow than man, a face with two dark holes for eyes and a slash of a mouth.

Apollo tugged her closer to his side. "Don't pay those posters any attention."

"Is that really how Lord Jacks looks?" Evangeline knew Apollo had called him a monster, but she hadn't expected this.

"It's a rough sketch. He looks more human than that, but barely." Something like hate poured off Apollo as he said the words.

It was the type of emotion that made Evangeline want to curl away from him. She imagined Apollo had every reason to feel spiteful, but for a second, she felt the urge to run. Although perhaps that was because of the poster of Jacks?

Evangeline's thoughts kept going back to the shadowy image until she briefly lost track of where they were and where they were going. Suddenly she found herself climbing a narrow spiral of stone stairs.

There was no rail on one side—just a terrifying drop to the bottom of the tower. If Evangeline had been in full possession of her senses, she'd never have started climbing.

She craned her neck, but there were so many steps ahead that she couldn't see the top, and they were too narrow for her and Apollo to walk side by side.

"Where do these stairs lead?" she asked uncertainly.

"I think it's better if it's a surprise," Apollo said. He was right behind her. She could hear his footsteps. But her steps and his were the only ones. The guards must have remained at the bottom of the stairs, and Evangeline soon found herself envying them.

"Can I just have a hint of where we're going?" she asked. "Is there a tower up here you're planning to lock me in?"

The sound of Apollo's footsteps halted.

She immediately knew she had said the wrong thing.

"You're not a prisoner, Evangeline. I would never lock you up."

"I—I know. I was only jesting." And Evangeline wanted to believe that she was. She didn't really think Apollo would lock her up in a tower like a cruel fairytale king. Yet her heart had started beating differently. *Danger. Danger. Danger,* it seemed to say—but it was too late to turn around.

They were nearly at the top. A few steps ahead, she could finally see another door, a simple rectangle without any adornment.

"It should be unlocked," Apollo said.

Nervously, Evangeline opened the latch and was promptly greeted by a dark night and whistle of cold wind that whipped her hair across her face.

Please don't abandon me up here, she thought.

"Don't worry, I'm here," Apollo said tenderly.

Evangeline didn't know if he'd sensed her fear, or if she'd actually said the words out loud. But he immediately came behind her, blocking some wind and providing a solid wall of warmth for her back.

As her eyes adjusted to the dark, she saw that the night wasn't quite so black as she had thought before—there was light from the windows of the castle below illuminating a short crenellated wall that surrounded the top of the tower. Beyond the castle, the world was dark, save for sprays of stars forming unfamiliar constellations.

"Is this what you wanted me to see?" she asked.

"No," Apollo said softly. "It should just be a couple more seconds."

A moment later, the bells of a tower clock rang out.

Ding.

Ding.

Ding.

Ding.

Ding.

Ding.

Ding.

Ding.

Ding.

Ding.

With every chime of the bell, pops of light burst to life in the distance. There were just a few at first—far-off embers of glow appearing here and there like bits of fallen stars. But soon there was more light than dark. A world of bright, as if the sky and the ground had switched places and now the Earth was covered in shimmering stars.

"What is all this?" Evangeline asked.

"It's a gift for us. It's called a Firenight. It's an old Northern blessing," Apollo said, voice softer than before as he moved closer, pressing his warm chest more firmly to her back. "Usually this happens before a king goes to war. Bonfires are lit across the land and people burn words of blessing. Wishes for health and for strength and for stealth and for safe returns home. When I found out there would be a Firenight tonight in honor of us, I thought you'd want to see. Every bonfire down there is for us. Subjects from all over the Magnificent North are burning words of blessing for our health and our marriage as we speak."

"It's a like a fairytale," Evangeline murmured. But even as the words came out, they didn't feel true.

It wasn't *like* a fairytale. It *was* a fairytale. It was *her* fairytale.

Would it really change things if she remembered exactly how she'd gotten here, how she'd met Apollo, how they'd fallen in love and married? Or would she just feel differently? Perhaps even if she had all her memories, Apollo would still make her nervous.

As the wind whipped around her and fires burst to life below, Evangeline slowly turned around and looked up at the prince. *Her* prince.

"You're looking in the wrong direction." He grinned, slow and cocky.

Her heart pounded faster and faster. *Danger, danger, danger,* it seemed to say again. But Evangeline was no longer sure she could trust it—or maybe she just liked the danger.

"Perhaps I prefer this view." She brought her hand to Apollo's jaw. It was a little rough against her palm as she tilted his face.

She wasn't sure if she was doing this right; all she felt were nerves as she rose up on the tips of her toes and pressed her mouth to his.

"Finally," Apollo growled. Then he took her lower lip between his teeth as he kissed her back.

Fireworks burst to life in the distance. Evangeline could hear them explode as Apollo's hands slid beneath her cloak, pushing it aside as he pulled her closer.

She wasn't sure if they were spinning toward the edge of the tower or if it was just her head going dizzy. But she could feel the wind rushing at her back, and she knew that the prince's arms were the only thing that kept her from falling.

6

Evangeline

The world had altered overnight, and it wasn't merely because Evangeline felt butterflies every time she thought of kissing Apollo.

The season appeared to have changed while she'd slept, turning from winter into spring. Instead of looking out her window to see blankets of white, she found eager green trees, happy shrubs and mosses, and glittering rocks. All of it was coated in a fine mist of silver rain that pitter-pattered outside her window.

While it rained that morning, another physician checked in to see if she had remembered anything, which she hadn't. After that, the seamstresses returned, but they didn't linger for long.

It seemed there was another appointment on Evangeline's

calendar, although she was unaware of it until an entirely new visitor arrived.

"Hello, Your Highness, I'm Madame Voss. It's a pleasure to meet you." The woman dropped into a perfect curtsy, the hem of her emerald-green skirt brushing against the stone floor. Madame Voss's hair was a beautiful shade of silver and her long face was full of deep smile lines that gave Evangeline an immediate impression of warmth.

"I'm going to be your tutor on all things royal. But first, let's start with all things *you*." Madame Voss set a beautiful blue book in Evangeline's lap. Inside, the pages were gilded in a shimmering gold that matched the book's decorative title.

Evangeline read it aloud. "*The Greatest Love Story Ever Told: The True and Unabridged History of Evangeline Fox and the Prince of Hearts.*"

Madame Voss gasped. "Oh, botheration!" Then she swatted at the volume in Evangeline's lap until finally the title changed to read: *The Greatest Love Story Ever Told: The True and Unabridged History of Evangeline Fox and Prince Apollo Titus Acadian.*

"My apologies for that, Your Highness. This book was freshly printed. I was hoping that since it was so new, it would be immune to the story curse." She gave the book a chastising look. "Hopefully it's only the title that's finnicky."

"Please, don't be sorry," said Evangeline.

Until that moment, Evangeline hadn't really thought much about the North's story curse, but her mother had told her all about it when she was a little girl. Every fairytale in the Magnificent North was cursed. Some stories couldn't be written down, others couldn't leave the North, and many changed every time they were shared, becoming less and less true with every telling. It was said that every Northern tale had started as actual history, but over time, the Northern story curse had twisted them until only bits of truth remained.

"Where I'm from, books just sit quietly on shelves," said Evangeline. "I find this delightful."

She stared at the cover a little longer. This was the first time she'd ever seen the words on a book change before her eyes. Madame Voss treated it like a nuisance, but to Evangeline it was magic. Because it *was* magic.

But it was also curious that the first title mentioned the Prince of Hearts.

In the Meridian Empire, where Evangeline was from, the Prince of Hearts was a myth—a character found inside decks of fortune-telling cards—not a real flesh-and-blood person. She wondered if here, perhaps, the Prince of Hearts could be another nickname for Prince Apollo?

She felt an uncomfortable jolt at the thought and wondered what else she didn't know about her husband, even as she told herself it didn't matter. She and Apollo would make new memories, as they had last night.

And yet Evangeline couldn't shake the strange wedge of discomfort inside her as she opened up Madame Voss's book.

The end pages were stunning full-color portraits of Evangeline and Apollo staring into each other's eyes as fireworks exploded in the background. Apollo was pictured dressed in a fine royal suit, a cape, and a great gold crown adorned with large rubies and other gems.

For a second, Evangeline thought she saw a third person in the picture—another man appeared to be watching from the edge of one page. But like the book's original title, this image was there and then gone.

There were more illustrations on the second page, and nothing moved. The top of the page was decorated with images of a sun and a moon and a sky full of stars that hung above the words:

Once upon a time,
a girl who believed in fairytales
stole the heart of a prince
who had sworn to never love.

"Is this true?" Evangeline asked. "Did Prince Apollo swear to never love?"

"Oh yes! Some people thought it was only a jest, but I didn't think so," said Madame Voss. "It was a little alarming, really. We have this tradition in the North—a terrific ball called Nocte Neverending."

Evangeline knew a little about Nocte Neverending, but she didn't say a word. She still knew nothing about her first meeting with Apollo, and she'd never gotten back to asking him about it last night.

"Apollo had said that once the ball started, it would never end, as he had no plans to find a bride," Madame Voss went on. "Then he met you. It's such a shame you don't remember. It was truly love at first sight. I wasn't there, of course. The dinner was very exclusive, and the two of you met in a private clearing, protected by an arch."

She said the word *arch* differently than all the others, as if it were a bit of magic instead of what Evangeline was probably imagining.

"I take it arches are special?" Evangeline said.

"Oh yes," Madame Voss replied. "They were built by the Valors, our first king and queen, so that they could travel any-where in North. But arches are also excellent for guarding things. The prince has one that guards the most magnificent phoenix tree. You should really get him to show it to you some-time. Ah, wait." She looked down at the book. "I'll bet there is a picture in here."

The tutor turned the page, and indeed there was a stunning portrait of Apollo lounging across a tree branch in one of the most magnificent trees that Evangeline had ever seen. Every leaf seemed to sparkle. Half of them were a symphony of warm har-vest colors—yellow and orange and russet—but the rest looked like real gold. Glittering, shimmering, dragon treasure gold.

"That's the phoenix tree," said Madame Voss. "Once it's grown and in full bloom, it takes over a thousand years to mature as the leaves slowly turn into real gold. However, if one leaf is plucked before all the leaves have changed, the entire tree goes up in flames. *Poof!*" she said with a dramatic hand gesture before giving Evangeline a warning look.

"Don't worry, I wouldn't dream of picking a leaf," Evangeline said.

But Madame Voss had already turned the page.

It was Apollo again, but this time he rode a white horse and was dressed more ruggedly in wood-brown breeches, an open-collared shirt, and a fur vest with crisscrossing leather straps that fixed a golden bow and a quiver of arrows to his back.

"This was when he proposed to you," said Madame Voss. "It was the first night of Nocte Neverending and he was dressed up like a character from a most beloved tale, *The Ballad of the Archer and the Fox.*"

"I know that story," Evangeline said. "It's my favorite . . ."

Or it always had been. As she said the words now, they didn't feel quite so true.

"That's wonderful," Madame Voss replied. "Hopefully you can picture it then. Prince Apollo looked so dashing as he rode into the ball on a mighty white horse. He was dressed just like the Archer—"

Suddenly Evangeline couldn't hear any more words. Her head hurt. Her chest hurt. Her *heart* hurt, every heartbeat seemed to pierce her like an arrow—a thought that also some-how pained her. She fought to remember why memories from her favorite fairytale would trigger so much misery. But all she found was . . .

nothing . . .

nothing . . .

nothing . . .

The harder she tried to remember, the more her heart ached. The sensation was similar to how she'd felt two days before, when Apollo had found her curled up on the ground in a strange and ancient room. Only now she didn't want to cry. This pain felt raw, angry—like a scream living inside her that threatened to rip her in half if it wasn't let out.

Once again, she remembered that there was some*thing* she needed to tell some*one*, only now the thought of it was even more painful than before.

Madame Voss's eyes went wide. "Your Highness, are you all right?"

No! Evangeline wanted to scream. *There's something I've forgotten and I need to remember.*

Last night she'd convinced herself she could just let her memories go. But now it was clear that she'd been kidding her-self. She knew Apollo had warned that regaining her memories would only hurt her, but some things were worth hurting for, and Evangeline believed this was one of those things.

She *needed* to remember.

"I'm sorry, Madame Voss," Evangeline finally managed to say. "I'm suffering from a bit of a headache. May we postpone this lesson?"

"Of course, Your Highness. I'll return tomorrow. I can tell you the rest of the story then. And we can have our first lesson on royal etiquette, if you're feeling up for that."

Madame Voss gave Evangeline a parting curtsy before quietly making her exit.

As soon as the tutor left, Evangeline started reading the book again, wondering if it might elicit any more feelings or memories. But the story inside—her and Apollo's love story—was more of a picture book that read like a toothless fairytale, one without a villain.

Evangeline had always loved tales with love at first sight, but love at first sight was mentioned so many times that she half expected the story to end with an advertisement for bottles of Love at First Sight Perfume: *Tired of Looking for Your Happy Ending? Stop Searching and Start Spritzing!*

The book, of course, did not end that way. It also did not provoke any memories. Not even an itch of one.

Evangeline finally put the book down and paced in front of the fire. She racked her brain for any story her mother might have once told her about memory loss, hoping it might help her find a cure. While she couldn't remember any, she did remember the stranger from the other day who had given her a little red calling card and said, *If you'd ever like to talk, and perhaps answer some questions, I might be able to fill in a few blanks for you.*

Evangeline searched for the little red card. It didn't seem to be anywhere in her rooms. Fortunately, the man had a memorable name.

Just then Martine, the young maid who, like Evangeline, was from the Meridian Empire, entered the room with a tray of piping tea and fresh raspberry cookies.

"Martine," Evangeline said, "have you ever heard of Mr. Kristof Knightlinger?"

"Of course!" Martine's heart-shaped face lit up. "I read him faithfully every day."

"Read him?"

"He writes for *The Daily Rumor*."

"The scandal sheet?" Evangeline had read the paper just that morning. She could still recall some of the dramatic headlines. *Where Is Lord Jacks and What Terrible Deed Will He Commit Next? Impostor Heir to the Throne Still at Large! Just How Heroic Is the Guild of Heroes?*

From what she'd gathered, Mr. Knightlinger peppered his scandal sheet with personal opinions. His article about Lord Jacks had been quite similar to what he'd written the day before, but she'd been entertained by his other stories. Mr. Knightlinger's comments, particularly about the impostor heir to the throne, had been highly amusing. He'd painted a picture that made Evangeline think of an excitable puppy that had stolen a crown simply because it was shiny and pretty and fun to play with. Then Mr. Knightlinger had gone on to speculate that the impostor might be a vampire!

All of this made Evangeline suspect that Mr. Kristof Knight-linger might not be the most reliable source of information. But she did imagine that whatever he said would be a little more varied than the "love at first sight" book from Madame Voss, and perhaps Mr. Knightlinger might finally prompt a memory.

7

Evangeline

Evangeline liked having a plan. Her current plan was thin—in fact, it was more of a day trip than a plan. Evangeline wasn't even sure it would take an entire day to visit Mr. Knightlinger. Still, she wanted to set out as early as possible.

It had been late in the afternoon when the tutor had left the day before. After an initial burst of excitement, Evangeline had lain down for quick nap, only to find herself waking up the following morning.

Although Evangeline still couldn't find Mr. Knightlinger's little red card, Martine had told her that the *Daily Rumor* offices were located in the Spires, a place the palace guards should easily be able to take Evangeline.

"You'll just love the Spires! They have all kinds of adorable shops and dragon-roasted apples! And you'll *love* the little dragons," Martine exclaimed as she looked for a pair of gloves to match Evangeline's dress.

Evangeline had chosen an off-the-shoulder violet day gown with a fitted bodice covered in iridescent pearls and gold-embroidered flowers that also dotted the hips of her flowing skirt.

"Here you go, Your Highness." Martine handed Evangeline a pink cloak and a long pair of sheer violet gloves. The gloves wouldn't do much against the chill, but they were very pretty. And Evangeline always felt a little happier wearing pretty things.

Four guards with neat mustaches, all dressed in polished bronze armor topped off with burgundy capes that flowed from their shoulders, waited on the other side of her door.

"Hello, I'm Evangeline," she said cheerfully before asking for their names.

"I'm Yeats."

"Brixley."

"Quillborne."

"Rookwood."

"It's a pleasure to meet you all. I am hoping to visit the Spires today. Do you think one of you could arrange transportation?"

A beat of silence passed as three of the guards turned to the one who'd said his name was Yeats. He appeared to be the oldest, with a smooth-shaven head and a very impressive black mustache.

"I don't think going to the Spires is a good idea, Your Highness. What if we gave you a tour of Wolf Hall instead?"

"Why don't you think it's a good idea? My maid told me they are mostly shops."

"They are, but Prince Apollo asked us to make sure you stay on the castle grounds. It's for your safety."

"So are you saying that the four of you fine gentlemen aren't strong enough to keep me safe if I leave the castle?" Evangeline needled shamelessly.

The younger guards responded exactly as she'd hoped.

They puffed out their chests and looked ready to prove her wrong.

But Yeats spoke up before they could say anything. "We are loyal to Prince Apollo's wishes. Right now, his wish is that you remain here on castle grounds, where he knows you are at no risk of anything or anyone coming after you."

Evangeline might have laughed if the guard hadn't looked so serious. The way he spoke made it sound as if everything in the North might try to kill her. "Where exactly in Wolf Hall am I allowed to go?"

"Anywhere. As long as you don't leave the premises."

"Is Prince Apollo currently in Wolf Hall?"

"Yes, Your Highness."

"Excellent. Please take me to see him," Evangeline said

calmly, hopeful that this was simply a misunderstanding. Two nights ago, Apollo had said she wasn't a prisoner and he'd never lock her up. In fact, he'd looked deeply hurt when she'd mentioned it. Clearly, these guards were mistaken.

"I'm sorry," said Yeats evenly, "but the prince is currently occupied."

"Doing what?" Evangeline asked.

Yeats's mustache twitched in annoyance. "It isn't our place to say," he grunted. "What if we took you to one of the gardens instead?"

Evangeline finally let her smile fade. Until now she'd tried to be polite and pleasant, but these men clearly had no respect for her.

Maybe before she'd lost her memories, she would have been less troublesome. She might have been eager to simply wander the castle and the gardens and to be seen as an easy-to-please princess. But right now she really didn't care about being a princess or being pleased or easy. She needed to *remember*. And that seemed unlikely to happen if she was confined to a fortified castle where people thought she was better off leaving the past forgotten.

"Did my husband tell you that he didn't want to see me?"

"No. But—"

"Mr. Yeats," Evangeline interrupted, "I'd like to see my husband. And if you tell me no or suggest that I walk through another garden, I'm going to assume you believe either that my husband can be replaced by flowers or that you're in a position to give me orders. Do you believe either of those things, Mr. Yeats?"

The guard gritted his teeth.

Evangeline held her breath.

Finally Yeats answered, "No, Your Highness. I don't think that."

Evangeline tried to hide her relief as she looked at the others and asked, "What about the rest of you?"

"No, Your Highness," they each muttered quickly.

"Splendid! Let's go see Apollo."

The guards made no move to leave. "We won't stop you from looking for him, but we won't take you to him," said Yeats.

Evangeline had never been much for cursing, but she wanted to do it just then.

"I'll take you to the prince," called a new guard from a few feet away.

Evangeline looked at this young man askew.

He wore the same guard's uniform as the others, but his armor appeared more scratched, as if he'd actually seen battle. There were a few scars on his face as well. "My name is Havelock, Your Highness."

He waited a beat.

Evangeline had the immediate sense that he was hoping she would remember him, which just added to her frustration when she didn't feel so much as a glimmer of recognition.

"It's all right," Havelock said. Then he nodded toward the cloak draped over her arm. "You won't be needing that. The prince is in his receiving room. The fireplace takes up an entire wall. No one needs a cloak in there."

Havelock did not lie.

The receiving room looked like the sort of place where children might gather on the night before a holiday to listen to a grandparent tell tales before the fire. Rain fell on the other side of the room's wall-to-wall windows.

When Evangeline arrived, she watched the rain pour down in silver curtains, soaking the dark green needle trees and hitting hard against the windows. Inside the room, the great fire crackled as logs broke, setting off a quick riot of sparks and filling the room with a new burst of heat.

Even though her shoulders were bare, she was suddenly warm.

Apollo stood with an unfamiliar figure near the far mantel. This person was as tall as the prince but was entirely concealed by a dark hood and a long, heavy cloak.

Evangeline felt a fresh flicker of unease as she recalled the words *No one needs a cloak in there.* They echoed in her head as she stepped deeper into the room. "I hope I'm not interrupting."

Apollo's eyes lit up as soon as he saw her. "No, you're just in time, darling."

The hooded figure continued to gaze into the fire.

Evangeline knew it was probably breaking some sort of rule to take a closer glance at the stranger beneath his hood, but she couldn't help herself. Not that it did much good. She discovered that the person beneath the cloak was male, but little else. A thick beard concealed the bottom half of his face, while a black mask covered the upper half, leaving her to gaze at nothing but a pair of slightly narrowed eyes.

Apollo gestured toward the man. "Evangeline, I'd like to introduce you to Garrick of the Greenwood, leader of the Guild of Heroes."

"It's a pleasure to meet you, Your Highness." Garrick's voice was rasping and low, and did nothing to quell Evangeline's growing sense of foreboding.

She'd never heard of Garrick or the Greenwood, but she had read about the Guild of Heroes yesterday morning.

Quickly she tried to remember what the scandal sheet had said. She thought it had started with something about the impostor heir who'd been on the throne when Apollo had been proclaimed dead. Apparently, this impostor was more concerned with parties and flirtations than with ruling the kingdom, and thus a band of warriors had taken it upon themselves to keep order in some areas of the North. They called themselves the Guild of Heroes. However, according to Mr. Knightlinger, it was debatable as to whether these warriors were heroes or mercenaries profiting off a series of unfortunate circumstances.

"Garrick is leading an effort that will take the hunt for Lord Jacks outside of Valorfell," said Apollo.

The hero cracked his knuckles and flashed a chilling smile at Evangeline. "My men and I are excellent hunters. Lord Jacks will be dead within a fortnight. Possibly sooner, if you're willing to help us."

"What could I possibly do to help you?" Evangeline asked. For a moment she had a flash of being tied to a tree and used as bait.

"Don't be alarmed, sweetheart." Apollo took her hand. "This will only hurt for a moment."

"What will hurt?" She pulled her hand free and tripped on the full skirt of her dress.

"There's nothing to be afraid of, Evangeline."

"Unless you don't like blood," muttered Garrick.

Apollo glared at him. "You're not helping."

"Neither are you, Your Highness. Not to be rude," Garrick said in a clearly rude tone. "But this will take an eternity if you mollycoddle her. Just tell her about the damn mark."

"What mark?" Evangeline asked.

Apollo's lips pressed into a tight line. Then his eyes dropped to her wrist.

Evangeline didn't even need to follow his gaze. As soon as he looked toward her sheer gloves, she could feel the broken heart scar on her wrist begin to burn. Her heart started to race as well.

She remembered then the seamstress who'd covertly left the room after seeing the scar yesterday, and Evangeline had a terrible feeling that she now knew where the woman had gone. She'd left to see Apollo.

"Lord Jacks made that scar on your wrist. It's his mark. It signifies a debt you owe him."

"What kind of debt?" she asked.

"I don't know what you owe," Apollo said. "All we can do is try to stop him from collecting it." He looked at her grimly now. His skin—normally a lovely olive—had gone a little gray.

"How?"

"By finding him before he finds you. The mark he gave you links you to him, making it possible for Jacks to locate you anywhere."

"But it can also help us find *him*," Garrick added. "The same link that allows him to track you should allow us to hunt him. But we need your blood."

Somewhere in the room, a bird cawed, loud and unnerving as Garrick flashed his teeth. *Bloodthirsty* was the word that came to mind.

Evangeline didn't like the idea that she owed Jacks a debt, but she also didn't want to give this stranger her blood. In fact, she had a powerful urge to run from the room and keep running until her legs gave out. But she had the impression that Garrick of the Greenwood was the sort of man who would chase anything that fled him.

"May I think about this?" she asked. "Of course I want you to find Lord Jacks, but this bit about the blood makes me rather uncomfortable."

"Very well then." Garrick snapped his tattooed fingers twice. "Argos, it's time to go."

A bird that looked like a raven swooped down from one of the beams above. It flew toward Garrick in an elegant arc of blue-black wings. Evangeline felt one of its feathers brush her face and—

"Ouch!" she yelped as the bird bit her shoulder. Two sharp pecks left two brilliant wells of blood. She tried to stop the bleeding with her hand, but Garrick moved faster. He moved nearly as fast as his bird as he clapped a cloth over the wound, quickly collecting her blood.

"Sorry, Highness, but there's really not time for you to think, and we've already done that bit for you." Garrick pulled the bloody cloth away and strode toward the door, whistling as his raven perched on his shoulder.

Evangeline seethed as she continued to bleed. She wasn't sure who she was more upset with: the mercenary who'd just attacked her with his pet bird, or her husband.

Two evenings before, that night at the tower, Apollo had been so sweet. He'd been caring, he'd been thoughtful. But today, between what she'd watched happen with Garrick and Apollo's instructions for her guards, the prince felt like another person. And Evangeline didn't know him well enough to know which version was really him. Earlier she'd thought what had happened with her guards was merely a misunderstanding, but now she wasn't so sure.

"Did you know Garrick was going to do that? That he was going to take my blood regardless of whether I gave my permission?"

Apollo worked his jaw. "I don't think you understand how much of a threat Jacks is."

"You're right. You keep saying Jacks is the villain. Yet you just let a man attack me with his pet bird in order to hunt another man down and kill him. You also told my guards—who aren't very nice, by the way—not to let me leave the castle, despite promising me you'd never lock me up. So, no, I don't know how much of a threat Lord Jacks is, but I'm starting to see you as one."

Apollo's eyes flashed. "Do you think I want to do any of this?"

"I think you're a prince and you do whatever you want."

"Wrong, Evangeline." His voice shook as he spoke. "None of this is what I want, but it's not just Jacks I'm trying to protect you from. There are people in this castle, people on my council, who believe I shouldn't trust you. They believe you worked with Jacks to assassinate me. And if these people believe my judgment is compromised and that you're still working with him, then even I won't be able to save you."

"But Jacks took all my memories," Evangeline argued. "How could anyone still think I was working with him?"

Apollo's frightened gaze darted back to her wrist, the one with the broken heart scar. "The current theory is that Jacks took your memories so that you couldn't betray him."

"Is this what you believe?" Evangeline asked.

For a long moment, Apollo just looked at her. His gaze was no longer fearful or angry, but it wasn't the warm, adoring gaze she'd grown used to. It was cold and distant, and for a second, she felt a tremor of fear. Apollo was the only ally she had in the

Magnificent North. If it wasn't for him, she'd have nothing, no one, and nowhere to go.

"I'm not working with Jacks," Evangeline said finally. "I might not remember anything, but I know that I'm not that kind of person. I have no plans to meet with him or to betray you or anyone else in this castle. But if you treat me like a captive or a pawn or if you let anyone else attack me with their pet bird, I will refuse to behave. But it's not because I'm not loyal."

Apollo took a deep breath and the cold left his eyes. "I know, Evangeline. I believe you. But my thoughts aren't the only ones that matter." He reached down and stroked a finger along her jaw. His eyes lowered, and she knew that he was going to kiss her. He was going to finish this argument with his lips on hers— and part of her wanted to let him. She couldn't risk losing him. He was all she had in this new reality.

But just because he was all she had didn't mean that she needed to give him all the power. "I'm still mad at you."

Apollo slowly moved his hand from her jaw into her hair. "Do you think you can forgive me? I'm sorry about the blood, and I'm sorry about your guards. I'll assign you new ones. But I need you to trust me and to be careful."

Evangeline raised her chin defiantly. "You mean you need me to stay in Wolf Hall?"

"Just until we find Lord Jacks."

"But—"

Before he could finish, the door to the receiving room swung open and the same guard who'd brought Evangeline there announced, "Lord Slaughterwood is here to meet with you. He says he has information about Lord Jacks."

8

Apollo

Havelock's timing was perfect, but Apollo wished he hadn't mentioned information about Jacks. Evangeline's reaction to the potential news was immediate. Her expressions were always so easy to read. Earlier he'd seen her unease; then he'd seen her fear, her anger; and now as she bit down on her lower lip, he could see her curiosity. She was the moth and Jacks was still the flame.

"Havelock, show Lord Slaughterwood to my study. I'll meet him there."

"May I join you?" Evangeline asked. "I'd like to hear what he has to say."

Apollo pretended to consider her request. But it was mostly

to make sure she wouldn't leave too soon and run into Lord Slaughterwood in the hall.

When Apollo had been under the Archer's curse and everyone had believed him dead, he'd read in a scandal sheet that Evangeline had attended Lord Slaughterwood's engagement party. So far she hadn't reacted to his name, but Apollo couldn't risk a run-in with the man that might jog any memories—or that Slaughterwood might say something to her about Jacks, who Apollo suspected she'd attended the party with.

"I'm so sorry, darling, but I don't think that would be a good idea. Remember what I said about people believing you're working with Jacks? If any of them were to find out you were in a meeting where his whereabouts were revealed, they would blame you if he were to elude us again."

Evangeline pinched her lips shut. She would argue with him, he had no doubt. But whatever she said next didn't matter. This was all to protect her.

He stroked her cheek. "I hope you understand."

"I do understand, and I hope you understand that as long as you treat me like an untrustworthy captive, I will act like one instead of like your wife."

She pulled away from Apollo and without another word turned her back and walked out of the room, pink hair swishing behind her.

He had an urge to chase her, a remnant of the Archer's curse that made him want to stop her before she reached the door and forbid her from leaving. He didn't. Apollo knew it was better that she left right now, and there was only so far she could go.

Evangeline might have decided that she didn't want to act like his wife, but it didn't change the fact that she *was*. She was his. And one way or the other, eventually she would want him as much as he wanted her.

A few minutes later, Apollo met Lord Slaughterwood in his private study.

Robin Slaughterwood had always had the sort of good-humored nature that drew people to him like a magnet. But he wasn't smiling today. His eyes had dark circles, his mouth was drawn, and his face was sallow. He looked as if he'd aged five years since Apollo had last seen him.

"You look excellent, my friend. Being engaged suits you well."

"You're as smooth a liar as ever," Slaughterwood grumbled. "I look like hell, and the engagement is over. But I'm not here to talk about that."

"You have a lead on Jacks?" Apollo asked.

"No," Slaughterwood said quietly, stepping closer to the fire. "I just didn't think you'd want me mentioning Vengeance Slaughterwood's cuff."

"Did you find it, then?" Apollo tried not to give too much of his excitement away. The cuff was an old story, a fairytale, the kind he'd never put too much faith in. But he'd learned recently that some of the old stories held far more truth—and more power—than he'd previously believed.

"No," Slaughterwood said bluntly. "If it exists, my family doesn't have it. But I did find something else that I thought might be of interest to you." He handed Apollo a heavy scroll bound up with a thin cord of leather. "Be very careful with this. And whatever you do, don't throw away the ashes."

9

Evangeline

Although Evangeline was forbidden from leaving the castle to visit Mr. Kristof Knightlinger, one of his scandal sheets was delivered with her breakfast tray the following morning.

It was not what Evangeline wanted. She still wanted to pay Mr. Knightlinger a personal visit and ask him to tell her everything he knew about her past.

She would have even settled for the gossip columnist coming to see her at Wolf Hall. However, as Mr. Knightlinger hadn't responded to the letter she'd written him yesterday, she curled up on the sofa to read his scandal sheet instead.

The Daily Rumor

MIDNIGHT EXiT

By Kristof Knightlinger

Yesterday Wolf Hall was abuzz with news that Garrick of the Greenwood, leader of the Guild of Heroes, had a private meeting with Prince Apollo. I of course was not surprised to hear that Apollo was meeting with the mysterious hero to find the dastardly Lord Jacks. What I did find surprising, however, was the news of Apollo's mysterious midnight exit hours later.

My keen sources said that the prince was seen riding from the castle at the stroke of midnight with only one of his trusted guards.

Where was he going?

As far as I know, he has yet to return, so one can only wonder. Has he decided to hunt for Lord Jacks himself? Or is there another mystery that would pull him away from Wolf Hall and his beloved Evangeline Fox?

Evangeline didn't *want* to be curious. She wanted to stay frustrated with Apollo—and she was. Her shoulder still hurt from where Garrick's bird had gouged her skin, and her heart ached whenever she thought about how the sweet Apollo from the rooftop was only who the prince was sometimes. And yet she also couldn't help but wonder where he'd gone.

As she dressed in a diaphanous peach gown dotted with little pink, white, and violet flowers, Evangeline asked Martine if she knew anything of the prince's departure. But like her, the maid had learned about it from the scandal sheet.

She'd have to ask her guards, then. Evangeline adjusted the

ribbons securing her gathered sleeves and braced herself for a potential battle before stepping toward the doors to her suite. They opened to the outer hallway, where two new guards in shining armor stood waiting.

"Hello, Your Highness." The guards greeted her instantly with deep bows and intense attention.

"I'm Hansel."

"And I'm Victor," said the other.

Evangeline imagined they must have been brothers—they had the same cleft chins, the same thick necks, and even the same red mustaches. She wondered briefly if having mustaches was a requirement for guards.

"What can we do for you?" Hansel said with a smile.

Evangeline briefly forgot why she had opened the door. Both guards were new, and so far they appeared to be *nice*.

Apollo had kept his word.

It was no doubt an easy thing for him to change a few guards. Apollo probably had thousands of guards at his disposal. And yet Evangeline felt her heart soften just a little.

"Can either of you tell me where Prince Apollo has gone?"

"We're sorry, Your Highness. His Highness didn't tell us where he was going," said Hansel.

"But we do have a message for you," said Victor. "Your tutor just stopped by and said to give you this." He handed Evangeline a scroll tied with wine-colored twine.

There wasn't a wax seal, and therefore the letter was not private. And just like that, her heart put up its guard once more.

She almost didn't read the note from the tutor—a proper prisoner wouldn't have been eager to obey any instructions. But she'd already undone the twine, so she read the message.

Your Highness,
I thought for today's lesson we might see a bit of the royal gardens. Shall we meet on the half hour before noon at the Well of Wishes?
I will of course try to be there on time, but if I'm late, don't hesitate to make a wish.

After signing the missive, the tutor had drawn a painstaking map of the Wolf Hall gardens. Then in handwriting so small that Evangeline nearly missed it, she'd written the words *Please come!*

Evangeline didn't know if it was the word *please* or the exclamation mark that struck her. Perhaps it was the combination of both that made her feel this request was perhaps a bit more than it appeared on the surface.

Tower bells rang in the eleventh hour right as Evangeline stepped outside the castle.

The sky was velvet gray and full of swirling clouds that

threatened more rain and told her to move quickly down the cobbled paths lined in hedges with pops of bright purple flowers.

There were four major gardens on the Wolf Hall grounds—the Sunken Garden, the Water Garden, the Flower Garden, and the Ancient Garden. Tucked away within each of these gardens were the four minor gardens—the Fairy Garden, the Moss Garden, the Secret Garden, and the Wishing Garden.

According to the tutor's carefully drawn map, the Wishing Garden with its Well of Wishes was situated in the center of the Flower Garden. It appeared to be a walled garden, surrounded by a moat and reachable by a bridge.

It should have been easy enough to find. The map was quite good, and the Flower Garden was manicured to perfection.

Yesterday's rain had left the castle grounds full of rich, damp colors so deep that Evangeline imagined that were she to touch any flowers, their petals would stain the tips of her gloves. It was lovely in a way she almost wished it wasn't. Evangeline didn't want to be ensorcelled by the beauty. It felt too close to being dazzled once more by Apollo.

But it was hard not to feel just a little bit enchanted. The silver fog swirled around the grounds like magic, adding misty sparkles to all the trees and shrubs. It was such a lovely fog that Evangeline didn't notice how dense it had become until she took a step and realized she could see nothing but the stone path a couple of feet directly before her. The fog was so thick she couldn't even make out where her guards were behind her.

She almost called out to see if they were still following. But then she thought better of it.

Evangeline didn't really want to be followed by guards and . . . a wild idea struck her.

Perhaps losing the guards was the tutor's plan. Maybe she wanted to see Evangeline alone. The woman was supposed to be an expert in all things Wolf Hall and royal, so she must have expected that the garden would be concealed by fog. Perhaps the tutor had arranged this to tell Evangeline something she did not wish others to hear.

It was perhaps too much to hope that this *something* would also help Evangeline find her memories, and yet she found herself quickening her steps.

"Princess, could you slow down?" called Hansel. Or maybe it was Victor. She couldn't distinguish who was yelling, only that they both were calling after her.

"We seem to have lost you!" one of them cried.

But Evangeline moved faster, stepping off the path so her boots wouldn't click and the guards wouldn't be able to easily follow her. The ground was damp and soft underfoot. Fallen petals clung to the edges of her cloak and to the tips of her boots.

Ding-dong!

In the distance, the tower clock chimed half past eleven.

Evangeline feared she was going to be late, but then she saw the bridge to the walled Wishing Garden. She quickly crossed it, leaving a trail of mud and flowers that would make it easy for the guards to find her once they got closer. But she'd hopefully get at least a few moments alone with Madame Voss.

The fog dissipated slightly at the end of the bridge, revealing a rounded door speckled with age. Evangeline had the impression it had once been a brilliant bronze, but that its color had faded over time, like a memory that would one day disappear altogether.

The door handle had a green patina that reminded her of a story she'd once read about a doorknob that could feel the hands of everyone who touched it and tell what sort of heart the person had. It was how the doorknob knew who to let inside.

Evangeline couldn't remember who the doorknob had been protecting, but she knew that someone with a wicked heart had tricked the doorknob by removing their own heart. She forgot what happened after that, but she didn't want to take the time to stop and remember. She needed to enter the garden before the guards caught up.

Fog swirled around her boots as she stepped inside. Unlike everything else on the royal grounds, this square of space was wild with rebellious flowers and drunken vines that curled around the garden's abundant trees and dangled from their branches like ribbons at a party. The path was entirely covered in bluish-green moss that stretched before her as if it were a carpet, leading to a little well that somehow remained untouched by all the overgrown plants.

It was white with an arch of stones that held a length of rope and a dangling golden bucket. Drops of rain began to fall again as Evangeline started toward it.

She looked around for her tutor. Her eyes darted about the trees and back to the strange door, but she didn't see or hear anyone. The garden was quiet, save for the growing drumming of the rain. What had started as a sprinkle was quickly turning into a storm.

Evangeline huddled under the hood of her cloak and willed her tutor to arrive. Then she remembered the end of the note.

I will of course try to be there on time, but if I'm late, don't hesitate to make a wish.

Evangeline's first thought was to wish that the tutor would get there soon. But that would be a silly thing to waste a wish on. She also wondered if perhaps the tutor was not being literal.

Maybe there was something on the well she wanted Evangeline to find. She took a closer look, in search of a clue. There appeared to be something carved into its bricks.

She could just make out the words *Instructions for Wishing,* but the other words were so faded she had to lean closer—

Hands pushed her from behind.

Evangeline screamed and tried to grasp the well. But the shove was forceful, and she was caught off guard.

She pitched forward like a stone and fell . . .

Evangeline

Evangeline had heard countless stories about girls falling through time and through cracks in the earth, and it always sounded magical. She pictured them like leaves, gentle and graceful and somewhat lovely as they drifted down, down, down.

Her fall was not like this. She plummeted hard. The air was knocked from her lungs as she hit the icy water and continued to sink. Her cloak and boots were like bricks, pulling her deeper and deeper.

Evangeline had never learned how to swim. She could tread water, but barely.

Frantically she undid her cloak—it was so much easier to kick this way. Her boots still weighed her down, but she feared drowning if she tried to untie them. It took all her effort just to break through the surface of the water. Thankfully, there was a piece of driftwood that she was able to use to stay afloat.

"Help!" she gasped. "I'm down here!"

From up above, she heard cawing birds, gusts of wind, and the relentless fall of rain against the well, but there wasn't so much as a footstep.

"Is anyone up there?"

In between cries, she fumbled with the ties of her dress. The wood was keeping her afloat, but barely.

It was a little easier to kick in just her chemise, but it was *so cold*, it was freezing. Her legs were losing strength, and without the kicking, she wasn't sure the wood would support her.

"I'm down here!" she yelled louder, but somehow her voice sounded weaker. "Help . . ."

It was getting harder to cry out. And it was so, so cold. Her kicks were growing weaker.

Evangeline should never have lost her guards. She probably shouldn't have gotten so close to the well, but she never thought someone would *push* her. Who would have done this?

She hadn't seen anyone, but she wondered blearily if her attacker had been one of the people that Apollo had warned her about.

She used what remained of her strength to kick toward the side of the well. She tried to grip a stone to climb out, but it was too slick and her fingers were numb. She fell back into the freezing water with a splash.

"Evangeline!" someone cried. The voice sounded male and unfamiliar. "Evangeline!"

"I'm . . . down . . . here . . ." she tried to call, but it came out like a whisper.

The stranger cursed.

Evangeline attempted to see up and out of the well. But she had fallen too far, and the walls were too high—all she could see was the golden bucket, lowering toward her.

"Grab it," commanded the voice. It was the sort of voice she would have obeyed even if her life hadn't depended on it. It wasn't kind, but it was full of power and sharp as an arrow's tip.

Evangeline wrapped her frozen hands around the bucket. It was more difficult than it should have been. Her fingers were so cold they could barely grip.

"Don't let go!" demanded the voice.

Evangeline shivered violently, but she obeyed. She closed her eyes as she held on to the bucket while the stranger worked the rope, lifting her from the water and up, up, up toward the top. Her wet chemise clung to her skin. Then there were arms—powerful, solid arms—wrapping around her waist.

"You can let go of the bucket now." He yanked her a little roughly, pulling her from the well.

Evangeline continued to shake, but her rescuer held on to her like a promise he intended to keep. His arms encircled her waist, keeping her close to his chest. She could feel his chest. *Pounding. Pounding. Pounding.*

She felt a strange, possibly delirious need to reassure him. "I'm fine."

He laughed, the sound a little raspy, broken. "If this is fine, I'd hate to see your definition of half dead."

"I'm just cold." She shivered against him as she craned her neck to see his face. Wet hair covered her eyes and rain obscured her vision. But when she finally glimpsed her rescuer, the world was suddenly brighter.

He was beautiful. Inhuman. A warrior angel with blue eyes and golden hair and a face that made Evangeline think that writing poetry should be her new hobby. He almost appeared to be glowing. It made her wonder if he was right, if maybe she really was half dead and he was the angel taking her to heaven.

"I'm not taking you to heaven," he muttered as he hauled her farther away from the well. His heart was still pounding against her.

Then her world was spinning. The rain whipped around her like a cyclone, blurring the garden and her golden angel until she was somewhere else—she was inside a memory that looked like a soft candlelit corridor.

He held her so tightly it hurt, but this pain she didn't mind. She'd let him crush her, let him break her, just as long as he never let her go. This was what she wanted, and she refused to believe that he didn't want it, too.

She could feel his heart pound against her chest as he carried her into the room next door to hers. It was a mess. There were apples and

cores all over the desk. The sheets on the bed were thrashed. The fire
was burning more than just logs.

The memory was so real Evangeline almost felt warm from
the fire.

Until, just as suddenly as she was plunged into the memory,
she was taken out of it by the feeling of hard wet ground beneath her, followed by the gruff sound of voices.

"What happened?"

"Who did this?"

The rain-drenched faces of two unfamiliar guards hovered
over her. Water dripped from their mustaches to the ground.

She looked past them for signs of the golden-haired angel
who had pulled her from the well, but there was no one else there.

All the blankets and the fires in Wolf Hall couldn't ward off
Evangeline's chills. The cold had seeped into her bones and her
veins.

After Evangeline had been carried into her room, her maids
quickly helped her out of her soaking slip. There was some de-
bate after that as to if they should put her in a hot bath, but
Evangeline had feared just the thought of being submerged in
more water. She'd opted for a soft robe and the bed.

But now, as she lay there shivering, she wondered if that was
a mistake.

"A doctor will be here soon," said Martine. "And Apollo's
been called back to the castle."

Evangeline burrowed deeper into the covers. She almost said she didn't want to see Apollo, but she wasn't sure if that was true. It seemed he really had been right about the danger she was in here.

At first she hadn't told anyone she'd been pushed into the wall. She'd lied and said she'd fallen. The lie had made her feel incredibly foolish. She had seen the faces of the guards on patrol who'd rescued her, twisting with looks that made it appear they were both thinking, *What kind of idiot falls into a well?*

The kind who doesn't want to give her husband another excuse to take away more of her freedom, Evangeline had thought, while out loud she'd tried to continue the charade through chattering teeth.

Not that it mattered. As the guards insisted on carrying her back to the castle, she realized that they hadn't actually believed her story about falling anyway. There were too many questions about whether she'd seen anyone. Did she still have the letter from the tutor? And did she know where her own personal guards, Victor and Hansel, had gone?

Evangeline felt silly as she realized how trusting she'd been. Although maybe the problem hadn't been that she was trusting, but that she'd trusted the wrong people. She should have believed Apollo when he had warned her that she was in danger.

Dr. Stillgrass paid her a visit and prescribed her hot tea and blankets. But when she sipped the tea, it tasted ... strange. She imagined it had some sort of sedative in it and dumped it in a potted plant as soon as she was alone again.

She didn't want to be sedated. She already felt exhausted. But once Evangeline was all alone, she found it impossible to sleep.

Every sound made her jump. Each crackle of the fire and creak of the floor left her feeling tightly coiled, like a jester in a box just waiting to explode. When she closed her eyes, she swore she could hear her heartbeat pounding.

A gust of cold swept through the room and she burrowed deeper into the blankets.

Perhaps she shouldn't have sent the maids away.

The floor creaked again. She tried to ignore it.

Then instead of a creak she heard footsteps, loud and confident. Evangeline finally opened her eyes.

Apollo stood next to her bed. His velvet cloak was damp, his dark hair was windswept, his cheeks were ruddy, and his brown eyes were glassy with concern. "I know you probably don't want to see me right now, but I had to make sure you're all right."

He looked as if he wanted to reach for her. But then he raked a hand through his hair instead.

Evangeline sat up carefully in the bed. Her fingers clung to the edge of the quilt. And she found she wanted to reach for him, too. She wanted a hug, she wanted to be held, and she knew if she asked, Apollo would do both.

She reminded herself why she couldn't. But her reasoning felt thin. It was hard to be angry at Apollo when it seemed the protection he'd said she needed was necessary.

Tentatively she reached out her hand, touching the tips of

his fingers. They were cold, not quite like ice, but near enough that he must have come straight to her from his travels. She'd refused to trust him yesterday, but that hadn't stopped him from coming to her when she needed him. "I'm glad you came."

"I'll always come. Even when you don't want me to." He took a step closer to the bed and slid his fingers through hers. He was shaking a little, just like he had been the morning he'd found her after her memories had been taken.

She looked up and smiled reassuringly. But instead of seeing Apollo, she pictured the warrior angel from the well, the beautiful golden-haired guard with the arms that held her like bands of steel. It was only a flash—but her cheeks felt flushed.

Apollo smiled, clearly thinking he was the reason. "Does this mean I'm forgiven for yesterday?"

Evangeline nodded. And in her daze, she must have said something, for he grinned wider and replied, "I'll always protect you, Evangeline. I meant what I said when I first returned from the dead—I'm never going to let you go."

11

Jacks

Jacks had always considered himself more of a sadist than a masochist. He enjoyed inflicting pain, not receiving it. And yet he couldn't bring himself to leave the shadows of Evangeline's bedroom.

It wasn't an obsession.

One visit wasn't an obsession.

Jacks just needed to make sure she was still alive. That she wasn't bleeding. In danger. Unhappy. Cold. She was safe in her bed. She'd be even safer when he left her. But he was too selfish to leave just yet.

He leaned against the bedpost and watched as she slept. He'd never understood why someone would watch another person sleep ... *until her.*

Castor did it. He said it was how he helped manage his urges.

It did the opposite for Jacks.

The dying fire smoldered in the hearth. He considered setting the room ablaze just so that he'd have a reason to pick her up and carry her out, to save her one last time, before he left her for good.

Of course it wouldn't really be saving her if he was the one who put her in danger by starting a fire.

"Wake up, Princess." Jacks tossed a leather vest at her sleeping form.

Evangeline squinted and rubbed her tired eyes as she pulled the garment away. She hadn't clearly seen him yet. But in the past, she wouldn't have had to see him. She would have known his voice or sensed his presence even before he spoke, and he'd have seen her body react. Her cheeks would have gone red or she might have shivered and then pretended that there was a draft. That it wasn't him.

She was better off not knowing him. But he was enough of a bastard to hate that she'd forgotten.

Even if it was his fault she'd lost her memories.

This is not a small mistake to fix. If you do this, Time will take someone else equally valuable from you, Honora had said.

Jacks had thought Time would take something from him. He hadn't thought it would take it from her.

Evangeline's lost memories seemed like an inconsequential price to pay when compared to her *life*. But even though she was alive again, Jacks would never forget seeing her die, feeling her go lifeless in his arms. It made him realize how fragile she really was. He thought she'd be safer in the castle with Apollo—and she would be, once Jacks got what he needed. Then he could leave her for good.

"Can you move any faster?" he drawled, tossing another garment. "I don't really feel like waiting all day."

She pulled away the shirt he'd just thrown and attempted a scowl as she mumbled, "It's still dark outside."

"Exactly." Jacks threw the last of the clothes at her.

"Will you stop that!"

"Will you finally get dressed?"

She shoved all the clothes from her face. He watched her bemused expression as her eyes fought to adjust. She still looked half asleep. Her eyes were bleary and tired. And he still couldn't tear his gaze away from her.

From that first day in his church, Jacks had wanted to watch her. He wanted to know what her voice sounded like, what her skin felt like. He'd followed her, listened to her prayer—hated her prayer. It had been one of the most god-awful prayers he'd ever heard. And yet even then he hadn't been able to walk away. He wanted a piece of her. To keep her. To use her for later.

At least that's what he'd told himself.

She was only a key.

A human.

She wasn't an obsession.

She wasn't his.

He brought a black apple to his mouth and took a wide, sharp bite.

Crunch.

Evangeline jolted at the sound and gripped the edge of her sheets.

"I didn't know you were afraid of apples."

"I'm not afraid of apples. That's ridiculous."

But she was lying. He could see the pulse jump in her neck. He'd frightened her, which was good. She *should* be scared of him.

But it seemed Evangeline still didn't have a sense of self-preservation. She had fully woken up now, but she didn't call for her guards or take up a defensive posture. Instead, her eyes went wide. And for a second it was painfully clear just how much she had forgotten, because she looked at him as if he could do no wrong.

"It's you," she breathed. "You saved my life."

"If you want to thank me, hurry up and get dressed."

She flinched a little at the bite in his voice. He knew he was being a bastard again, but by the end of this, it would hurt her more if he was kind.

"Why are you here?" she asked.

"You need to learn how to defend yourself against the next person who tries to kill you," he said brusquely.

She eyed him skeptically. "You're an instructor?"

He shoved away from the bedpost before she could look too closely at him. "I'll give you five minutes. Then dressed or not, we start."

"Wait!" Evangeline called. "What's your name?"

You already know, Little Fox.

But once again, his thoughts weren't projected loudly enough for her to hear.

Instead, he gave her the name he'd planned on. He knew she wouldn't remember it, and he needed to make sure he didn't forget it. "You can call me Archer."

12

Evangeline

Evangeline found Archer in the hall, leaning against the stone wall, arms crossed firmly over his chest, as if waiting was not a thing he was comfortable with. His jaw tightened as she stepped out of the room.

Something inside her tightened as well, right around her chest. The sensation was knifelike, biting, and uncomfortable. It felt even sharper as his eyes raked over her, darkening as he took her in.

She'd put on the clothes he'd given her. Although if she'd been more awake, she wouldn't have. The full white skirt was actually the most practical of the items, as the other bits weren't practical at all. The pale pink blouse was too sheer, the leather vest was too tight, and it felt even tighter as Archer's eyes lingered on it.

She wondered then if following this guard was a good idea.

Just standing near him made her feel as if she'd already made a bad decision.

He'd saved her life, yes. But he didn't seem much like a savior anymore. There was an almost inhuman sharpness to him, one that made her imagine she might slice her finger were she to accidentally graze his jaw.

His clothes looked a little too careless for a royal guard. He wore tall scuffed boots, fitted leather pants that hung low on his hips, and two belted straps securing a number of knives. His shirt was loose and undone at the throat with sleeves shoved up past his elbows, revealing lean, strong arms. She could still remember the powerful way they'd wrapped tightly around her, how good it had felt to have him hold her. And for a prickling second, she was jealous of anyone else he might ever hold.

This was definitely not a good idea.

And—where were her other guards?

"There was a threat," Archer said upon noticing the shift of Evangeline's eyes as they darted up and down the low-lit hall. "They went to investigate."

"What kind of threat?" she asked.

Archer shrugged a shoulder. "It sounded like a screeching cat to me, but your guards seemed to feel differently." One corner of his mouth slowly tugged up into an almost smile. In that second, his entire face changed. He'd been handsome before, but now there something almost uncomfortable about how beautiful he was.

But Evangeline didn't want to think him beautiful at all. She had a feeling he was making fun of her, or that his smile was part of a private joke that she was not privy to.

She scowled.

This only made him grin wider. Which was worse. He had dimples. Unfair dimples. Dimples were supposed to be sweet, but she sensed this guard was anything except for that.

Evangeline asked herself one last time if it was wise to go with him. But then she decided not to answer the question. Because the truth was, she wanted to go with him. Maybe she was still delirious from her fall down the well or from lack of sleep, or maybe something besides her heart had been broken during the time she couldn't remember.

"Have we met before?" she asked. "Do I know you?"

"No. I don't usually play with things that easily break." He uncrossed his arms and shoved off the wall.

Archer moved through the castle like a thief, his steps elegant and quick as he darted through halls and rounded corners. It was difficult to keep up in the ridiculously full skirt he'd tossed at her.

"Hurry it up, Princess."

"Where are we going?" she asked when she finally caught up with him at the bottom of a set of stairs.

She was slightly winded, while he looked almost bored as he lazily opened a door that led outside.

Evangeline hugged her arms to her chest as a burst of frigid air blew past her. "It's freezing out there."

Archer smirked. "You don't get to choose the weather when someone attacks you."

"Is that why you gave me such impractical clothes?"

His only answer was another frustrating smirk before he started down the path into the dark.

The air was even colder when Evangeline stepped outside after him. It must have been an hour shy of sunrise. The night was as black as a well of ink, save for the intermittent lampposts that lined the garden path, revealing large pools of water on either side.

He'd taken her to the Water Garden.

She could hear the bubbling fountains and tumbling water-falls in the distance. In the day she imagined it was rather whimsical, but right now, during the darkest, coldest part of the night, all she could think about was how it would feel if she fell into those waters. She doubted any of them were as deep as the well she'd almost died in the day before. Yet for a second, she couldn't move.

"Come on, Princess," called Archer.

But he was too far ahead for her to see him. Evangeline felt nervous once again, remembering what had happened the last time she'd lost a guard.

All she could hear now was the quick sound of steps.

After an anxious second, she followed the sound. It led her

to a rickety suspension bridge. It was the sort she would have loved as child, made of old wood and rope and probably more than a dash of recklessness, as it felt wildly unstable. If she'd had a coin her pocket, she would have tossed it in the rushing river below and said a quiet prayer for safe passage.

She could hear the water smash against the rocks. But she couldn't hear Archer's steps.

"Archer?" she called.

No one answered.

Had he lost her on purpose? She didn't want to believe that. She had known following him was a bad idea, and yet deep down, she'd hoped it was a good one.

But maybe it was time to head back to the castle.

The bridge wobbled beneath her as she turned around. Then cold arms suddenly wrapped around her, pinning her arms to her sides.

"Don't scream," Archer whispered into her ear, "or I'll toss you off this bridge."

"You wouldn't dare," she gasped.

"You want to test me, Princess? Because I would dare to do even more."

He easily dragged her toward the side of the bridge and bent her forward over the meager rope railing until her hair was dangling above the water rushing below. Evangeline had a feeling that even if she didn't scream, he still might throw her over just to watch her fall.

"Are you mad?" She wriggled against him.

He laughed under his breath. "You'll have to do better than that."

"I thought you were supposed to teach me what to do!"

"I want to see if you know anything first." He leaned over her back until his mouth was right at her ear. She thought she felt his teeth, nipping her as he spoke.

Her heartbeat pounded faster. Clearly he was mad after all.

She tried to butt his head with hers.

He quickly pulled back. "Easy to dodge."

She stomped, aiming for his foot, but all that did was rock the rickety bridge.

"I'm starting to feel as if you don't want to escape." He definitely nipped her ear this time, teeth sharp as they scraped her skin. She wondered if he liked to hurt everyone, or if it was just her. Something about this was starting to feel personal. Although the nip of teeth at her ear didn't hurt so much as it unsettled her.

"Do you want me to toss you over the edge?" he taunted.

"Of course not!" she yelled.

"Then why aren't you fighting?" He sounded angry.

"I'm trying my best."

"And I'm not, which means you need to try harder. Kick me."

Evangeline gritted her teeth and kicked backward. She aimed between his legs, but only managed to ruffle the back of her ridiculous skirt.

"Good job, Princess."

"Are you mocking me?"

"Not this time. You made me adjust my stance. Any kick like that and most assailants will bring their legs closer together. This allows you to change your position. Step out with your right leg," he commanded. "Then move your left leg so that it's behind me."

"What will that do?"

"Just do it. I'm not letting you go until you've earned it." Archer tightened his cold arms as a raindrop fell, followed by another and another. Within seconds her thin shirt was soaked. So was his. She could feel it clinging to her back in the places that her vest didn't cover as he continued to tighten his grip until it almost hurt.

Evangeline finally did as he had told her. She stepped to the right with one leg, then moved the other behind him. He was right. It shifted her position, but it seemed only to further entwine them.

"Now grab me," he ordered.

"My arms are pinned!"

"But your hands are free."

They were, but she still felt hesitant to grab him.

"Do it," he repeated, "then use your hip to leverage my weight and flip me over."

Archer held her tighter. He banded one arm firmly around her ribs, the other he circled just below her waist, almost on her hips, his fingers splayed in a way that felt less like he wanted to restrain her and more like he just wanted to touch her—to hold her on that bridge in the dark where it was only the two of them and the rain and the feel of too many heartbeats racing between them.

Finally she grabbed his legs. Everything was wet and slick. Her fingers slipped against his leathers as the bridge rocked.

She lost her footing. The slat that had been beneath her was gone.

"No—" Evangeline cried.

Archer moved ridiculously fast. He shielded her, turning her body as they fell. When they landed just shy of the broken slat, it was his back that hit the bridge with a loud crack.

She heard him grunt, as if the air was knocked from his lungs, but he didn't let her go. If anything, he held her tighter.

She could feel his ragged breathing against her neck as they lay there on that broken bridge. Her shirt had ridden up in the fight, and his fingers were now on her bare stomach.

The rain pounded harder. Every single inch of her skin was soaked. But all she felt were his fingertips as they slowly traveled lower toward the band of her skirt.

"This is where you break free," he said softly.

"I don't want to," she said, but the words came out wrong, breathless. And despite all the cold and the damp, she could feel herself go hot from her cheeks all the way down to the bare skin beneath Archer's hands. "I mean, I just need to catch my breath."

He made a scolding sound with his tongue. "You don't get to catch your breath. If you stop fighting, you lose." He moved one icy hand up to her throat and she felt the sharp tip of a knife against her neck.

Evangeline went very still, or she tried to. It was surprisingly hard not to move with a blade to her throat and a hand intimately wrapped around her stomach. "Are you insane?"

"Undoubtedly." He slowly moved the dagger, drawing a careful line over her pulse. He didn't pierce her skin, but the effect was still dizzying.

"*Never* imagine you're safe," he scolded. His knife traced a line from the hollow of her throat to the center of her chest all the way down to the laces of her vest.

Her breathing hitched. The tip of the blade hovered just beneath the laces. All it would take was one little flick and they would be undone.

No.

She wasn't sure if he thought the word or if she did. It almost sounded like his voice in her head.

Then in one impossible move, Archer hauled her to her feet and released her just as quickly.

She staggered back on quivering legs.

Across from her, Archer was soaked. Water dripped from his golden hair to his pale cheeks, but he didn't even shiver. He just stood there, gripping the knife he'd just held to her throat. His knuckles were white, but that might have just been the cold. "We'll try again later."

"What if I don't want to try later?" she panted.

He smirked, an expression that said it was cute that she

thought she had a choice. "If that's what you want, then you'll need to do a better job of fighting me off when I come into your bedroom. Until then you carry this. *Everywhere.*"

Archer tossed her his dagger.

It flipped, handle over tip. Jewels sparkled in the light, and suddenly Evangeline saw an image of this knife. But it wasn't in the air, it was on a dark floor. And this wasn't just a picture, it was a memory.

Many of the gems were missing, but the knife's hilt still glittered in the torchlight, pulsing blue and purple, the color of blood before it was spilled.

The memory was quick.

As it faded, she looked at the knife in her hand. It was definitely the same blade. It had the same blue and purple gems, down to the ones that were missing.

She didn't know if it had always been his, or if it had once been hers, but one thing she was certain of was that Archer had lied about knowing her.

She wanted to ask him why, and she wanted to ask him about the knife.

But once again, he was suddenly gone.

13

Apollo

Apollo stood in front of the fire of his private study, hands clasped behind him, chin tilted up, eyes down. It was a pose he'd frequently struck for portraits, like the one that currently hung above the fireplace mantel. Of course, he had been younger in that portrait. It had been painted before he'd met Evangeline, before he'd died and seen himself replaced within a week by an impostor. And an unimpressive one at that.

Apollo knew he was still young. He'd lived only twenty years—and they'd been twenty peaceful years, which made it rather hard to live a life that inspired bards and minstrels. He liked to think that had he lived a little longer before his supposed death, his legacy wouldn't have been so quickly discarded.

Yet Apollo was still disappointed in himself that he'd squandered so much time.

Coming back from the dead had given him an edge in building a legacy that would not be so easily forgotten. But he knew that this alone wasn't enough to forge the future that he wanted, to ensure that no one would curse him again or use him in any other way to harm Evangeline.

He had to do more.

Apollo unrolled the scroll that Lord Slaughterwood had given him two days ago. Just as before, it began to catch fire, not enough to burn him, but enough to destroy the page and render it into ashes. It started with the words at the bottom of the scroll; they always caught fire before he could read them. But he'd read enough of the story. He knew exactly what he had to do.

But first Apollo had to make sure Evangeline was safe.

The knock on the door came precisely on time.

Apollo took a deep breath, bracing himself for what he feared he would have to do next.

"You may enter," he said, turning down his mouth as the door to his study opened and Havelock stepped inside.

The guard immediately noticed the burning page in Apollo's hand and the ashes on the ground. "Have I interrupted something?"

"Nothing important." Apollo dropped the smoldering page on the floor. Like all stories in the North, it was infected with the story curse. This particular story set fire to itself every time it was opened.

The page would burn until it was just a pile of ash. Then it would re-form—much like what Apollo was doing with his life and Evangeline's.

"What news do you have about the attack on Princess Evangeline?" Apollo asked.

The guard bowed and took a beleaguered breath. "The princess's tutor continues to maintain that she's innocent. Madame Voss swears she never sent the princess a letter to lure her out to the well. She claims the guards are lying."

Apollo ran a hand through his hair. "What are Victor and Hansel saying?"

"They stand by their story. They say there was a letter from the tutor and they lost Evangeline in the fog when she tried to meet her. They swear that they aren't part of any plot."

Apollo grimaced. "Do you think they're telling the truth?"

"They seemed sincere, Your Highness. But it's difficult to tell. The tutor seemed sincere as well."

Apollo sighed and looked down at the floor where the page was almost done burning.

"Victor, Hansel, and the tutor are probably all working together," Apollo said.

He wanted to take the words back as soon as he'd spoken them.

But it was too late now. It had been too late ever since he'd told Victor and Hansel to give Evangeline the falsified note from the tutor, to pretend to lose her in the gardens, and then to push her in the well. But Evangeline had given him no choice.

She'd refused to believe that she was in danger. He had to show her that she was wrong.

He hadn't meant for the lesson to be quite so traumatic. He'd expected the guards on garden patrol to find her sooner. That had been a mistake, but he hadn't wanted to involve more people than necessary in his plan.

"Continue to torture the tutor—I feel as if there's a chance she could crack. Especially if you tell her that you've killed Victor and Hansel."

Havelock paled.

Apollo clapped him on the shoulder, and once again, he was tempted to change course. To tell Havelock just to leave Victor and Hansel in prison. He hated to lose these particular soldiers. They'd proven themselves quite admirably. But he couldn't be sure how long their loyalty would last. And the last thing he needed was whispers getting out that he had been the one to orchestrate the latest attempt on Evangeline's life. "I know Victor and Hansel were your friends, but they betrayed Evangeline. We need to do this as an example."

Havelock nodded bleakly. "I'll make sure it's done tonight."

Apollo felt a pang of something like guilt. He hated to do it, and he hated that things had come to this, that Evangeline's lack of trust in him had forced him to take such drastic action. But he was doing the right thing.

He was protecting his wife from everyone, including herself.

14

Evangeline

Archer was not an angel or a savior. He was unhinged, possibly unsafe, and yet, he felt like Evangeline's greatest hope for getting her memories back.

Once more Evangeline looked at the dagger Archer had given her. What she remembered of it didn't give her much to go on, so perhaps it was more like a bread crumb than a proper piece of a memory, but every lover of fairytales knew that bread-crumb trails were always worth following.

And Evangeline planned to follow this one wherever it led.

One memory could be shaken off as a coincidence.

But she'd seen Archer twice, and twice he'd brought back vivid memories, and along with them her hope.

After waking before dawn and spending the darkest hours struggling in the rain against Archer, Evangeline should have crawled back in bed, exhausted.

Instead, she was exhilarated. It felt as if she'd found a bit of her old self. And it was one of her favorite pieces. It was the part of herself that loved to hope. She'd forgotten how hope could make colors brighter and feelings warmer, how it could shift thoughts from what *wasn't* to what *was* possible.

Her memories were not gone forever, they were merely lost, and Evangeline now had every hope that she would find them.

Since Archer had already prompted two memories, it made sense to hope that when she saw him again, he'd bring about more. And if he didn't, she was at least going to get him to tell her how they knew each other.

But this time she wasn't going to wait for him to find her.

Evangeline planned to ask for a tour of Wolf Hall—one that included the quarters where the guards and soldiers lived. She knew that Archer had said they'd have another lesson later, but she didn't want to wait until whenever *later* happened. She wanted to find him again today.

"Pardon me, Your Highness," squeaked Martine. "Before you leave, you might want to take a look at this. It arrived as you spoke with the physician's apprentice." The maid handed Evangeline a cream-colored note with Apollo's seal in the wax, which Evangeline swiftly broke before reading the letter.

My sweet Evangeline,

I'm sorry that my many royal duties are keeping me from you today. Would you do me the honor of meeting me for dinner one hour past sunset in the Court of Columns?

I look forward to seeing you then, and to introducing you to a few special guests as well.

With all my love,
Apollo

"We should start getting you ready straightaway!" exclaimed Martine, not even attempting to hide that she'd been reading over Evangeline's shoulder.

"Do I really need to start dressing for dinner right now?" It was just shy of noon, which should have given her at least a few hours to search for Archer. "It's just a dinner."

"Nothing is just a dinner if it's in a castle," said Martine. "When a prince says dinner, he really means *banquet*. Everyone will be there. Every courtier, every noble, every Great House, every guard—"

"Every guard?" Evangeline asked, her thoughts immediately going to Archer.

If he was at the dinner, she wouldn't have to look for him now. And if this dinner was as large a gathering as Martine made it sound, then surely it should be easy to sneak away for a private chat.

15

Apollo

Apollo should have chosen a different location for dinner.

The Court of Columns was one of Wolf Hall's more impressive rooms, with a three-story domed glass ceiling that provided an excellent view of the stars. Eight enormous columns formed a circle in the center of the room. The columns were carved in the likenesses of the Forgotten Saints. Apollo thought they were far more spectacular than the carvings of the Valors that sat in the bay, as these statues still had their heads. They were also carved of rare starstone, which glowed at night, adding an otherworldly quality to the court that he hoped would delight Evangeline.

But now he regretted the choice.

He should have thought more defensively.

The columns were impressive, but they also obstructed his view of the entire court and the doors leading out. Guards were there, of course, to look for any hint of Jacks. But by the end of the night, half the guards would be as drunk as the guests. It was how these things always went.

Apollo was never too strict with his guards during festive dinners. The greatest danger at these things was usually that the toasts went on too long, and letting the guards imbibe was an easy way to keep them loyal. Apollo didn't want to risk losing any of that loyalty now—especially since he'd had to lose Victor and Hansel. He'd just have to keep Evangeline close to him all night.

He felt it as soon as she stepped into the court. A buzzing across his skin, pleasant and uncomfortable all at once, like the pull he felt toward her. It was a leftover effect from the Archer's curse. Although when he'd been under the curse, it had been much stronger—like a fire burning his skin that he felt only she could put out.

He turned to find her as she entered the room, and everything else went out of focus.

The tables of food, all the guests in their finery, the columns, and the great candles that surrounded them became hazy for a moment, like a watercolor painting blurred by the rain.

In the midst of it all, Evangeline sparkled, graceful and innocent and beautiful.

Once the party returned to focus, Apollo could see every other eye had turned to her as well. He couldn't look too long at the way other guests watched her. Some were merely curious, but certain gazes put him on guard, and a few made him want to slit throats.

He tried not to get too angry—she was the most beautiful woman in the room. He couldn't blame others for looking at her that way.

But he wanted to make it clear that she belonged to him.

Evangeline didn't see him as he approached. She moved quietly through the room, eyes wide with wonder as she looked up toward the glowing columns.

Her hair had been swept up and her dress was low-cut, with thin little straps that Apollo imagined he could break with a snap of his fingers. Maybe if he played this right, she'd let him do so later that night.

Quietly he stepped behind her.

"You look beautiful," he whispered. Then because she was his, and because he could, he pressed a soft, lingering kiss to the back of her neck.

He felt her skin go warm against his lips. But then she stiffened.

He hoped he hadn't triggered a memory.

Slowly he put a hand on the small of her back and came to stand beside her. "I hope I didn't frighten you."

"Not at all," she said. But her voice was strangely high. "I just didn't expect to see so many people here." Her eyes darted around the room.

Apollo couldn't quite tell if she was merely nervous or if

she was searching for someone. The latter shouldn't have been possible, since she didn't remember anyone . . . or she wasn't supposed to.

In the distance, the minstrel began singing. His lyrics spoke of Apollo the Great and Jacks the Dreaded Soon to Be Deaded. "He's a monster among men, a walking deadly sin. He'll slaughter your children, steal your wife, let him too close and he'll ruin your life."

People nearby swayed to the sound of the tune, but Evangeline looked visibly uncomfortable. She had stopped searching the room with her eyes, and now Apollo wondered if she *was* just nervous about all the people.

He'd never thought his bride was shy, but he remembered she'd been anxious the day of their wedding.

"I wish tonight could have been more intimate, but the court all wanted to be here, and it's important they know that we're happy and well." He removed his hand from the small of her back and laced his fingers with hers. "Don't worry, just stay close to me tonight."

He kept her at his side as they began greeting the guests one by one.

Apollo always hated this part. But Evangeline seemed to warm up as people greeted her with smiles and hugs, complimenting her on everything from the sound of her voice to the brightness of her cheeks and the rose-gold curls of her hair.

He wished the conversations were a little more inspired, but he supposed it could have been worse. It was during one of the conversations about her hair that Apollo stole away for just a minute to procure a goblet of wine. These things were much better with a drink in hand, although it seemed he'd picked the wrong moment to step away.

When he returned to his blushing bride, Evangeline was laughing at something Lord Byron Belleflower had said. Belleflower issued another quip and she laughed again, her smile wider than any Apollo had seen all night.

Bastard.

In the council meeting, Belleflower had practically called for her head. Now he was trying to charm her.

"It seems I can't turn my back for a second," said Apollo as he smoothly stole Evangeline's hand and pulled her closer to his side.

"No need to feel threatened, Your Highness. I have no wish to steal away your wife. I was merely telling her some stories about the two of us as boys. I thought she could use some entertainment after the week she's had." Belleflower put a hand to his heart as he turned back to Evangeline. "I also wanted to say, I heard about your fall yesterday, Your Highness. I'm so glad you were found in time and that the guards responsible for endangering your life have been put down like the dogs they are."

"Put . . . down?" Evangeline repeated. All the laughter vanished from her face as her gentle eyes went wide with alarm.

Apollo could have killed Belleflower then.

"I thought my guards were merely wanted for questioning?" she asked, turning to him.

"There's no need to fret, my sweet," replied Apollo with what he hoped was a reassuring smile. "I think our friend Lord Belleflower has been receiving his news from the scandal sheets. The only thing that has been put down tonight is the beast we're having for dinner. Now, if you'll excuse us."

He pulled Evangeline closer as he steered her away from the scheming Lord Belleflower.

But it seemed the damage was already done. The glimmer of light he'd seen before had left her eyes, and her fingers now felt cold in his.

Quickly Apollo stopped a servant passing out silver goblets of wine.

"Here, darling." He grabbed a chalice and handed it to Evangeline. "I think it's time we have a toast, don't you?

"Friends!" Apollo called out loudly, drawing everyone's attention. "I fear that my court has forgotten how to celebrate. Much of what I've heard tonight are bland compliments and uninspired rumors. So let us lift our glasses to the glory of coming back from the dead and the magic of true love!"

16

Evangeline

It was the sort of dinner party Evangeline had pictured when her mother had told her fairytales as a child—a beautiful ballroom full of charming people wearing dazzling things. And she was one of those people now. Dressed in a sparkling gown, on the arm of a prince—or she had been, until he'd raised his goblet to make a toast.

Apollo kept his wine high above his head as people gathered round and raised their goblets as well.

Evangeline did the same, although she didn't feel much like drinking after hearing that Hansel and Victor were dead. They had seemed so kind, and it was still difficult to believe that they could have had anything to do with the attempt on her life.

But that was one of the problems with having missing gaps of memory—it made so many things difficult to believe.

She tried to covertly look around the gathering of courtiers and guards in search of Archer. Earlier, she swore Apollo had caught her looking and had seemed to become a little upset, almost jealous.

Now he was occupied with his toasting, which gave her another chance to glance around the room. It was much like when she'd first entered—all glowing columns and elaborately dressed guests.

She didn't glimpse anyone who looked like Archer as Apollo cried, "May all those in this room who seek true love find it, and may those who stand in its way be cursed!"

The crowd all clinked their goblets and cheered with Apollo. "To love and to curses!"

Evangeline lifted her goblet to her lips. But she couldn't bring herself to drink. She understood toasting to love, but not to *curses*. It was disturbing that no one else seemed to feel the same way. The heady scent of wine filled the court as the party-goers drained their goblets and stained their lips.

And for just a second, Evangeline had a fleeting thought that if this was happily ever after, she was no longer sure she wanted it.

"You're smart not to drink to a toast like that," chimed a musical voice.

Evangeline turned slightly away from Apollo to find the source.

If she had thought her world to be strange moments ago, it was about to become even more peculiar.

The girl who came up beside her truly looked like a fairy princess from a fairytale, the sort in which people toasted to things like honor and valor instead of careless curses. She had a heart-shaped face, bright bottle-green eyes, and hair the shimmery color of violets.

With locks the color of rose gold, Evangeline was used to being the only girl in the room with unusual hair. She half expected to feel a small bolt of jealousy—but when this girl smiled, it was so incredibly sweet, Evangeline felt a sort of kinship instead.

"Did you know," mused the violet-haired girl, "there's an old Northern story that says you don't need magical spells to enact a curse? It was believed that when the North first came into being, it was so full of magic that sometimes the word *curse* was enough to enact one—as long as the people who heard it believed what was being said."

"Is that what you believe happened tonight?" asked Evangeline.

The girl sipped her goblet with a catlike smile. "I believe that magic fortunately died long ago. But I also believe anything is possible." She winked. "I'm Aurora Vale, by the way, and it's a pleasure to meet you, Your Highness."

The girl dropped into a perfect curtsy and whispered, "Now you get to meet my parents."

The air changed as two more people approached. Moments ago, everything had been cheers, clinking glass, and the tart scent of plum wine. But now, as Aurora's mother and father approached, it all went strangely quiet. Glasses stopped clinking, footfalls ceased, people paused conversations to look at the pair curiously.

Evangeline felt curious as well. As with their daughter, this couple made Evangeline think of another era where blood was spilled more often than wine, and even the softest of people had to be hard in order to survive.

Aurora's mother moved unlike everyone else. Instead of doing her best to shimmer and shine and show off her gems—which wouldn't even have been possible, as she wore no gems—the woman glided through the crowd like an arrow through the night, graceful and sure. She gave Evangeline the impression that she was used to walking through battlefields instead of ballrooms.

Aurora's father appeared as rugged as his daughter was beautiful. His shoulders were broad, his beard was full, and the scar that ran down the right side of his face looked so brutal, Evangeline wasn't sure how he'd survived the cut that produced it.

She watched as the man clapped Apollo on the shoulder with one bearlike hand. "Thank you for inviting us, Your Highness."

"Of course," said Apollo. His grin was wide, but it also looked somewhat tight around the corners, as if he, too, sensed the power of this couple and it made him nervous. "Evangeline, let me introduce you to Lord and Lady Vale and their daughter, Aurora, whom it seems you've already met."

"It's a pleasure," said Evangeline.

"The pleasure is all ours," said Lady Vale, who immediately wrapped Evangeline in a hug. She was a fraction of her husband's size, but her hug was unexpectedly ferocious and quite warm. "I've heard such wonderful things about you from your beloved prince, I almost feel as if I know you."

It might have been a trick of the room's shimmering candlelight, but it looked as if Lady Vale's eyes filled with tears as she pulled away.

Evangeline wanted to ask if she was all right.

But then Apollo, who still looked a little uncomfortable around the family, spoke up before she could. "The Vales have come to Valorfell from the far reaches of the North," he said. "They're bravely taking on the immense task of rebuilding the Merrywood."

I know that name, Evangeline almost said. But she didn't know it, not really. It had just sounded familiar. Maybe she had heard it mentioned earlier that night. Or perhaps she was remembering. . . .

"What's the Merrywood?" she asked.

"The Merrywood encompasses all the lands that belonged to a former Great House. There's a forest, a village, and a manor that burned down hundreds of years ago," explained Apollo.

Evangeline had a flash of a ruined house where all that remained was a smoldering staircase. It was probably just her attempt at imagining, but for a second, she wondered if it really could be a memory. Maybe this was why Apollo was nervous about this family, because they were rebuilding a place that was somehow connected with her missing memories.

"How did the manor burn down?" she pressed.

"No one really knows," Apollo said. "Most of the story has been lost to time and the story curse."

"Not entirely lost," said Aurora brightly. "Although I can imagine why it doesn't get repeated much. It's quite tragic."

"Then maybe you shouldn't repeat it, either," said Lord Vale.

"But the princess asked about it," protested Aurora.

Both Lord and Lady Vale peered at their daughter with looks that bordered on scolding, as if they didn't want to make a scene but they also did not wish to have this particular conversation.

"I did ask," Evangeline said, not wanting to get Aurora into any trouble. But she was also eager to know more. To see if it helped her remember.

"It's not really a tale for a party," said Lady Vale, who now looked distinctly uncomfortable.

"I'd still like to hear it," Evangeline said. "I don't know nearly as much Northern history as I'd like."

"Well then, let me educate you," said Aurora.

Her parents both appeared nervous, but Aurora wasn't to be stopped. "Vengeance Slaughterwood of House Slaughterwood was once engaged to the most beautiful girl in all the North. Only this girl didn't love him. Her parents refused to let her out of the engagement, but she refused to marry without love. On the day of the wedding, she ran away. Of course Vengeance couldn't let her go—he had a name to live up to, after all. And so when Vengeance heard a rumor that this beautiful girl loved Lord Merrywood's only son, Vengeance razed Merrywood Manor, Merrywood Village, and Merrywood Forest, thus living up to his terrible name." Aurora finished cheerfully, the way someone else might end a toast, yet her face was no longer smiling.

Across from her, Lady Vale had gone extremely pale, and Lord Vale had turned an angry shade of red.

In all her life, Evangeline's father had never looked at her the way Lord Vale looked at Aurora right now. Of course Evangeline had also never looked at her father in the defiant way that Aurora did now. It made Evangeline wonder if maybe she was wrong about this family being connected with her missing memories. Perhaps it was just the tension among them that made Apollo so uncomfortable. That was all the story seemed to bring about. It didn't elicit a flicker of anything else.

"Hopefully our rebuilding of the Merrywood will help to restore some of that which was lost," Lord Vale announced, in a clear attempt to change the subject.

This time Aurora didn't seem to mind. It appeared she'd said all she wanted to on the matter. "I do hope you and your prince can join us for the rebuilding festival. I'm *so* excited to get to know you better."

Aurora hugged Evangeline and whispered, "I have a feeling we are going to be *great* friends—ouch!" She pulled back with a pained flutter of her lashes.

"What's wrong?" Evangeline asked.

"I didn't realize you had a dagger on your person." Aurora cocked her head, inclining it toward Archer's jeweled knife, which Evangeline had tucked into her belt.

A crease formed between Apollo's brows and his gaze turned unusually dark. "Where did you get that?"

Evangeline protectively put her hand over the dagger's hilt. "I found it in the gardens," she lied.

She regretted it immediately—Evangeline had never been a liar—but she couldn't bring herself to stop.

Apollo looked suspicious as he eyed the knife. It was the same way he'd looked earlier when he'd caught her searching the room, but this time the jealousy was unmistakable. His eyes narrowed, a muscle throbbed in his forehead, and Evangeline was glad that she hadn't told the truth, that another young man had given her the blade. She still feared Apollo might take it anyway.

Quickly she made up a slightly ridiculous story about finding it in the well just before she'd been pulled out. "I feel as if it's a bit of a lucky charm. But I'm sorry it hurt you, Aurora."

"It was really nothing. In fact, now that you've said it's good luck, I'm rather glad you have it. But you might want to be more careful with your weapons. I know it's your charm, but with so many guards around, do you really need it?"

"She's right," Apollo said. "I—"

"Ahem." Someone cleared their throat loudly behind them. Evangeline's relief was immediate. She was almost certain Apollo had been about to take the knife.

Now his attention was on a new guard who stood at the edge of their circle.

"Your Highnesses, I'm sorry to interrupt, but there's a matter of great urgency that I need to speak with the prince about."

"And this couldn't wait another minute?" Apollo turned to the guard with a glower.

The young man visibly paled. "Believe me, Your Highness, if it wasn't important, I wouldn't have interrupted." The guard leaned in close and whispered something to Apollo that made the prince go gray.

"I'm sorry, but I'm afraid my attention is needed elsewhere." He looked down at Evangeline. "I hate to leave, but I'll find you later tonight."

Before she could ask where he was going, Prince Apollo strode away.

17

Evangeline

Evangeline didn't touch her wine, although she seemed to be the only one abstaining. The merriment of the dinner party continued after Apollo left. Soon it wasn't just the courtiers who were drinking; a number of the guards were imbibing as well.

There wasn't a clock in the Court of Columns, but she could tell from the movement of the moon overhead that some time had passed since Apollo had left, enough time to tell her that whatever had pulled the prince away was significant.

Evangeline briefly wondered if they had found Lord Jacks. But she supposed that news would have made the prince happy, and he had not looked glad before he'd exited. No, it must have been something else.

She continued to wonder through the dinner's third course until someone halfway down the table made another toast. Northerners, it seemed, were quite fond of toasting. This particular toast was to the archer who'd felled the birds they were feasting on, and suddenly Evangeline remembered. *Archer.*

Her insides did a quick somersault. She looked around the court once more, hoping that he'd finally stepped inside. But there was still no sign of him.

Now Evangeline had never thought of herself as a reckless person. Others might argue with this. But Evangeline would say to them that she was merely hopeful of what could be, whereas others were fearful as to what could go wrong.

Evangeline knew that especially given recent events involving a well, sneaking away from the dinner without her guards in search of Archer may have posed a bit of danger. But Evangeline also imagined that with Apollo gone and so many people distracted, this was perhaps the perfect time to try to find Archer again and hopefully regain her memories.

She pondered the different distractions she could cause in order to sneak away. First she considered tugging on the tablecloth to topple the platters of food. She imagined spilling the wine. Then another toast began, and she realized that this was her opportunity.

Lord Vale was giving the toast. He was actually doing a rather spectacular job of it, vividly explaining his desire to rebuild the Merrywood in an effort to rally others to his cause. Even Evangeline found it difficult to look away from him.

Lord Vale drew every eye as he stood and raised a glass high above his burly head. "This restoration is for the entire North!" he declared with a voice like thunder. "We rebuild to banish the ghosts of our pasts that dare to keep haunting us. For we are Northerners! We are not afraid of the myths and the legends! We *are* the myths and the legends!"

The room erupted in shouts. "We are the legends!"

"Who will join me in this rebuilding?" Lord Vale cried.

"Count me in!"

"My House will be there!"

The room exploded in a cacophony of impassioned voices as men and women and even guards all over the court raised their glasses and cheered.

"We will begin right after the Hunt!" Lord Vale bellowed.

Evangeline chose this moment to slip from the table and through the closest set of doors. She focused on being quick more than being quiet. The riot of the court was loud enough to drown out the sounds of a war.

And so it wasn't until a few minutes later that Evangeline heard the footsteps echoing behind her.

She quickly reached for Archer's dagger and spun around.

"It's only me." Aurora Vale raised her hands defensively. "Sorry, I didn't mean to frighten you. When I saw you slipping away, I thought I would join. My father's toasts can go on for days. I remember a particular wedding where he toasted from sunset until sunrise."

"Didn't anyone try to stop him?"

Aurora laughed. "No one tries to stop my father. I don't imagine tonight's toast will go on that long, as he seems to have rallied enough of the dinner party to his cause. But we should move on before anyone notices." Aurora bounced forward, swishing her violet hair. "Where are you going? Do you have a secret lover? Or perhaps you're off to see your personal witch who tells the future?"

"Oh no," Evangeline replied quickly. "I don't have a lover or know any witches. I was just planning on going back to my suite."

"Well, that's disappointing." Aurora sighed. "Still, I suppose walking you back to your room is better than listening to my father." She linked her arm with Evangeline's.

Earlier, Evangeline had liked Aurora, but now there was something about the girl that didn't feel right. Or maybe it was just that she was ruining Evangeline's plans to find Archer.

"Thank you for the offer," Evangeline said carefully, "but I'd actually prefer to be alone."

Aurora gave her a dubious look before she flashed a brilliant smile. "So you do have a secret lover after all?"

"No," Evangeline repeated calmly. "I'm married."

Aurora twisted her mouth. "That usually doesn't stop other people. There's really not a guard or handsome stableboy who has caught your eye?"

"There's only Apollo," Evangeline said firmly. Although, even as she spoke, her thoughts flashed to Archer. She pictured him standing there on the bridge in the rain, shirt clinging to his chest as his eyes clung to her. But she didn't want him as a lover. He was reckless and uncivilized and he'd lied about knowing her. She only wanted to find him so he might spark a new memory.

But it seemed that wouldn't be happening tonight.

Footsteps had begun to pound down the hall. Aurora had waylaid Evangeline long enough for her guards to notice her absence and finally catch up.

Disappointment made Evangeline tired. As her guards had walked her to the room, she kept looking over her shoulder for Archer. She didn't know if she really thought he could appear, or if she just wanted him to arrive so much that she thought she could will it to happen.

She imagined colliding with him in the hallway and regaining all her memories in a sudden rush that made everything in her upside-down world make sense.

But alas, after an uneventful journey, she was returned to her room, where she found herself undressing for bed and thinking words like *alas*.

She didn't know when she crawled into bed exactly, or how long she'd been there. She was somewhere between asleep and awake when she heard the floor creak beside her. It didn't sound like Apollo's confident stride. It sounded like someone sneaking in. Evangeline dared to imagine it was Archer as she opened her eyes—

A broad hulking figure loomed over her bed.

Not Archer or Apollo.

She tried to scream.

But the assailant moved faster. In the time it took her to open her mouth, he was on the bed, slamming a large gloved hand over her lips and pressing her down with the weight of his body.

He smelled like sweat and horses. Evangeline couldn't see his face—he wore a full mask that left him with only a pair of dull eyes exposed.

She tried to scream again. Tried to bite his hand. Archer hadn't taught her what to do in this position. But she could hear his words from this morning. *If you stop fighting, you die.*

She kicked, aiming between her assailant's legs.

"It'd be better if you stayed still." The assassin flashed a knife the length of her forearm.

Help! Help! Help! she cried wordlessly, frantically fighting to buck him off.

He lowered the knife, parting the top of her nightgown. Then she felt the blade's sharp tip carve a painful line beneath her collarbone.

"You've got to be kidding me," growled Archer.

Evangeline hadn't even noticed him enter the room, but suddenly he was there—golden and glowering and possibly the most beautiful thing she'd ever seen. He ruthlessly grabbed the assassin by the neck, yanked him from the bed, and pinned him to a bedpost, holding him aloft so his legs dangled as uselessly as a doll's.

Evangeline scrambled off the bed. "I tried to fight him."

Blood streamed down her chest as she tightened her robe with hands that wouldn't stop shaking.

Archer's eyes narrowed on the blood and Evangeline swore they flashed from blue to molten silver. He looked back at the assassin and snarled.

The sound that came out of his mouth was purely animal. He ripped off his mask, pulled out a knife, and brought the blade to the man's left eye. "Who hired you to harm her?"

The assassin paled but gritted his teeth.

"I'll ask you one more time, then you lose the eye. And I almost hope you don't answer, because I'd love to cut out your eye. *Who* hired you to kill her?"

"It was anonymous," the assassin rushed out.

"That's too bad for you." Archer lowered his knife.

"I swear, I don't know," the man spit out. "I was just told to make it slow and painful and bloody."

Evangeline went numb all over. It was one thing for someone to want her dead, another to learn they wanted to torture her.

"Did they say why?" Evangeline asked.

The assassin clamped his mouth shut.

"Don't be rude. The princess asked you a question." Archer lifted the man higher and roughly shook him by the neck until his head rocked to the side. "Answer her."

"I dunno why," the man spit out. "I was just told to make it hurt."

Archer's nostrils flared.

"You're lucky that I'm kinder than your employer." He cocked his golden head, looking almost thoughtful. "This will hurt, but not for long." Then he took his knife and stabbed the assassin in the heart.

18

Evangeline

The assassin fell to the floor with an ugly thud. He twitched, convulsed—Evangeline wasn't quite sure of the proper words, only that he didn't die immediately. It was all rather horrifying, but she couldn't say she was sorry. She could still feel her own blood staining the robe she held to her chest. It had been such a pretty gown, periwinkle blue and lined in delicate cream lace that was turning dark with the welling blood.

The assailant made a few gurgling sounds that resembled curses.

"You're wasting your last words," said Archer. "I'm already damned." He leaned down and twisted his knife. When he pulled it out, blood spattered on his dark cloak and the pale shirt he wore beneath it, but he didn't appear to care.

He stepped over the body and stalked along the edge of the bed, glowering at Evangeline.

"Why is it that people are always trying to kill you?" His voice was low, on the edge of something deadly. "You need to be more careful."

"How is this my fault?"

"You have no sense of self-preservation." Archer took another angry step. "If someone labeled a bottle *poison,* you would drink it. You take warnings as invitations. You can't seem to stay away from all the things that will hurt you."

Like me.

She swore she heard the last two words in her head as he took another step toward her until he was standing so close, she could practically feel the hot fury pouring off him.

She needed to back away, to call her for guards, to tell him to leave. Her heart pounded impossibly fast.

But she found herself saying, "You're not here to hurt me."

"You don't know that." A muscle ticked in his jaw. "This morning I nearly tossed you over the side of a bridge."

"You also just killed someone to save my life."

"Maybe I just enjoy killing people." Archer wiped his bloody blade on the sheets, but his blazing eyes never left hers. He still looked furious and feral. There was blood on his hands, and his eyes were shot through with it as well. Yet she'd never wanted anyone more.

She must have lost her mind sometime during the night because she wanted him to move closer. She wanted his hands on her. She wanted him holding her, restraining her, teaching her to fight. She didn't care, as long as they were touching.

She told herself it was just the fear, the excitement, the blood rushing through her. It would fade in a minute. But the mad part of her didn't want it to vanish.

Before she could think better of it, Evangeline reached for his hand.

The touch was electric. As soon as her fingers found his, the world started spinning. Her room turned into a kaleidoscope of night and sparks, and suddenly she was elsewhere.

She was in another memory.

It was dark and wet and for a second, she couldn't breathe.

The icy water hit hard as earth. She thrashed on instinct, but someone held her tightly. His arms were unyielding, dragging her up through the crushing waves. Salt water snaked up her nose, and the cold filled her veins. She was coughing and sputtering, barely able to suck down air as he swam to the shore with her in tow. He held her close and carried her from the ocean as if his life depended on it instead of hers.

"I will not let you die." A single bead of water dripped from his lashes onto her lips. It was raindrop soft, but the look in his eyes held the force of a storm. It should have been too dark to see his expression, but the crescent moon burned brighter with each second, lining the edges of his cheekbones as he looked at her.

Evangeline's entire world tilted as she recognized his face as Archer's.

The crashing ocean felt suddenly quiet in contrast to her pounding heart, or maybe it was his heart.

Archer's chest was heaving, his clothes were soaked, his hair was a mess across his face—yet in that moment, Evangeline knew he would carry her through more than just freezing waters. He would pull her through fire if he had to, haul her from the clutches of war, from falling cities and breaking worlds.

Evangeline's mind spun as the memory ended. Days ago, when she'd glimpsed the last part of this memory, she'd thought the person who'd been carrying her was Apollo.

But she had been wrong. It had been Archer.

The day at the well had not been the first time he'd met her. She also doubted this new memory was of their first encounter. He'd held her with too much intensity.

As Evangeline's senses returned to the present, the first thing she noticed was that Archer had crossed the bedroom. He was standing at the door and he wasn't looking at her the same way he had in the memory, as if he'd walk through fire to save her. The hand she'd been touching was fisted at his side and he looked at her as if he wanted nothing more than to get away.

And she wanted nothing more than for him to stay.

She had so many questions, and not just about this new memory. She thought about how she'd reacted when Madame Voss had mentioned *The Ballad of the Archer and the Fox.* She'd thought the story had triggered her, but now she knew it was just the name. *Archer.*

It was him.

"I'll make sure the guards clean this up and keep it quiet. But in case anyone asks, tell them that *you* killed the man who attacked you."

Archer turned to go.

"Wait!" Evangeline called. "Don't leave!"

He didn't stop.

He was already out of the room.

But this time she chased after him.

19

Apollo

A pollo's boots were going to be ruined. There was so much blood. Blood stained the carpets, the walls, and now his boots. Not that he was actually mad about the boots. Apollo could easily get more boots—he didn't care about his footwear, not really. What truly bothered him was that his wife had been carrying around a dagger that had once belonged to Jacks.

Apollo would have loved to have gone out and hunted the bastard that very night, but he had to deal with this mess instead.

"You said there was one survivor?" he asked.

"Yes, Your Highness," replied the guard assigned to this particular scene.

"I'd like to speak with him privately." Apollo marched out into the hall, stepping in more blood as he moved. He'd seen death before, but it had never been this grisly.

Down the hall, he heard another guard heaving into a pot.

Apollo was thankful he hadn't had the time to eat before arriving, or he would have done the same.

Upstairs the mood was grim, but at least the air no longer held the coppery scent of blood.

It smelled of beeswax candles. Their soft light cast a glow over the flowery paper covering the walls. There were also a number of framed watercolor paintings and pencil sketches. Someone in the family must have been an artist, for none of the paintings were that good at first. But as he ventured farther down the hall, the art grew quite a bit better. Some of the sketches appeared to be faithful renderings of the family members who now lay strewn dead across the floor downstairs.

Finally the guard stopped in front of the door that must have led to the massacre's sole survivor.

"I'll enter alone," said Apollo.

"But, Your Highness—"

"That's an order. This victim has been through enough torment tonight. I don't want him to feel as if he's being interrogated."

The guard dutifully stepped aside.

Apollo entered the dim room and shut the door behind him.

A boy who looked to be about fourteen sat curled up on a large sleigh bed, holding his knees as he rocked back and forth.

He was skinny, most likely going through a growth phase rather than malnourished.

The Fortunas were one of the Great Houses. Even if they lost half their fortune, they would always have more than enough to eat.

That's why Apollo had been called here tonight. It wasn't often most of the members of a Great House were massacred in a single night. Word of what had happened here would get out, and when it did, the Crown needed to be in control of what was said.

This sort of news could either cast a further pallor on Apollo's reign or make it stronger.

"Hello there," Apollo said as he sat gingerly on the edge of the bed.

The boy curled tighter into himself.

"I'm not here to hurt you."

"Doesn't matter," said the boy, voice cracking. "Nothing could hurt more than this."

"No," Apollo agreed. "I've never seen anything so horrific, which is why I'm here. I want to make sure whoever committed this atrocity is caught so that it can never happen again."

"You can't catch him," the boy murmured, rocking back and forth. "He's not human."

"Why do you say that?"

The boy finally looked up. The terror on his face was so raw he looked like a skeleton with skin painted on. "He moved so fast. I was up here when I heard the first scream. It was my sister.

She's always so dramatic. I ignored it at first. Then there was another and another."

The boy brought both hands to the sides of his head and covered his ears as if he were still hearing the wails.

"I knew it was bad—evil. I ran downstairs, but as soon as I saw all the blood, I hid in the closet."

"Did you see who did this before you hid?"

The boy nodded shakily. "He looked feral."

"Did he look like Lord Jacks?"

"No."

"Are you certain?" Apollo asked.

He didn't actually believe it was Lord Jacks. Only one type of creature could cause this sort of devastation. But he wanted the boy to say it was Jacks. It would make everything so much easier.

"It wasn't him. I would have recognized him. Lord Jacks was friends with my grandmother before she passed. This man—I don't think he was even a man . . ."

The boy brought the palms of his hands to his eyes and quietly cried.

Apollo, never having been comfortable with crying, pushed up from the bed and took a quick survey of the room. There was a desk near the window with an easel to the side of it. It seemed this boy was the family artist. Propped against the easel was a half-finished watercolor that looked rather nice. On the desk there were even more drawings and sketches and notebooks.

He seemed to favor animals and people. Although there was one drawing of an apple.

Apollo hated apples.

Just the sight of the fruit brought his anger back to the surface. He looked from the outline of apple to the blood on his boots to the boy still crying on the bed.

There was nothing he could do for the boy or about the blood. But all the artwork and the apple made Apollo realize there was something he could do about Jacks.

"You're quite talented," Apollo told the boy. "Some of this art is good."

"Thank you." The boy sniffed.

"Do you think you could draw something for me?" Apollo picked up a notebook and a pencil, then he handed the items to the boy.

"You want me to draw you something now?"

"Yes. Art is supposed to be good therapy for the soul."

Apollo told the boy what he'd like him to draw.

The boy replied with a quizzical look, but he made no attempt to argue with the prince. Most people usually didn't, though it might have been better for this boy if he had.

As it was, the boy quickly went to work on his sketch, bowing his head over his book as he feverishly outlined and shaded and did whatever it was that artists did. When he finished, he carefully tore out the page and handed it to Apollo.

"Excellent," Apollo said. "This is really good work, young man."

"Thank you."

"Do you feel any better now?"

"Not really," muttered the boy.

Apollo clapped him on the shoulder. "I truly am sorry for your loss," he whispered, "but soon you won't feel any pain at all."

Then Apollo took his knife and stabbed the boy in the heart.

Shock and pain briefly crossed the boy's face before he fell back on the bed, as dead as the rest of his family.

Apollo felt a moment of sadness. He wasn't really a monster. He just did what had to be done. A boy this trusting and this cowardly wouldn't have made it long in this world; his family was all dead now, anyway. And Apollo would make sure his sacrifice was put to good use.

The prince wrapped the boy's hands around the dagger, making it look as if the death was self-inflicted for whoever found him later. Then, after a quick glance in the mirror to make sure his shirt didn't have any blood on it, Apollo stepped into the hall and quickly shut the door behind him before the waiting guard could see inside the room.

"How did it go, Your Highness?" asked the guard.

Apollo shook his head mournfully. "Such a tragedy. The boy feels guilty for surviving. I fear he'll never be the same. But he did draw me a picture of the man who murdered his family."

Apollo handed the drawing to the guard. "Have new wanted posters drawn up. Mention this massacre and then add this picture of Lord Jacks."

20

Evangeline

Evangeline ran out of the door right as two guards burst through into her room. She quickly dodged past, expecting them to give chase. But she was the only one running. Her bare feet clapped against the cold hard stones as she ran after Archer and cried again, "Wait—stop!"

He couldn't have gone far. She could hear the fall of his boots around the corner. Hall after hall after hall she heard him in the distance. But every time she turned a corner, Archer wasn't there. All she saw were portraits of Apollo that looked far more accusatory than she remembered.

The prince's painted eyes watched her as she ran down a particularly narrow hallway. Some of the lights had been snuffed out, making it darker as well, until she reached another portrait of her husband. The sconces flanking this picture seemed especially bright, glistening off the golden frame as if to make up for the lights that had gone out.

It looked like another portrait of Apollo in the magical phoenix tree, lounging across the branches. Although it was difficult to be sure. The portrait had been slashed down the middle.

Archer stood beside the mutilated picture, cape tossed back behind his shoulders, arms crossed over his chest, as he eyed the mangled portrait. "I think I like this one best."

Evangeline didn't see a knife in his hand, but there was a sharpness to Archer's gaze that felt like a blade. If anyone could cut with a look, it would be him.

"Did you do this?" she asked.

"That wouldn't have been very kind of me."

Evangeline's eyes drifted toward the blood spattered on his pale shirt. "Would you describe yourself as kind?"

"Not at all. But I think you already know that." He shoved off the wall and stalked closer to her. The hall was quite narrow, so it wasn't much of a walk. Two steps and he was there, near enough that everything smelled of apples and her head felt suddenly light.

Yesterday morning when she'd met Archer in the hall outside her room, just standing next to him had made her feel as if she'd made a bad decision, yet she had still wanted to follow him. She had supposed herself delirious from lack of sleep. But she wasn't delirious now. She wasn't mad. It was just him.

Standing this close to Archer made her feel as if she couldn't catch her breath, as if her blood was made of champagne bubbles all rushing to her head.

"What are you to me?" she asked.

Archer's eyes locked with hers. "Nothing."

But it didn't feel like nothing when his fingers reached down and he took hold of the sash that kept her robe tied together. He held it as if he couldn't decide if he wanted to untie it or tug her closer to him.

"Why are you lying?" she asked.

"I thought we'd already established that I'm not very kind." Archer tugged on the sash, enough to loosen the knot.

Evangeline quickly stole it out of his hands and pulled her robe tighter.

He laughed softly. "Am I making you nervous now?"

He said it as if he hoped he was. Or maybe he was just trying to keep her from asking questions. When he was this close, it was hard to think clearly, hard to remember why she'd chased him down the hall. There was something about Archer that made her just want to be there, with him.

She knew it was wrong. She was with Apollo. *Not just with Apollo,* she reminded herself, *married.* Apollo was her husband.

Archer couldn't be anything to her. And he'd just told her that he was nothing to her. But he'd also said he was a liar.

"Just tell me one thing that's true," she said, and then she promised herself silently that she would walk away from him, and from these feelings. "I know we met before you rescued me at the well. Were you my guard?"

He worked his jaw.

For a second, she didn't think he would answer.

Then he shook his head. "No. I'm generally better at doing damage than protecting." He looked down toward the blood staining the front of her robe.

She hadn't really looked at the cut that had caused all the blood since she'd first been injured. It was shallow enough that it had already closed. It would not need stitching. But the blood left behind looked something awful—*she* probably looked awful as well.

"You could never look awful," he said faintly.

She looked up again. For a second, he looked almost shy and incredibly young, barely older than her. Blond locks of hair fell over his eyes as he slowly leaned in closer.

She didn't know if he was trying not to frighten her away, or if he was maybe frightened. He seemed uncharacteristically nervous as he reached toward her cheek. He slowly took an errant pink strand of hair between his fingers and tucked it behind her ear. He was so careful, his fingers didn't even brush her skin, but he looked as if he wanted to.

There was a different kind of pain tightening his jaw and making the muscles in his neck pulse as he stood there, holding her gaze as if he wished he could be holding her instead, crushing her to him like he had in her memory.

Married.

Married.

Married, she reminded herself.

She was married to Apollo. She was nothing to Archer.

"I should go," she said. "My guards—they're probably about to ring an alarm. I'm surprised we're not hearing bells right now," she babbled, hoping to find more words so that she'd have a reason to stay, even though she knew she needed to leave.

She imagined that there were still more memories of him that she'd forgotten. But now she was a little afraid of what she might remember, if remembering more meant feeling more than she already did.

It was hard enough to stand there across from him, not touching in a way that almost felt more intimate than touching. It looked as if it was taking all his strength not to reach out and graze her fingers with his. As if one brush of their skin might set off a riot of sparks or blow out every light in the hall.

She waited for him to walk away.

But Archer didn't move.

For a second, neither did she. She couldn't shake the feeling that if she left him now, if she turned her back, she might not ever see him again.

She'd felt butterflies when she'd kissed Apollo, but Evangeline had a feeling that kissing Archer would be earth-shattering.

Married, she reminded herself one more time.

And this time she finally turned to leave.

As soon as she moved, Evangeline felt as if she'd just made

a mistake. Although she had no idea if the mistake had been getting too close to Archer or turning and walking away.

Evangeline tried not to think about Archer as she practically ran back to her suite. She looked over her shoulder only twice. He wasn't there either time.

Upon returning to her suite, she found all evidence of the crime gone.

It was actually a little bit unnerving. It should perhaps have been more than a little unnerving, but after the events of the night, Evangeline wasn't really capable of feeling more than she felt. Or asking too many questions about the oddness of it all.

There were guards waiting at her door, but at her arrival, they didn't even ask her about where she'd gone or the man who'd been dead on her floor. A man that they'd clearly seen, for they'd already cleaned up the body.

When Evangeline stepped inside her suite, it was as if nothing foul had ever happened.

Her bed was once again covered in a fluffy quilt as pure as snow. There were no stains to be seen, not even on the floor, where a new white-and-gold carpet had been placed. Everything was crisp and pure and clean—except for Evangeline.

Archer had said, *I'll make sure the guards clean this up and keep it quiet.* But this was all remarkably clean and quiet. Either the guards were exceptionally loyal to him, or . . .

Evangeline didn't actually have any words to go after the *or*.

Now that she was back in her room, she was feeling more of the shock that she should have experienced earlier.

Her pink hair was a riot; her eyes were overlarge, stuck in a state of fright; and there was blood on her nightgown and smeared across her cheek. She looked a mess.

Her hands shook as she cleaned the blood from her person and changed into a fresh pink gown. She tried to stop her thoughts from flickering back to Archer. He wasn't hers to think about, and yet she kept picturing the way he'd looked in the hall, and how for a second, he'd seemed almost shy, almost scared, and almost hers.

Ding. Ding. Ding.

The tower clock chimed three o'clock in the morning.

Evangeline startled back to the present. She closed her eyes, shook away the memories of Archer, and then returned to her main room—only to be startled again at the sight of Apollo.

He looked as if he'd just stepped inside the door to her suite. His eyes were hooded, his shirt was wrinkled, and there was blood spattered on his boots. It was only on his boots, but there was so much of it, soaking through the tan leather until they were practically red all over.

Death. It seemed to be everywhere tonight.

"Are you all right?" Evangeline quickly crossed the room. "What happened?"

Apollo pulled a shaking hand through his hair and closed his eyes, as if the memory of whatever had occurred was simply too much for him. "I'd rather not talk about it."

When he opened his eyes, they were bloodshot, and his jaw was covered in a layer of stubble that she'd never seen before. Apollo was always immaculate. The perfect fairytale prince. But in the few hours since she'd seem him last, something appeared to have changed.

Evangeline felt wrung out. She'd thought she wasn't capable of experiencing more emotions, but she must have cared for Apollo more than she realized. She didn't know what had happened, but she wanted to try and make it better.

"Is there anything I can do for you?" she asked.

He looked as if he was about to say no. Then his eyes dropped. They moved to her mouth and lingered there, as if maybe he could think of one thing.

Her heart thudded nervously.

He didn't move right away, as if he knew this wasn't the sort of help she was offering. But maybe deep down it was; maybe this was what they both needed.

He needed comfort and she needed clarity.

He leaned in closer.

Her body trembled. She didn't know why this felt so wrong when it should have felt so right. It should have been easy to lean into him, to put her hands on his chest as his arms went around her waist.

His fingers were shaking, which made her feel a little better. As if maybe nerves were normal.

The first press of his lips was soft, and so was the slide of his palms as they moved lower on her body. Wearing only her thin gown, she could feel so much more of him than she ever had when they'd kissed before.

Soon she was a little lost in the taste of his tongue and the press of his body against hers as they tumbled together toward the bed. Then her world was spinning sideways, plunging her into another kiss from another time.

She could feel a breeze at her back and the pressure of Apollo against her chest.

Evangeline's heart became a drum, beating harder and faster as he pressed in closer. There were layers of clothing between them, but she could feel the heat coming off him. More heat than she'd ever felt. It was almost too hot, too hungry. Apollo burned like a fire that consumed instead of warmed. And yet there must have been a part of her that wanted to be scorched, or at the very least singed.

She wrapped both hands around his neck. Apollo's mouth left her lips and dropped to her throat, trailing kiss after kiss down her—

A cold hand clamped on her shoulder and wrenched her free of the prince's grasp. "I think it's time we go."

Archer pulled her toward the balcony stairs with supernatural swiftness. One moment, Apollo was all Evangeline could feel and then she was tucked underneath Archer's hard arm, pressed close to his cool side as he ushered her toward the steps . . .

Archer.

Apollo quickly broke away from the kiss. "What did you say?"

Evangeline's throat went suddenly tight. She must have accidentally said Archer's name out loud.

"I just had a memory," she blurted, and then of course she instantly regretted it. She could not tell Apollo she'd had a memory with Archer. She could maybe tell him about the first part, the kiss. But then he would probably ask why she'd said Archer, and she didn't want to mention that he pulled her away afterward.

Although suddenly Evangeline was intensely curious as to why Archer had done that. And how could he have? Apollo was a prince. But she didn't have time to wonder about the why of it all—not when Apollo was staring at her as if she'd betrayed him.

Jealousy far worse than what she'd seen earlier burned in his eyes. She could feel it in his hands as he clenched his fist in the back of her nightgown.

Evangeline scrambled for something to say. Anything that would change the way Apollo was looking at her now. Then she remembered the engagement story from Madame Voss. She could tell him this was what she remembered.

"I had a memory of you. It was the night you proposed. We were at a ball and you were dressed like the Archer from the old fairytale, *The Ballad of the Archer and the Fox*."

As she spoke, Evangeline had a picture in her head that might have been a memory, too.

Apollo went down on one knee.

She abruptly forgot how to breathe as the crowd around them increased, caging Evangeline and Apollo in a circle of ballgowns and silk doublets and shocked faces.

Apollo took both of her hands in his warm grip. "I want you,

Evangeline Fox. I want to write ballads for you on the walls of Wolf Hall and carve your name on my heart with swords. I want you to be my wife and my princess and my queen. Marry me, Evangeline, and let me give you everything."

He brought her hand to his lips again, and this time, when he looked at Evangeline, it was as if the rest of the celebration didn't exist.

No one had ever looked at Evangeline like this before. All she could see was the longing and the hope and the hint of fear swirling in Apollo's expression.

And yet it wasn't nearly half as powerful as the way that Archer had looked at her in the memory she'd had earlier, as if he'd haul her from the clutches of war, from falling cities and breaking worlds. She could picture him again, looking down on her as a drop of water fell from his eyelashes onto her lips.

But that was all in the past.

In the present, she was married to Apollo. Whatever feelings she'd had for Archer didn't matter. If she could forget a year of memories, she could forget those feelings as well. But the problem was, she wasn't sure she wanted to. Not yet, at least. Not when she still didn't know the entire story.

She knew it was wrong to hold on. But she also realized tonight just how little she truly knew her husband. She hadn't known that he was jealous and that he liked to toast to curses. She didn't know why he had blood on his boots right now.

And after telling him she'd regained a memory of his proposal, she would have expected him to look happy. But Apollo looked unmistakably alarmed.

21

Jacks

Jacks had seen enough.

If he stayed on the balcony any longer, if he kept watching, he'd kill Apollo, or at least make it impossible for him to touch Evangeline ever again.

Jacks reminded himself she was safe with Apollo. As a princess, she'd have anything she ever wanted.

But she wasn't supposed to want to kiss him. It wasn't fair of Jacks to hate her a little for it. But feeling hateful was the only thing that made it possible for him to leave. And he really needed to leave.

Evangeline was safe. That was what mattered.

If Jacks stayed, if he stormed in the room and used his powers to make Apollo watch as Jacks told Evangeline that she wasn't nothing to him. That she was *everything*. That he'd turned back time to keep her alive, and he would make the same choice again. If Jacks made her remember that *he* was the one she should have wanted to kiss. She wouldn't be safe anymore. She wouldn't even be alive.

If Evangeline was going to have any future, Jacks could not be a part of it.

Quietly he leaped from the balcony. His boots made no sound as he landed in the darkened courtyard below. Although he should have timed it better. He could hear two guards on rounds approaching.

Normally, he'd have used his abilities to control their emotions so that they might turn around. But he was a little drained from all the guards he'd controlled earlier. He could also hear the conversation of these guards, and the words *blood* and *massacre* caught his attention.

Jacks moved closer to the stony walls of Wolf Hall and hid in the shadows as the guards drew closer and the taller one said, "Quixton was there and he said it wasn't possible that one person could kill so many people. He said it was like a demon did it." The guard paused to shudder. "I don't have any love for the family of House Fortuna, but no one should have their throat ripped into and their heart ripped out."

Jacks disagreed with his last statement. But he was less concerned that a royal guard could have such an irrationally soft heart than he was about this guard's use of the word *demon*.

Demons didn't exist.

But Jacks did know of a creature that humans often mistook for one, especially in the North, where the story curse made it nearly impossible for tales about vampires to properly spread. When they did, the curse prevented humans from being reasonably fearful. So whenever a human was truly afraid, they usually referred to the vampires as demons.

And Jacks feared he knew exactly which bloodthirsty demon these guards were speaking of tonight. *Castor*.

The Valors had originally cast the story curse to protect their son, Castor, when he'd first been turned into a vampire. It was supposed to affect only stories about vampires. But the curse had been cast out of terror, and curses that come from a place of fear always turn out a little twisted or become far more terrible than intended.

Jacks wondered if the Valors would attempt to reverse the curse now that they were back. It would be interesting to see if Honora and Wolfric would choose to reshape the North, or if they would simply live a quiet life in the rebuilt Merrywood Manor.

He had yet to visit them there. He'd seen most of the Valors after the arch had been opened, but he'd been half dead at the time, thanks to Castor's appetite. Since then, Jacks had seen only Aurora. He knew she wouldn't turn him in to Apollo or his soldiers. He was less certain about her parents, Wolfric and Honora.

First, there was the matter of honor, which they both had. Then there was Apollo, who had bestowed the status of Great

House upon their new name and gifted them Merrywood Forest, Merrywood Manor, and Merrywood Village.

The forest, the manor, and the village weren't much of a gift
in Jacks's opinion. Their history was as ugly as they were. Most
people simply said they were cursed or haunted. Even Jacks
didn't like traveling through those lands.

But he thought again about the guards talking about a murderous demon. Then he pictured that same murderous *demon*,
ripping into Evangeline's throat, killing her, again.

Jacks mounted his horse and rode hard for the Merrywood.

He could already sense a change as soon as he reached Merrywood Forest. He could hear the life teeming on either side of
his path. Rabbits, frogs, birds, deer, and trees as they began to
grow again.

The Valors might have returned only a few days ago, but there
was a reason they were the Valors, a reason that even when
they'd been long dead, the stories about them had lived and
grown, transforming them into beings that sometimes sounded
closer to gods.

Jacks knew they weren't.

The Valors could bleed and die like everyone else, but they
didn't live like everyone. They weren't content merely surviving. He wasn't even sure they were capable of it. Before they'd
been locked away in the Valory, they'd started a kingdom that
spanned half a continent. Jacks didn't know what they would do
now that they were out, but he had no doubt the Valors would
create another indelible shift in the world.

He hopped off his horse and tied it to a post just outside Merrywood Village. The Valors hadn't started their rebuilding of the manor yet. They were beginning with the village first. Jacks imagined they'd all be staying somewhere in the vicinity, and therefore Castor would most likely be nearby instead of at his old crypt in Valorfell.

Like the forest, Merrywood Village was also returning to life. The air smelled of fresh-cut lumber as Jacks entered the square. It was an old square, built around a large well that had once upon a time been surrounded by shops—a smithy, an apothecary, a bakery, a butcher, a candlemaker—and the daily fruit and vegetable market.

For a second, Jacks remembered sneaking out at night and meeting his friends on the apothecary's rooftop. They'd lie back, watch the stars, and brag about all the things they would do someday, as if their days were guaranteed instead of numbered.

He looked up, not expecting to find Castor on the apothecary rooftop now, but he also wasn't surprised when he did.

One of the downfalls to being immortal was a propensity to remain tethered to the past, to the time before the immortal had stopped aging. No matter how many days Jacks lived, those days when he was a human were always the clearest to him and never seemed to fade with time. It was another downfall of being immortal—these endless, haunting memories that always gave humanity the illusion of being far more vibrant than immortality. It made Jacks hate humans at times, but he imagined it made Castor want to become one.

"Are you going to come down or do I need to set the apothecary on fire?" called Jacks.

"That threat might work better if you actually had a torch," Castor replied. A second later he easily dropped down to the ground and casually leaned an elbow against the wall of the crumbling old apothecary. With the helm off and his family back, he was more like Castor, the noble prince without a care, than like Chaos, the long-suffering vampire with a helm, who couldn't feed.

For a second, Jacks felt a pinprick of envy.

"What has put you in such a foul mood?" Castor asked. "Were you watching Evangeline again?"

"I'm not here because of her," Jacks snapped.

"Well, you're certainly snippy about her."

Jacks glared. "And you're in a disturbingly good mood for someone who just slaughtered an entire family."

Castor's expression immediately darkened. Heat seeped into a gaze that looked less like hunger and more like a threat.

If Jacks had more regard for his own life, he might have been frightened. But Jacks wasn't feeling much these days unless the feelings involved Evangeline, and he was trying his best to avoid those at the moment.

Anything that helped take his mind off her was pleasant in comparison—except for maybe this. Castor was his oldest friend, so Jacks didn't want to hate him, but when he looked at him, he could still see his teeth in Evangeline's throat as he ripped her life away.

Castor had no idea that version of their history even existed.

It wasn't entirely fair to judge him for it. But Jacks hadn't cared about being fair for a very long time.

"If you're here to lecture me," said Castor, "I don't want to hear it."

"Then I'll keep this short. You need to control yourself. Or your parents are going to find out and maybe this time, instead of placing a helm on you, they'll just place you in a grave."

Castor worked his jaw. "They wouldn't do that."

"They're still human, Castor. Humans do a lot of stupid things when they're scared."

Jacks had. And the worst part was, he'd thought he'd been doing the right thing. As when Castor had died.

Jacks had been the one who'd told Castor's mother, Honora, to bring him back from the dead.

Castor and Lyric had been Jacks's best friends, more like his brothers. Lyric had just died, and Jacks couldn't lose Castor, too.

He hadn't thought about what it would cost to return him to life. He hadn't imagined how much blood would be shed. One of the reasons Jacks had allowed himself to be turned into a Fate was so that Castor wouldn't be alone. Then he'd started the rumor that Castor was Chaos and that Chaos was a Fate, so that the world wouldn't figure out he was the last remaining Valor.

"I'm just trying to look out for you," Jacks said. "You finally have the helm off and your family back. I don't want to see you destroy this chance."

Castor scoffed. "I'm not the one about to destroy my life."

"What's that supposed to mean?"

"I talked to my sister. Aurora told me what you want and what you're willing to exchange for it."

"Your sister—" Jacks stopped himself. Even he knew better than to insult the twin of a vampire with control issues. Although it was tempting. He could feel his hands clenching into fists, but Castor wasn't the one he really wanted to punch. "I know what I'm doing."

The vampire gave him another hard look. "If Evangeline ever gets her memories back, she'll never forgive you for this."

"At least she'll be alive to hate me."

22

Evangeline

The Hunt..."

"...the Hunt."

"...the Hunt..."

Normally Evangeline did not hear her guards talking, but these two words kept sneaking through her door, as if just the name of this hunt had more power than other, more ordinary words. She'd heard mention of it before, but she'd thought it had just been a reference to the hunt for Lord Jacks. Now she wasn't so sure.

She would have asked her maid, but Martine had stepped out to return her luncheon tray. After all that had happened last night, Evangeline had slept half the day away.

As she sipped a cooling cup of starmire tea, she reached

for that day's scandal sheet, hoping it might have an answer for her. And it did—only it wasn't an answer to her questions about the Hunt.

The Daily Rumor

MURDER! MURDER! MURDER!

By Kristof Knightlinger

Bolt your doors! Don't travel alone! Be on your guard! No one is safe! Last night Lord Jacks committed another heinous crime. During the early hours of the evening, he viciously slayed the entire family of House Fortuna—makers of the beloved Fortuna's Fantastically Flavored Water. One guard that I spoke with said he'd never seen so much blood.

There was one lone survivor, young Edgar Fortuna. Unfortunately, the grief of it all was too much for poor Edgar. He died by his own hand shortly after the massacre. Edgar did, however, provide us with a sketch of the killer, which we are printing in this morning's paper.

I urge anyone out there who has seen Lord Jacks to please alert the Royal Order of Soldiers immediately. No clues are too small. This heartless murderer must be stopped before he kills again.

Evangeline turned the page. This time there was no shadowy image. There in freshly printed black and white was a drawing of Archer. He wore a devil-may-care grin and tossed an apple in one hand, looking nothing like a murderer—and everything like what Evangeline secretly wanted.

"No," Evangeline breathed.

No. No. No. No.

"This can't be," she said, her words coming out more frantic this time.

This had to be a mistake.

Maybe Archer just looked like Lord Jacks. Or perhaps this was the wrong drawing. Archer couldn't be Lord Jacks. He was a guard. He'd saved her life—twice.

"Your Highness," said Martine as she stepped back into the room, "you look a bit pale in the cheeks."

"I'm fine. I just saw something in the paper that alarmed me." She held up the page for Martine to see. "Is this really what Lord Jacks looks like?"

"That is him, Your Highness. I can see why you've gone all pasty. He's just awful, isn't he?" But her voice came out like a sigh, and Evangeline swore there were hearts in Martine's eyes as she looked at the black-and-white image, which was anything but awful.

Jacks looked like a happy ending that was just out of reach, and Martine was clearly bewitched by him. Just like Evangeline had been, only she was afraid her feelings for him had been a lot deeper than bewitchment.

Even now she could feel *things* just looking at this picture.

She didn't want to believe it. Evangeline still wanted to think the paper had gotten it wrong. Archer—rather, Lord Jacks— had been with her last night.

But he hadn't been with her *all* night. He'd found her only after Apollo had been called away. But . . .

She tried to make another excuse. She once again reminded herself Archer—*Jacks*—had saved her life, so he couldn't be a killer. Yet last night, he'd as much as confessed to her.

Maybe I just enjoyed killing people, he'd said. And instead of being horrified, she'd felt—Evangeline couldn't actually think about how she'd felt last night. Now she just felt sick and foolish and stupid and absolutely furious with herself.

She should have known. She should have put it together that Archer was in the memories Apollo wanted her to forget. Apollo had warned her. *Jacks has done atrocious, unforgivable things to you, and I think you might be happier if those things stay forgotten.*

And he was right, because Evangeline felt awful.

She still didn't want Archer to be the villain. She didn't want him to be Jacks. And she definitely didn't want to have feelings for him.

Her cheeks flashed with something like shame.

Martine looked at her with concern. Evangeline wanted nothing more than to smile and burn the paper and pretend none of this had happened. But even if she could pretend away her feelings—which she doubted, since feeling was what Evangeline did—she could not pretend away all the people Jacks had murdered last night.

She needed to tell Apollo that she had seen Jacks in Wolf Hall masquerading as a guard named Archer.

Evangeline grabbed the first dress she could find—a gown with a moss-green velvet bodice, a sweetheart neckline, and slender straps lined in pale pink flowers that matched the gown's long gauzy skirt.

Martine handed her a pair of matching slippers, which Evangeline quickly pressed her feet into. Then she started toward the door before she lost her courage. She didn't want to think she would, but she needed to act quickly.

Jacks needed to be stopped before he murdered more innocents, and Evangeline hoped her confession might help. If Jacks was sneaking in and out of the castle, obviously there were people here who were loyal to him, like her guards from last night. Unless they were also naive like her.

With a deep breath, Evangeline finally opened the door from her rooms into the long hallway.

Her guards from late last night were not there. Instead, Joff and Hale, the same soldiers who'd found her at the well, waited on the other side, wearing shining bronze armor and friendly smiles. Like all the other guards, they had mustaches—another thing Archer had not possessed.

"Good morning, Your Highness," they said in perfect unison.

"Good morning, Joff. Good morning, Hale. Could you please take me to see Apollo? I need to speak with the prince right away."

"I'm afraid he's already left for the Hunt," said Joff.

"Then take me to the Hunt," Evangeline said.

The day was already halfway gone and she could feel more minutes rapidly slipping away as she stood in the hall. She might have told these guards she had news on Lord Jacks—surely they would listen to that. But she wasn't certain who in this castle she could trust. She imagined a number of the guards had to be loyal to him or he would not have been able to sneak in and out of Wolf Hall without notice.

Hale frowned. "Your Highness—"

"Don't say you're not allowed to take me off the castle grounds."

"Oh no. We wouldn't pass up an opportunity to go to the Hunt."

Hale said the word *Hunt* with a combination of both reverence and excitement, and although Evangeline felt as if she really didn't have time to waste, she couldn't help but ask, "What *is* this Hunt?"

Hale's and Joff's square faces both brightened.

"It's only the most thrilling event of the year!" said Joff.

"Everyone looks forward to it," echoed Hale.

Evangeline didn't have any brothers, but if she had, she imagined they might have been a little like Joff and Hale. Both young men were so animated, they finished each other's sentences and echoed each other's words as the two went back and forth to explain the wonder of the Hunt.

"It's a tradition almost as old as the North itself," said Hale.

"It was started forever ago by the Valors," added Joff. "The story goes that one of their daughters—the pretty one—"

"They were all pretty," Hale interrupted.

"Well, the prettiest one," Joff continued, "had a pet unicorn, you see, and once a year, after the first rain of spring, they'd send this unicorn out into the Cursed Forest and everyone would hunt it."

"And this was supposed to be fun?" asked Evangeline.

"Don't worry, they weren't trying to *kill* it," Hale promised. "It's terrible luck to kill a unicorn. And they're far more useful alive."

Joff nodded and added, "Whoever caught the unicorn was granted a half wish."

"What's a half wish?"

Both men shrugged.

"No one quite knows," admitted Joff.

"There aren't any more unicorns," finished Hale. "But now, every year, someone volunteers to dress up like a unicorn for the Hunt. One year Joff almost did it!"

Joff nodded proudly. "I would have, but then that onionhead Quixton beat me to it."

"May I ask," said Evangeline in what she hoped was a polite tone, as these men clearly held a high regard for the Hunt, "why would anyone want to volunteer for this?"

"If you're the unicorn," Hale explained, "and you can make it through two nights and three days without being caught, you get a proper knighthood and a squire and a pile of gold."

"And if you get caught?" Evangeline asked.

"Well," said Joff a little less enthusiastically, "whoever dresses up like the unicorn usually gets maimed pretty badly if captured. And whoever catches them is the one who gets the title—if they need it—along with the pile of gold and the squire."

"So . . . people love the Hunt because of the prizes at the end?"

"There's also a big celebration afterward," said Hale.

"And," added Joff, "it's the only time of the year anyone is allowed to enter the Cursed Forest."

Evangeline had never heard of the Cursed Forest. "And people want to enter this forest?" she asked.

"Oh yes, the Cursed Forest is a *special* kind of cursed. But you should really change into sturdier shoes and put on a cloak or two before we go," said Hale. "It always rains on the path, which was what I was trying to warn you about before."

Evangeline

Once upon a time, the Cursed Forest was supposedly not cursed at all. It was said to have been the loveliest forest in the Magnificent North. The sort of forest that the best parts of fairytales were born from, full of friendly forest folk willing to guide lost travelers back to their paths or help wounded ones find aid. This forest was filled with flowers that produced light at night and birds that sang music so sweet even the hardest heart wept at hearing it.

It was believed to have been a favorite forest of the Valors, and the Valors were said to be the forest's favorite family.

Thus when the Valors were all beheaded, the forest grieved for its beloved family. It grieved so deeply that it transformed into something else entirely. Something *cursed* that in turn cursed all those who dared to enter it.

Some say this curse was the forest's way of trying to make others love it the way that the Valor family had loved it—for the curse of the forest was a peculiar sort of curse. At first it didn't even seem like a curse, it seemed a bit like a wonder. Until more and more Northerners went into the forest and never came out.

And so in true Northern fashion, it was decided that all paths to the Cursed Forest should be cursed as well, so that Northerners would stop disappearing inside of it.

Unfortunately, there were disagreements on how best to bewitch the roads, so several sloppy spells were all cast at once.

Evangeline was unaware of this history. But as soon as she reached the path she'd chosen to take with her guards, she immediately saw the evidence of such spells. It began with a sprinkle that was not too bad at first, but the rain grew heavier as the road went on. Suddenly there were gusts of wind and lashes of rain that pelted her sideways and slantways.

Soon she was soaked. She wasn't sure how long the road was, but it felt like the rain beat down on her forever. It was so tempting to turn around. But she had to tell Apollo that Jacks had been sneaking into the castle to see her.

The only weapon Evangeline had was the jeweled dagger Jacks had given her. It was tucked into a little green velvet belt that circled the waist of her gown, and she told herself if she saw him again, she wouldn't hesitate to use the blade. And yet, a part of her feared she might not actually be able to stab him. There was also a twisted part of her that was scared she might never see him again. Her stomach clenched as she remembered how she had turned her back on him last night and how he hadn't chased after her.

She knew Jacks was the enemy, but a part of her still felt bewitched by the thought of Archer. On her own, she would never defeat him. Evangeline needed Apollo and his army and whatever else he had, and tromping along a rainy path was a tiny price to pay for that.

"Just keep going," Joff said as the wind whipped his cape around his face and spattered his boots with mud.

Evangeline was grateful the men had not let her leave the castle wearing only slippers or they would surely have gotten stuck in the path, like so many others had before her. Instead of cobblestones, bits of the road were entirely paved with shoes. Then there were the overturned carriages that lined the way—all of which appeared to be very old. It seemed most Northerners were now familiar with the spells that prevented all manner of transportation, save for one's own feet, into the Cursed Forest.

"We're almost there," called Hale. As he spoke, a sign popped up on the side of the road.

ONE HUNDRED STEPS
TO THE CURSED FOREST—
You Can Still Turn Around!

The rain poured harder as Evangeline passed it, making loose bits of hair stick to her face. She was barely able to make out another sign a few moments later:

WHY HAVEN'T YOU
TURNED AROUND YET?

The rain became angrier, falling in sheets until she reached a final sign that read:

WELCOME TO
THE BEST DAY
OF YOUR LIFE!

The wood was pink and the words were gold and it was the most peculiar thing. As soon as Evangeline reached the sign and read its words—which happened all at once—the rain suddenly ceased. She could still hear the harsh pound of its fall against the ground. But when she turned around to look at the path she'd just trod, it appeared as dry as a valley on a hot sunny day.

"There's no rainfall *in* the Cursed Forest," said Joff. "That's the other reason all the paths in and out of it are spelled. If you get lost, the rainfall is the one way you can be sure you're out of the forest."

"So we're in the forest now?" Evangeline asked, looking at all the camps surrounding them.

After the difficult road to get here and all the warning signs, she'd expected something a little more sinister. She'd pictured shadows, spiderwebs, and lots of creepy-crawlies, but all she saw was a dusky sky on the verge of sunset above a village of colorful silk tents festooned with flag bunting—as well as lots of men and women all dressed for an adventure. There were horses, too, a number of dogs, and quite a few falcons perched on shoulders.

Evangeline strained to see beyond the camps, looking for trees or even just leaves. But past the tents, all she saw was a misty blur of colors that made her think of the end of the rainbow.

"We're in the in-between," said Hale.

"You'll know when you're in the forest," added Joff.

"Evangeline! I mean, Your Highness!" cried Aurora Vale as she skipped forward, her perfectly curled violet ringlets bouncing.

While everyone else in the nearby campsites looked frazzled by the rain, Aurora appeared as fresh as a flower. Her light gray boots, which laced up to her knees, were pristine, as was her short armor-plated dress and the quiver of silver-tipped arrows at her back.

Hale stood straighter at the sight of her, while Joff quickly smoothed his unruly hair.

"I didn't know you were joining the Hunt!" Aurora said excitedly. "You can be on a team with me and my sister, Vesper."

"Thank you, but I'm only here to find Apollo."

"You could always join the lovely miss after you find him," offered Joff.

"I'm sure the prince wouldn't mind," added Hale quickly.

Evangeline wasn't sure she agreed. But she also wasn't sure the guards were quite in their right minds. Even before the lovely Aurora had dazzled them with her arrival, the men's faces had filled with adventurelust at the sight of all the flapping tents and sharpened weapons.

"Oh, please, do ask your prince to join! We would have so much fun together." Aurora looked up at Evangeline with an expression that was a bit like a puppy that hoped it could go out to play. Of course, puppies didn't usually have arrows at their backs, arrows that they planned to shoot at other puppies.

"I'll think about it," Evangeline said. "But I must find Apollo first."

"I can take you to him," Aurora said. "I just saw him over that way. His camp is beyond the collection of tents from House Casstel." She pointed north, where there was a stretching village of pale blue tents striped with silver and a number of rather tall men and women all dressed to match.

"I'm afraid the lady is mistaken," said a new voice that Evangeline didn't recognize, at least not at first. But as soon as she turned, she saw the friendly face of Lord Byron Belleflower.

He smiled kindly, just as he had last night when she'd met him at the dinner and he had regaled her with all sorts of humorous stories about Apollo. She wasn't sorry to see him again, but now was not the best time.

"I didn't even hear you arrive, my lord."

That wasn't all too surprising when Aurora Vale was captivating everyone's attention and Lord Byron Belleflower looked as if he'd dressed to be overlooked.

Today he wore brown pants, a leather vest, and a beige shirt with sleeves rolled up to the elbows. Unlike Aurora, Lord Belleflower didn't wear any arrows on his back. All he had was a small dagger at his belt and a knife at his hip.

"I thought we were friendly enough that you could call me Byron. And forgive me for startling you, Your Highness. I just came from seeing Apollo. He was speaking with the Guild of Heroes over there, right next to where his camp *actually* is." Byron indicated the opposite direction, past a row of food tents, where Evangeline spied a valley of dark green tents, surrounded by clusters of men and women who all seemed to either have a pet dog or bird of prey.

"That's impossible," said Aurora, a sudden flush rising to her cheeks. "The prince along with his royal camp are in the other direction. I was just there a few minutes ago, before I found Princess Evangeline here."

"Your Highness," said Byron calmly, "forgive me for insulting your friend, but I fear she's either addled or lying. The prince is not that way."

"I am not—"

Da-da-da-da! A host of trumpets sounded in the distance, interrupting Aurora's protests. A moment later, a nearby herald dressed in royal colors cried:

"Attention! Attention! The Hunt will officially commence in ten minutes. Ten minutes until the Hunt begins!"

Evangeline was running out of time.

"Well then, it looks like we should all be off," said Aurora, as if the argument had never even happened.

Joff and Hale immediately started to follow her with their heads held high and their shoulders back. They would have probably followed her into a volcano if she asked.

Byron was not as dazzled. He gave Evangeline a quick pleading look. "You're making a mistake if you go with her," he said quietly.

Evangeline quickly peered around the closest campsite, hoping to ask a passerby if they had seen the prince. But everyone was heading in the opposite direction toward the misty edge of the Cursed Forest, and Apollo was probably doing the same. She needed to make a decision if she wanted to tell him about Jacks before the Hunt began and Apollo entered the forest.

"I'm sure one of you must be simply mistaken," Evangeline said sweetly.

Although she didn't actually believe this. One of them was lying.

Both of them looked offended.

Aurora had stopped walking away. She looked as if she wanted to swear that she was virtuous and would never tell a lie, but then she simply pursed her lips and gave Byron a venomous look that turned her face from lovely to ugly in an instant.

Evangeline didn't trust her. Something about Aurora just didn't sit right with her. She'd started to feel suspicious after she'd drawn attention to Evangeline's knife and then waylaid her in the hall with accusations of an affair.

She wasn't sure she trusted Byron, either. After all that had happened within the last few days, Evangeline was feeling rather distrustful of everyone. But the young lord also hadn't given her a reason *not* to trust him.

"Joff, why don't you go with Aurora," Evangeline said. "If you find the prince first, tell him I'm looking for him and not to join the Hunt until I find him. It's important. Hale and I will head the other way with Lord Belleflower."

Hale looked dejected at having to leave Aurora.

"I'm sure we'll see her again," said Evangeline as they followed Byron toward the food tents, which actually appeared to serve far more ale than food.

Torches illuminated the people who lingered around them. Evangeline watched as a group clinked their glasses together and cheered, "To the Hunt!"

"Good luck, my friends!" said Byron with a wave.

The men and women all lifted their glasses and cheered again.

"Five minutes!" cried a herald in the distance. "Five minutes until the Hunt begins!"

This herald was farther away than the last one. Evangeline didn't even see him appear. She just heard his voice, fainter than earlier, before it trailed off entirely.

The tents they walked by now, apparently belonging to the Guild of Heroes, were quiet as well. It seemed all the heroes had already started toward the forest. All that lingered was a thin spiral of smoke from a freshly doused fire. The chatter, the laughter, the sharpening of swords had stopped.

Evangeline hoped they weren't too late. She didn't want to chase Apollo into the actual Cursed Forest, especially now that the sun was setting.

"Are we almost there?" she asked.

"It's just a little farther," said Byron confidently.

But as the sky darkened and tendrils of fog crept in around them, it seemed that they were moving closer to the edge of the Cursed Forest instead of toward a camp.

Evangeline feared she'd perhaps made a mistake to go with him. She pulled away, moving closer to Hale.

"You should stay by me." Byron took Evangeline's wrist, bringing her back toward him. The fog had grown thicker, turning from mere tendrils to a dense mist that came up to their knees, but it was Byron's hold that now made her nervous.

"Please, let me go," she said, and she tried to tear away. But Byron held on tighter.

"Lord Belleflower." Hale's hand hovered over the hilt of his sword as he spoke. "Princess Evangeline asked you to release her."

Byron's mouth tipped into a smile. It was one of those moments that moved slow and fast all at once. As Byron's smile slid slowly into place, he reached for his knife so quickly that Evangeline didn't even see it until it shot through the air and buried itself in Hale's throat.

Hale dropped to the ground and blood poured from his neck.

"*No*! Hale!" she screamed. "Hale!"

Byron quickly cut her off. He clamped one hand over her mouth and wrapped his other arm around her tightly. "Time to pay for what you did to Petra."

"Who is Petra?" Evangeline cried, not that the words came out. She thrashed, but Byron only constricted his grip on her and dragged her backward through the dirt. There were no more tents now, just heavy fog and the two of them—alone.

She tried to kick, to step out—to do everything Archer had taught her—but her feet were barely on the ground. Only the tips of her toes were scraping the dirt. She had no leverage.

She did, however, have a hand that was just close enough to grab the dagger wedged in her belt. She imagined she had only one chance to use it, one chance to save her own life.

She grabbed the dagger and thrust it up, slicing through Byron's wrist.

"You bitch!"

"That was for Hale!" Evangeline yelled as Byron's hands fell away.

Then she ran.

24

Apollo

A pollo wasn't a murderer—he didn't kill unless it was absolutely necessary.

But he was tempted to take his sword and run it through Joff's stomach.

There was no one else in the tent with them, and on a day like this, it would be easy to dispose of the body by simply leaving it in the Cursed Forest. Accidents always happened during the Hunt.

But Apollo needed answers, not more bloodshed. He leveled a cool look at the soldier. "Where is my wife?"

"She's with Lord Belleflower, Your Highness."

"Why on earth would you leave her with him?"

"She told me to, Your Highness. Princess Evangeline wasn't sure where your camp was, so she had Hale and I split up."

"Your job is to stay by her side," Apollo interrupted. "Regardless of what she wants."

"I know, Your Highness." Joff bowed his head. "I'm sorry I failed."

"Get out," Apollo said, "before I run you through with my sword."

"There's just one more thing, Your Highness." A bead of sweat dripped down Joff's brow. "The princess asked me to tell you not to join the Hunt until she found you."

"Did she say why?"

Joff shook his head. "No, but she seemed very determined."

"She's always determined."

"Your Highness!" cried a breathless, high-pitched voice as a small child burst into the tent.

"Stop, runt!" screamed a guard, but the child was quick.

"The princess, she's in trouble!" said the child. "I just saw a man trying to murder her. Now she's run into the Cursed Forest!"

25

Evangeline

Evangeline tore through the fog. She thought she'd headed back the way she'd come, toward the tents belonging to the Guild of Heroes. Only she saw no tents, just endless fog and night.

She might have turned around, but she could still hear Byron yelling foul names. Ones that made her wonder just what he thought she'd done and who Petra was.

It wasn't until she outran his voice that she finally allowed her legs to slow enough so that she could catch her breath and wipe the tears from her eyes.

Poor Hale. He hadn't deserved to die like that, or at all.

Evangeline knew it wasn't her fault—she hadn't thrown the knife at his throat—and yet it felt like her fault. With so many people who kept trying to kill her, she couldn't help wondering what she had done to bring all of this about.

Was it merely because she'd married a prince—or was it because of another event in her past that she'd forgotten?

It became harder to breathe as she jogged deeper into the dark fog. She hated this not knowing and this fear that she might never know.

Mud splattered her boots and the hem of her green velvet cloak until the ground turned hard. She stumbled briefly as the road underfoot changed abruptly to cobbled stones.

Then, as if a curtain had been parted, the fog was gone, along with the pitch-dark night. It disappeared entirely to reveal a street full of shops as bright as sweets in a jar. They all had cheery striped awnings, shiny bells, and doors painted in every color of the rainbow.

Evangeline's skin prickled as she passed the storefronts with their perky window displays. She knew she couldn't stop—she shouldn't stop. She was still running for her life, and she needed to find Apollo to tell him about Jacks.

But this wasn't just a pretty street. Evangeline *knew* this street. She knew the crooked lamppost at the end of it, the reason that it smelled of sweet fresh-baked cookies. And she knew that in the middle of the street, situated between Crystal's Candy Haven and Mabel's Baked Delights, she would find the one place in the world that she loved more than anyplace else, her father's shop: Maximillian's Curiosities, Whimsies & Other Oddities.

Her chest tightened painfully as she reached the front door. Suddenly nothing else mattered but this.

The shop was different than she remembered. Like the rest of the storefronts, it was fresher, shinier, *younger*. The paint was a shade of green so brilliant it appeared wet. The glass of the window was so clear, it looked as if there might not be any glass at all—Evangeline imagined she could simply reach through the window and snatch one of the curious items spilling out from the toppled-over purple top hat. A hat that, like the shop, Evangeline had thought she would never see again.

She might have believed this was all an illusion. There should have been no possible way that she could have run all the way home to Valenda—she wasn't even sure how to return to Valenda from the North, but she was fairly certain one had to take a boat.

And yet when Evangeline reached out her fingers toward the shop, she could feel the door, solid and wooden and sun-warmed underneath her hand. It was real. All of it was real. She could still smell the cookies from the bakery down the street. And then she heard a voice in the distance. "Get your lemonade! Fresh lemonade!"

The cry was followed by the appearance of bubbles at the end of the street and a perfect moment of euphoria.

When Evangeline had entered the edge of the Cursed Forest, the sign had read: *Welcome to the Best Day of Your Life!*

She'd thought the words were frivolous, but now it seemed that's exactly where—or *when*—she was.

This particular day had occurred the day before her twelfth birthday.

Evangeline had always had a love affair with anticipation. One of her favorite pastimes was to dream and to imagine. *What could be? What would happen? What if?* She particularly loved the rush of anticipation before special occasions, and her parents always made her birthdays extra-special.

On her ninth birthday, she'd woken up to find every tree in her mother's garden had branches full of lollipops tied to them with polka-dot strings. There were also gumdrops sitting in the center of the flowers, and overlarge pieces of rock candy laid among the blades of grass to make it seem as if the garden stones had turned to candy in the night.

"We didn't do this," her father had said.

"Oh no," her mother had agreed. "This was definitely magic."

Evangeline knew it wasn't—or she mostly knew. Her parents had such a way of doing things that there was always just a bit of wonder that lingered around the perimeter and made her ask if maybe it was magic after all.

And so on this day just before her twelfth birthday, Evangeline was full of hope for what magic her parents might make for her this year.

Evangeline had unshakable faith that her mother and father

had planned something marvelous. She could hardly wait for it, and yet it was the waiting that made the day so wonderful.

Evangeline's anticipation for what was about to be bubbled over. It touched everyone who entered her father's curiosity shop that day, turning each person's mouth to a smile and filling the store with laughter. Although no one even knew what they were laughing about. The happiness was simply contagious.

And maybe there was just a little bit of magic in the air, for by happenstance the baker down the street tried out a new recipe for stained-glass cookies that he decided to bring into the curiosity shop. He wanted to see what everyone would think, and the shop was clearly the place to be that afternoon.

The cookies were of course delicious, and they were made even better by the lemonade cart that had stopped in front of the shop. It was all yellow and white and had some mysterious mechanism underneath that blew out a constant stream of bubbles shaped like hearts.

Evangeline had seen lemonade carts before, but never one like this. It had four flavors that, according to the sign, changed every other day. That day's choices were:

Blueberry Lemonade
Lavender Lemonade with Honey Ice
Crushed Strawberry Lemonade with Basil Leaves

And then the most delicious of all,

Whipped Lemonade!

It was made of cream, lemons, and sugar, and topped off with a glittering dollop of vanilla cream.

Evangeline tried to savor the drink, but she also wanted to share it with her mother and father, who'd made the mistake of simply ordering the blueberry.

Evangeline could still remember sitting on the steps in front of the shop between her parents and feeling like the luckiest girl in all the world.

Evangeline didn't know how it was possible that she could have traveled back in time to this day, but she didn't need for it to be possible. She wanted it so much—*to be back at the shop, to be with her parents, to be safe*—she was willing to believe in the impossibility of it all.

A shadow moved in the shop. Evangeline saw it through the window, and although it was just a shadow, she knew who it must have belonged to.

"Father!" she cried as she stepped inside the curiosity shop.

It smelled just as she remembered—like the wooden crates that were always going in and out, and the violet perfume her mother used to wear.

Evangeline's boots clacked against the checkered floor as she went deeper inside, crying, "Father!"

"Sweetheart," called her mother, "don't come back here!"

Evangeline's knees went weak at the sound of her mother's voice. It had been so long since she had heard it. She didn't care what it said, no earthly force could have stopped Evangeline from following it.

She raced toward the back of the shop, where a door disguised as a wardrobe opened up to the rear storeroom. But her parents weren't there. There were only open crates, a half-finished window display, and piles of other whatnots that Evangeline didn't pay attention to. If she had remembered this particular day correctly, she'd find her parents in the attic filling up balloons for the following day.

The stairs were at the back of the room. But as soon as she reached them, her father's voice boomed from above: "Honey, don't come up here!"

"I just need to see you for a second!" She quickly climbed the stairs, her heart swelling with hope and fear that if she wasn't fast enough, she might be plunged back to the present, and that she might not see her mother and father ever again.

When she felt the doorknob beneath her hand, solid and real, she nearly cried. The door swung open to a room full of birthday balloons. Lavender and purple and white and gold, all bouncing on springy pink strings. They were the same ones from her birthday that year, only like everything else that day, they were brighter and bouncier and there were so many *more* of them than she remembered.

"Sweetheart, you're not supposed to be here," said her mother.

"You're spoiling the surprise," added her father. His voice

was clear and sounded near, but Evangeline couldn't see him or her mother through all the birthday balloons.

"Mother! Father! Please come out."

It felt like a dream that had turned to a nightmare as Evangeline shoved through the balloons. Every time she pushed one aside, another two popped into its place.

"Mother! Father!" She began popping balloons in between her cries, but more kept on appearing.

"Honey, what are you doing up there?" called her father.

Now his voice sounded as if it was coming from down the stairs.

She knew it was a trick, just like this awful room.

But the problem with hope was also what made it so wonderful. Once a bit of hope had come to life, it was difficult to kill. And now that Evangeline had heard her parents' voices, she couldn't help but hope that if she just ran fast enough, she would see their faces as well.

She nearly tripped on her skirts as she started down the stairs, rushing back into the room with the endless curiosity crates. As with the balloons, there were more crates than she remembered, an endless labyrinth. And just beyond, she could hear her mother saying, "Sweetheart, where are you?"

This time her mother's gentle voice made Evangeline's throat go tight. It was so close, and yet she had a feeling that was all it would ever be. Close, but never quite there.

"I'm sorry," said a new voice.

Evangeline jolted and glanced to her side. Only the young

man who'd just spoken didn't have a face meant for glancing at. One look made her breath catch. He had an incredibly handsome face, and the greenest eyes she'd ever seen, eyes so green it made her wonder if she'd ever seen green eyes before.

"Why are you sorry?" Evangeline asked. "Did you do this to me?"

The Handsome Stranger's mouth tipped down. "I'm afraid I'm not that powerful. This is how the Cursed Forest traps you. It gives you just enough to chase, but it never lets you find what you want."

"Sweetheart, where are you?" her mother repeated.

Evangeline looked toward the sound of her voice. She believed the Handsome Stranger was right. In a way, she'd feared all along that this was too miraculous to be true. People fell into holes and wells, not into the best day of their lives, and yet all she wanted to do was run through the crates and chase the sound of her mother's voice. She just wanted one last glimpse, one last minute, one last hug.

The Handsome Stranger didn't look as if he was going to try to stop her if she ran after her mother again. He stood so still he could have been one of the inanimate objects pulled from the crates.

He didn't blink, didn't twitch, didn't move so much as a finger. He was dressed a bit like a soldier in exquisite leather armor, but it didn't appear to be like any other armor she'd seen that day. And although he wore armor, she didn't notice any weapons on his person, nor did he have a mustache, so he couldn't have been one of Apollo's guards.

"Are you a trap of the forest, too?" she asked. "Are you here for some sort of bargain? You'll let me see my parents if I give you a year of my life?"

"Would you make that bargain?" he asked.

Evangeline considered it. There was something about being so close to her parents, about this *almost-place* she was in, that made the lonely ache in her chest hurt more than usual. It was tempting to give up a year of time just for a hug, just to be held by people she loved, who loved her back and who she knew without a doubt wanted nothing but the best for her. She wanted to forget for a moment that all she had was a mysterious husband, that people kept trying to kill her, and that the one person she was inexplicably drawn to was the most dangerous murderer of all.

A year didn't seem like such a bad price to pay to escape from all of it. But her parents would hate it if she did that.

"No, I don't want to make that deal," Evangeline murmured.

"Good," the Handsome Stranger said. "And no, I'm not another trap. I'm in a trap of my own."

He took a slow step forward, moving with a surprising amount of grace for someone so tall and powerfully built. "The Cursed Forest brings everyone into a place that replicates the best day of their life. Then it gives people just enough of that day to make them want to search for more."

"So you're in a different day than I am?" Evangeline asked.

The Handsome Stranger nodded. "The forest can change its setting, but it can't hide the people inside from one another. That's how I found you."

"Why would you want to find me? Who are you?"

"You knew me as Chaos. I'm your friend," he said. But there was something strange about the way he said the word *friend*, as if he wasn't entirely sure.

If Evangeline hadn't just seen one of her guards murdered by someone who had then tried to kill her, she might not have thought much of it. She didn't want to believe her luck could be so wretched that this Chaos person would try to kill her as well.

But she wasn't willing to risk it.

Evangeline took her dagger from her belt.

Chaos quickly threw up his hands. "You're not in danger. I'm here because a friend of ours needs help—your help. He's about to make a horrible decision and you need to change his mind before it's too late to save him. I'm not here to hurt you, Evangeline."

"Then why don't you get the hell away from her," growled Archer.

Evangeline hadn't heard him approach. She just turned and suddenly Archer—*Jacks*—was there. It was easier to think of him as Jacks as she watched him, striding swiftly in between the crates, glaring at Chaos with murder in his eyes.

"I don't want you near her. Ever." Jacks pulled out his sword, and before Chaos had time to speak, he shoved the blade right through his chest.

26

Jacks

Jacks's back hit the ground as Evangeline flung herself at him. "You monster!" she cried, and cursed.

He'd never heard her curse properly before. She wasn't very good at it, but she was trying furiously.

As they fell to ground, she landed on his chest with a force that ought to have knocked the air from her lungs, but it didn't stop her from wailing, "Why did you do that? You can't just go around killing people!"

She continued to thrash on top of him. Her knees were on either side of his waist as she whaled at him with her hands. Jacks couldn't tell if she was trying to hit him or stab him, and he suspected she didn't know what she was trying to do, either.

If she wanted to stab him, she was holding the knife in the

wrong direction as her fists continued to beat his chest. Another day, he might have been pleased that she was at least trying to protect herself. But as usual, Evangeline had no idea what sort of danger she was actually in.

Jacks trapped both of her wrists in his gloved hands and yanked them above her head before she could accidentally slice his throat.

"He's not really dead," he ground out. "The *actual* monster, the one I just stabbed, will come back to life. And when he does, we need to be gone."

"There is no *we*. I know who you are!" Evangeline finally tore her hands free, reared back, and pointed her dagger directly at his heart. This time, the blade was pointed in the proper direction. Her hands were shaking, but her voice was still furious and hurt. "I saw your portrait in the scandal sheets—along with a story about everyone you murdered last night!"

"I didn't murder anyone last night."

"You killed someone in front of me!"

"That wasn't murder. He was trying to kill you."

Evangeline screwed her mouth to the side. She knew he was right. But she didn't move the dagger. She kept it pointed at his heart. He could see in her eyes that she believed it was the right thing, to end him. And she wasn't entirely wrong.

"I deserve this," he said. "I probably deserve a lot worse. But this is *not* the day to kill me. I'm trying very hard to keep you alive."

Jacks grabbed her arms again and flipped her over, trapping

her beneath his body. He tried to be gentle, he tried not to hurt her. But he needed her to understand before he let her go. "Yes, I am a murderer. I enjoy hurting people. I like blood. I like pain. I am a monster, but whether you remember it or not, I'm *your* monster, Evangeline."

Her breath caught.

For a second, Jacks could have sworn it wasn't anger or fear he saw in her eyes. Her neck turned pink and her cheeks flushed . . . differently from before. He couldn't tell if she was finally remembering.

But he was selfish enough to hope that she was.

He debated keeping her trapped under him until she did. He knew it was a bad idea, but he wanted her to remember him. He wanted her to look at him, just once, and know him the way she had before.

It was cruel of him to want her to want him again. If she remembered, it would only hurt her more.

He was still haunted by the last time he'd seen her with her memories. It had been right outside the Valory. Hours before, he'd felt her die in his arms.

Evangeline had no idea what had happened, no clue that Jacks had already used the stones to turn back time for her.

She was trying to talk him out of using them to go back to Donatella. She'd asked him to come with her instead.

After everything, she'd still wanted him.

Jacks had so badly wanted to tell her that he couldn't even remember what Donatella looked like, that Evangeline's face was the only one he saw whenever he closed his eyes, that he would go with her anywhere . . . if he could.

But he couldn't see her die again. His first fox had believed in him, and she had died, just like Evangeline would. There was only one way their story ended, and it wasn't happy. Her hope might have been powerful, but it wasn't magic. It wasn't enough.

It was better to hurt her, better to break her heart, to do whatever he needed to do, to keep her alive and to keep her away from him.

That hadn't changed.

But today, Jacks was failing at letting her go. He wanted to keep her pressed to the floor beneath him. He would have set the world on fire and then let it all burn just to keep holding her like this.

He glanced to the side. Castor was motionless. His chest was still, his eyes were frozen open. He really did look dead. But it wouldn't be much longer until he returned to life.

Jacks had to get Evangeline out of here.

She was still flushed beneath him, her face red, her breathing heavy. He could see that she hadn't decided whether to trust him, but he couldn't waste any more time.

He jumped up from the ground. Then he grabbed her hand and yanked her to her feet before he reached for the rope in his belt.

"What are you doing?" she started, but Jacks didn't give her the chance to break away. He pulled her back to him and quickly tied her wrist to his.

27

Evangeline

Evangeline didn't even see where Jacks had taken the rope from. Suddenly it was just there in his expert hands, as if he always carried it around, in the event he needed to take a girl and tie her up. "How could I have ever been in love with you?"

It was an unkind question, but Evangeline was feeling overwrought. One second, she was on the floor with Jacks on top of her and now they were tied together, skin touching skin, which felt different than when there'd been a layer of clothing between them.

She imagined he could feel her pulse, racing against his.

Evangeline tugged on the ropes binding them, but instead of the ropes coming loose, little flowers started to grow on them, tiny white and pink buds on jewel-green vines that twirled around their arms, binding them even closer together.

"What are you doing?" Jacks demanded.

"I thought you were doing this!"

"You think I'd tie us up with flowers?" He scowled as a little pink bud burst into a blossom.

"It must be this place," he muttered.

It was then Evangeline noticed that they were no longer in the back room of the curiosity shop.

The confusion of crates was gone, and the shop had been transformed into a lovely cottage—or perhaps this peculiar place was an inn? The brightly lit entryway where Evangeline stood with Jacks looked a little too large for a family's cottage. There were at least four stories of rooms above them, full of doors with curious carvings on them, depicting things like rabbits wearing crowns, hearts inside glass cloches, and mermaids wearing seashell necklaces.

She felt instantly foolish for not immediately noticing, for being unable to see beyond Jacks.

Directly across from her was a rounded door, and beside it was the most wonderfully irregular clock. It was brightly painted with gleaming jeweled pendulums, and instead of hours, the clock had names of food and drink. Things like *Dumplings & Meat, Fish Stew, Mystery Stew, Toast and Tea, Porridge, Ale, Beer, Mead, Wine Cider, Honey Pie, Brambleberry Crisp, Forest Cakes.*

"Welcome to the Hollow," Jacks said softly.

Evangeline whirled on him. Or she tried to. Whirling wasn't exactly possible with the rope of flowers binding their arms. "You can't just tie people up and whisk them to wherever you want them."

"I wouldn't need to, if you would just remember." His voice was still quiet, but it was a dangerous sort of quiet, one that gave his words a bite.

Evangeline told herself not to care. But instead she felt compelled to argue. "You don't think I'm *trying* to remember?"

"Clearly not hard enough," Jacks said coldly. "Do you even want your memories back?"

"All I've been doing is trying to get them back!"

"If you believe that, then either you're lying to yourself or you've forgotten how to really try." His eyes burned as they met hers; it was a fire like anger. But she could see hurt as well. It came in threads of silver that moved through the blue of his eyes like cracks. "I've seen you try before. I've seen you want something more than anything else in the entire world. I've seen what you're willing to do. How far you were willing to go. You haven't even come close to that now."

Jacks ground his jaw as he stared at her. He looked angry and exasperated. He reached up, as if to run his free hand through his hair, but then he wrapped it around the back of her neck and dropped his forehead to hers.

His skin was cold, but the contact made her go hot all over. The hand at her neck slid into her hair and her entire body went boneless. He held her to him, fingers gentle and firm as they dug into her scalp.

This was so wrong, wanting the man who'd tied her to him and done countless other unspeakable things. But all she could think was that she wanted him to do even more.

He was like poisoned fairy fruit—one bite ruined a person for anything else. But she hadn't even bitten him, nor was she going to. There could be no biting. She didn't even know why she was thinking about biting.

She tried to pull away, but Jacks held tight, knotting her hair in his fist and keeping his forehead pressed to hers. "Please, Little Fox, remember."

The name did something to her.

Little Fox.

Little Fox.

Little Fox.

Two simple words. Only they did not feel simple at all. They felt like falling. They felt like hope. They felt like the most important words in the world. The words made her blood rush and her head spin until once again it was only her and Jacks. Nothing existed except for the press of his cool forehead, the feel of his strong hand tangling in her hair, and the pleading, broken look in his quicksilver blue eyes.

The combination of it all shuffled her insides like a deck of cards, until all the feelings she'd tried to shove away were back on top.

She wanted to trust him. She wanted to believe him when he said the Handsome Stranger he'd just stabbed wasn't really dead. She wanted to think that the murderous stories she'd been told about him were all lies.

She wanted *him.*

It didn't matter that moments ago, he'd told her he enjoyed blood and hurt and pain. Those things were on the bottom of the deck. And she didn't want to reshuffle.

Evangeline could have come up with reasons to justify this, reasons that went beyond just hearing a nickname.

But she didn't want to defend her feelings; she just wanted to see where they led. She no longer wanted to pull away; instead she wanted to go down whatever dark path he was about to take her. And that had to mean something. Maybe it merely meant she was a fool, or maybe it meant that her heart remembered things her mind did not.

She tried once more to remember anything else. She closed her eyes and silently repeated the nickname like a prayer.

Little Fox.

Little Fox.

Little Fox.

Just the thought of Jacks saying the words made her heart tumble, but they did not bring back her memories.

When she opened her eyes, Jacks's inhuman gaze was still locked onto hers. She could see something like hope in his eyes.

"I'm sorry," she said softly. "I can't remember."

The light went out of his gaze. Jacks quickly untangled his

fingers from her hair, straightened, and pulled away. All that touched now were their wrists and their arms where the vines bound them together.

He didn't try to cut the vines curling around their arms, and Evangeline was strangely glad of it. She might not have had her memories back, but it seemed her heart truly remembered him, because she felt it breaking a little as he looked at her with a gaze that had gone cool as shadows in a forest.

The uncanny clock in the hall struck *Mystery Stew,* and the body of the Handsome Stranger on the floor shifted. Evangeline saw his chest shudder with something that wasn't quite a breath. But it was definitely movement.

"We need to get out of here," Jacks said sharply. He tugged on the flowering rope that bound him to Evangeline and several pale petals fell from the flowers.

"Where are we going?" she asked. "And how did we even get *here?*"

"We're here because I tied us together," said Jacks. "If two people are touching skin to skin, then they're both brought into the illusion of the person with the strongest will. Otherwise we might lose each other. Since we were trapped in different illusions, you might encounter a wall, where I would have a door."

"So, this is your best day?" Evangeline asked. She wished she realized it sooner, or that she had more time to look around this curious inn, to see what it was that Jacks held dear.

But he clearly didn't want to linger. He didn't even respond to her question.

She didn't hear any voices calling for him, but she wondered if being here hurt Jacks the same way being so close to the memory of her parents had hurt her. If he, too, felt the pull of something he wanted but couldn't have.

He quickly opened the door leading out of the Hollow as if he couldn't get away fast enough. Yet Evangeline saw a flicker of pain in his eyes, as if it also hurt him to leave.

Outside, he rushed down one of the cheeriest paths she'd ever seen.

Hummingbirds flitted, birds chirped, and tiny blue dragons napped on polka-dot mushrooms. The poppies lining the path away from the inn were enormous as well. They were as tall as her waist, with deep red petals that looked like velvet and smelled like the sweetest perfume.

When they reached the end of the cobblestoned path, the air turned from flower-sweet to mossy and damp. There was still a path, but it was made of nothing but dirt and lined in enormous trees that turned the world from sunshine bright to shadowed and cool.

Evangeline could hear a stream trickling in the distance— along with the sounds of voices and pounding horse hooves.

The Hunt must have been close, which meant Apollo could have been near as well.

With all that had happened, she'd forgotten about him. She wondered if he was a part of the Hunt, or if he'd gotten her message from Joff about waiting to join until she'd found him. She hoped very much he'd gotten the message and was waiting outside of the Cursed Forest. She didn't want to imagine what would happen if he found her now, bound to Jacks.

"Where exactly are we going?" Evangeline asked.

"First we need to get out of this accursed forest before someone else tries to kill you."

"About that," she said, "someone else did try to kill me earlier, before I entered this place."

Jacks gave her a baleful look. "How is it that every day someone tries to kill you?"

"I wish I knew. Maybe then I could stop it from happening."

He appeared doubtful. "Who was it this time? Did you see them?"

"It was Lord Byron Belleflower. Do you know him?"

"We've met. Spoiled, rich, mostly useless."

"Do you know why he would want me dead? He said something about Petra?"

Jacks flinched. It was so quick, almost imperceptible, that Evangeline wondered if she'd imagined it.

When he spoke again, he sounded almost bored. "Petra was a nasty wench. She was Belleflower's lover until she died recently. But you had nothing to do with that."

"Then why does he want to kill me?"

"I have no idea." Jacks sounded slightly annoyed now. "At this point, I'm just assuming everyone wants you dead."

"Does that include you?"

"No." There wasn't even a second of hesitation. "But it doesn't mean I'm safe."

He looked at her then, meeting her eyes for the first time since he'd pressed his forehead to hers and pleaded with her to remember. He had the brightest, bluest eyes she'd ever seen. But as they stood there in the forest, his eyes looked paler than before, a ghostly shade of blue that made her think of lights on the verge of flickering out.

"I don't believe you're going to hurt me," she said.

The color of his eyes became dimmer.

You'll feel very differently soon.

The words were only in her head, but they sounded just like Jacks's voice, and for a second, there was a terrible falling feeling in her stomach.

A bird cawed above, loud and shrill.

Evangeline looked up.

A dark, familiar creature with wings circled above them.

Her heart skipped over a beat as she had a flash of the very same creature biting her shoulder. "Oh no!"

"What's wrong?" Jacks asked.

"That bird," Evangeline whispered. "It belongs to the leader of the Guild of Heroes. He's hunting you."

With his free hand, Jacks pulled a knife from the holster on his leg.

"No!" Evangeline quickly grabbed his wrist.

Jacks scowled. "Don't tell me I'm not allowed to kill birds now."

"It's a pet, and it shouldn't be condemned because of its master."

Jacks looked at Evangeline as if she made absolutely no sense to him. But he put away the knife. "Let's just hope this pet bird is living its best day full of fat rabbits and not focusing on us."

"Thank you," said Evangeline.

"I don't think I really did you a favor."

"But it was what I wanted."

Jacks looked as if he wanted to say something else about her *wants*, but then he tugged her forward through the forest by her wrist.

Evangeline didn't know how long they walked after that, but eventually the vivid forest turned to mist. The flowers and the vines binding them together disappeared, fading like a dream that could live only in the sun.

She could still see Jacks and feel his wrist pressed against hers, now tied with simple rope, but the world around them was growing dark. The sky was a swirl of gray and charcoal and hovering clouds about to break.

The first drop felt like a surprise. Then more rain began to fall in relentless silver-gray lines that muddled the stars and the dark of the night.

Evangeline quickly lifted the hood of her green velvet cloak, but the rain had already soaked her hair through. "Does this mean we're officially out of the Cursed Forest?"

"Yes."

"But where are all the tents for the Hunt?"

"We're on the other side of the forest now," Jacks said without pausing as it continued to pour.

Evangeline once again lost track of time as they trudged through the rain. It was dark when they'd escaped the forest and it was dark still. Jacks had grown very quiet, and she had become rather hungry.

She couldn't remember the last time she'd eaten or had anything to drink. It hadn't seemed to matter inside the Cursed Forest. But now her stomach was growling and her legs were tired, and every rock and acorn looked like something worth taking a bite of.

She was starting to feel the effect of going an entire day without eating or drinking. At least . . . she thought it had been a day. She wasn't entirely sure how much time had passed since she'd gone to the forest.

All she knew was that it was night again, her mouth was dry, and her legs felt as if they would collapse underneath her. Jacks kept pace beside her, but she imagined she was slowing him down.

Her cloak was drenched and starting to leak through to her chilled skin.

"We're almost there," he said. Rain dripped from the tips of his golden hair to his cheeks before running down his neck to his doublet. Unlike Evangeline, he wore no hood or cloak, just the rain—and like everything else, it looked good on him.

He glanced at her sideways. "You shouldn't stare at me like that."

"Then how should I stare?"

"You shouldn't stare at me at all." He abruptly looked away.

Evangeline felt a stab of something close to hurt. Jacks had tied her to him, he'd saved her life, and now he was saying not to look at him.

"What is it we're doing, Jacks?"

"We need to get out of the rain," he said.

As soon as he spoke, the inn appeared in the distance, like a picture in a pop-up book. A rainy pop-up picture book. But Evangeline didn't care as long as it was warm and she could get something to eat. Her shoes were soaked; her cloak was drenched and clinging to her person; even the rope tying her to Jacks was sopping wet. But as they drew closer, she could see that even in the pouring rain, the inn looked warm and cozy.

The building was all glistening redbrick with overflowing flower boxes full of fluffy fox-leaf flowers covered in fat drops of rain. The chimney on the moss-covered roof, with puffs of gray piping from it, filled the wet air with a woodsy sort of smoke, as the sign in front of the inn swayed with the wind.

Ye Olde Brick Inn at the End of the Forest: for Wayward Travelers and Adventurers.

Beneath this sign was another swaying sign that contained the word: *Vacancy.*

And then hooked beneath that was an even smaller sign that read: *One Bed.*

28

Apollo

Apollo had never participated in the Hunt.

It's an excellent way to get killed, his father had always said. *Be there at the start, give a rallying battle cry, and then get the hell out.*

Apollo had always done just that. He never even ventured beyond the perimeter of the royal camp to enter the Cursed Forest.

The one thing that could have drawn him into the Cursed Forest was Evangeline. As soon as the child had appeared in his tent and told him that someone had tried to kill her, Apollo had wanted to go into the forest to save her.

Then he'd realized this was the opportunity he'd been waiting for. The moment that would ensure he'd always be able to take care of her.

"Your Highness," called a guard. The front flap of his tent cracked open and the guard quickly slipped inside. "Lord and Lady Vale are here to see you."

"Let them enter," Apollo said.

The door to his tent swung wider and Honora and Wolfric Valor stepped inside.

The air stilled as they entered. The flames in his fire went low, as if the tent had taken a deep breath and held it.

Wolfric didn't bother with a coat. He simply wore an old homespun shirt with ties at the throat, heavy black trousers, and worn leather boots. His wife's clothing was equally plain. They should have looked like peasants, and yet some higher authority still clung to them. Before Apollo's guards had closed the tent, he'd caught them watching the couple with something close to reverence, despite not knowing who they truly were.

"Please, take a seat." Apollo motioned to the bench across from a low table covered in candles while he took a chair adjacent to them. As Apollo had planned to be here for days, he'd made sure that his tent possessed as many comforts as possible. Pillows, blankets, chairs—he even had a bathing tub in the corner.

"Thank you for coming tonight. It is good to see you both again, Your Majesties. Though I wish it were under better circumstances. I'm sure you know now that my wife is missing."

"My family will help however we can," said Wolfric.

"I'm glad to hear that, because I believe you may have access to the one thing I need."

Apollo pulled out the scroll that Lord Robin Slaughterwood had given him and carefully unrolled it. Instantly, the bottom of the page began to burn, just as it always did. Slowly, flames ate up the words line by line.

After Lord Slaughterwood had first given him the scroll, it had taken Apollo eight tries to read the page, and even then, he never managed to catch the last few lines—they always burned too fast. But he had read enough to know that he never should have wasted his time in search of Vengeance Slaughterwood's cuff. This story was the one that he should have been chasing all along.

"Do you know what this is?" he asked the Valors as the page continued to burn before them.

"No," replied Wolfric. "And you should know, I'm not one for theatrics. If you have a request, spit it out."

"It's not theatrics," Apollo said apologetically. "It's just the story curse." He worked to keep his voice from sounding condescending. If this was going to work, the old king could not see him as a threat. "This scroll contains a long-lost tale about a tree of which there is only one. The Tree of Souls."

Apollo paused long enough to take in Wolfric's expression, but the stoic former king gave nothing away. Neither did his wife, although the scroll didn't mention her, so perhaps she didn't know about it.

"I'd never heard of this tree until the day a friend gave me this scroll. According to the scroll, the branches of the Tree of Souls are filled with blood, and anyone clever enough to find the tree and brave enough to drink its blood will be human no more, but immortal."

"Sounds like quite the myth," said Wolfric.

"You would know," said Apollo. "This scroll also said that you were the only person who successfully grew this tree."

"I was," said Wolfric calmly. "I was also a fool to plant it in the first place. The Tree of Souls is evil."

"Sometimes evil is necessary."

For a second the former king's stony expression finally cracked. His lips curved. Apollo felt a brief flare of triumph.

Then Wolfric stood and looked down at him as if Apollo was nothing more than a simple child. "There is never necessary evil, just poor choices, and I fear you're about to make one, boy."

Apollo bristled at the word *boy*. But he managed to temper his voice as he said, "Evangeline is an innocent, and Lord Jacks is an immortal with immortal friends. I'll never best him and save my wife as long as I am merely human."

Wolfric snorted. "I heard your wife was taken by Lord Belle-flower, not Lord Jacks."

"That may be true, but mark my words, Jacks will have her by now."

"Then you should stop wasting your time in luxurious tents and go out like an actual leader and search for her," said Honora.

Apollo was more than a little taken aback and slightly

abashed. Wolfric's words had made him bristle, but Honora's put Apollo to shame.

"My wife is right," said Wolfric. "Go search for your princess, and if you value your life, forget all about the Tree of Souls."

29

Evangeline

Evangeline hoped Ye Olde Brick Inn would be warm. Impossibly warm. She hoped that the rooms were small and cozy, the fires were blazing, and there were quilts— piles of quilts. She pictured patchwork quilts on the benches, quilts lining the floors, and quilts covering the staircases.

She realized then that she perhaps was a little delirious. And it wasn't from Jacks this time. She'd grown used to the feeling of his wrist tied to hers. Although as they neared the inn, she felt his pulse begin to spike.

"Whatever you do, do *not* remove your hood."

It continued to pour as Jacks reached for her cloak and tugged its hood down so that it practically covered her eyes.

"I can barely see." Evangeline lifted her hood so that it wasn't a complete blindfold. "What about you? You don't even have a cloak."

"I don't need a cloak."

"You're just as recognizable as I am. And you have a woman tied to you."

"I'm very aware of that," Jacks grumbled. "Just follow my lead and go along with whatever I say."

Before Evangeline could ask another question, he opened the door.

The inn was not covered in the quilts Evangeline had imagined, but it was quaint and inviting from what she could see.

Wooden beams crisscrossed a ceiling covered in mismatched glass lanterns that looked like little lost stars as they illuminated stairs to right and to left, and then a hallway down the center that led to a quiet tavern full of grainy lantern light. It must have been quite late, for the tavern's only patrons were a couple talking quietly over half-empty mugs of ale and a fluffy white cat drinking milk from a saucer on one end of the bar.

"How can I help you two?" said the barkeeper.

"We need a room for the night." Jacks lifted their tied wrists, covering Evangeline's face. "I believe you've been expecting us. I wrote earlier this week to reserve a room for myself and my new bride."

Bride.

The word conjured a host of feelings, a fluttering of her chest, and a spinning of her head. She liked hearing him say the word *bride* more than she probably should have, but he'd also said that he'd written earlier this week.

Jacks had planned this—*and Jacks's plans never ended well.*

Evangeline couldn't remember why she felt this way. She tried to remember some things that Jacks had planned in the past. But all she could remember was how Jacks's pulse had raced just outside and how he'd told her before that she shouldn't stare at him. And she now had a sudden and terrible feeling about this plan.

"Ready, love? Or would you like me to carry you?" he said.

Now all Evangeline could hear was the word *love.* She told herself Jacks was only acting, playing a role for whatever scheme he'd put together. But Evangeline was a little breathless as he sliced the rope binding their wrists and then effortlessly lifted her into his arms.

Her heart thudded as he climbed the stairs. She loved the feel of his arms, but she couldn't shake off the feeling that something else she did not love was going on.

"Jacks, what are you planning?" she whispered. "Why did you bring me here? Why are we pretending to be married?"

"You ask a lot of questions."

"Only because you do a lot of questionable things."

He ignored her as they reached the second floor of the inn. Halfway down the hall, a door was cracked. Grainy candlelight spilled through into the hall. When Jacks stepped through, the other side looked anything but sinister.

The room was a cottage dream. Everything was green and gold and pink.

Flickering glass lanterns with emerald-green glass hung on either side of a bed with a headboard carved to look like a flowering tree. The coverlet on it was a soft shade of forest green and covered in pale pink petals. The petals were strewn on the wooden floor as well, and the mantel of a fireplace where a few logs quietly burned filled the room with a gentle glow.

Evangeline felt Jacks's chest move as he took a deep breath. His heart was racing again, and now so was hers. But she feared it was for a different reason than his.

Time seemed to slow as he carried her toward the bed. The air was warm from the fire and sweet from all the flower petals, and everything looked perfectly dreamlike.

Except for Jacks.

He wasn't looking at her. In fact, he seemed to be looking anywhere but at her as he carefully laid her down on the bed.

Then he was reaching toward the straps on his legs where he secured his knives.

"What are you doing?" Evangeline scrambled to her knees as Jacks retrieved a small pewter vial that she hadn't noticed before. "What is that?" she asked nervously.

He slowly worked his jaw. "I lied," he said. "I do wish that we could have had a different ending." He uncorked the vial. "Goodbye, Evangeline."

"Why are you saying goodbye?" She panicked as Jacks started to tilt the vial toward her.

She had no idea what was in it. She still didn't believe he would hurt her. But she had no doubts he would leave her.

Was he planning to put her to sleep? Did he have some sort of sleeping potion inside the ampule?

She surged off the bed and knocked the vial out of his hand. It went flying.

"No!" Jacks tried to move, but for once he wasn't fast enough.

Shimmering gold dust from the vial fell like a spell over the entire room. Evangeline could feel it dusting her cheeks, her lashes, her lips.

She told herself not to taste it. But whatever it was, it must have affected her upon contact. The bedroom was spinning enough to make the world seem pleasantly buzzy as all the gold dust shimmered around them. Jacks seemed to shine the most of all. In fact, he looked as if he was made to shine. His hair, his cheekbones, his sulky mouth were all beautifully golden and glowing.

It looked as if the powder might have been affecting him, too.

Evangeline watched as he tried to shake the shimmer from his hair, but his locks were still damp and the gold dust was stubborn. After a second, he gave up on shaking his hair and tried to scowl, but it just came across as petulant. Everything about Jacks that was usually sharp looked suddenly soft and just a touch bewildered.

"You are a menace," he grumbled as the gold swirled around him. "That could have been poison!"

"You would have poisoned me?"

"I've been tempted on more than one occasion . . ." His eyes darkened as they lowered to her lips and stayed there.

Evangeline's skin heated and she started to think that she and Jacks had very different definitions of poison.

Something prickled at the back of her mind. *Jacks's cruel mouth. Her lips. Death and kisses, and pairs of doomed stars.*

The thoughts felt like fractured pieces of a memory. She tried to grab on, tried to remember. If she could just remember, maybe she could make him stay. But everything was so hazy in her head from the golden dust.

The room was growing warmer, and for a second, all she wanted to do was close her eyes and lie down on the bed until everything stopped swirling. But she feared that if she closed her eyes, when she opened them again, Jacks would be gone. *For good this time.*

He'd just told her goodbye. He'd said he wished their story could have had a different ending, as if they'd already reached the final page.

But Evangeline wanted more pages.

When Jacks averted his gaze and turned to go, she grabbed his wrist with both her hands. "I'm not letting you leave. You said you were *my* monster. If you're mine, why bring me here just to leave me? None of this makes sense."

He gritted his teeth. "Being yours does not make you mine."

If the shimmering gold powder was still affecting him, Evangeline couldn't tell. All of his sharp corners were back as he stood there with his damp hair and his burning eyes. They were unearthly bright, almost fevered.

I can't stay with you. You and I aren't meant to be.

He pulled away—

But Evangeline held tight. She fought against the sleep over-taking her as she said, "I don't believe you, Jacks. I might not remember everything about you. But I know you. *I know that I know you,* and I don't believe there is anything you can't do."

"I can't do this," he said roughly.

This close she could see his eyes were glossy red around their edges. It almost looked like . . . blood?

He closed his eyes, as if he didn't want her to see, but doing so only made him look more lost. Close and far away all at once.

She heard a drop of water fall. She thought it might be a tear, but it was rain from his doublet, dripping onto the floor.

The fire and gold dust had removed most of the chill, but their clothes were still soaked all the way through.

Tentatively, she reached for the top button of his doublet.

Jacks's eyes flashed open. "What are you doing?"

"Your clothes are wet," she whispered as she slowly undid the first button with a soft click. It was a small sound, but somehow it filled the room.

Outside, the rain lashed hard against the thin window, shak-ing the glass, but Evangeline could still hear the sound of every button as she undid one after another.

"This is a very bad idea," Jacks murmured.

"I would have thought you liked bad ideas."

"Only when they're mine."

He stood very still as her fingers reached for the bottom button and carefully slid it through the hole. For a second, there was no rain, there was no breathing. There was just the two of them.

Carefully Evangeline parted the fabric of his doublet.

Then she felt Jacks's hand braceleting her wrist.

"My turn," he said hoarsely. And she swore she could feel his voice on her skin as he reached for the ties of her cloak.

His bare hands were hot from the gold dust. Evangeline could feel the burning tips of his fingers as he carefully undid the knot at her neck. He barely grazed her skin, but she was suddenly on fire as he pushed the cloak off her shoulders.

She wore a dress underneath, but it could have been nothing for the tortured way he looked at her. She didn't want to breathe. Didn't want to move, for fear that his hands would stop there, that he would leave her in the damp dress, that he wouldn't reach for the ties at her breasts.

He took a deep, ragged breath and then his hands were on her waist, gently guiding her onto the bed, pressing until she was lying on top of the quilt. She could feel the flower petals clinging to her damp skin as Jacks hovered over her, his knees on either side of her legs.

His eyes lowered.

Her stomach dipped as he reached for the straps of her gown and slowly slid them over her shoulders. She felt even more light-headed as his hand moved to the velvet bodice of her gown. He carefully undid the hidden clasps that held it to-gether, and eased it down over her hips, leaving her in nothing but a silky chemise. It should have made it easier to breathe, but instead she forgot how.

What was breathing? What were words? The only thing Evangeline knew was Jacks's hands were on her, hot and curious as they slid up her hips to her waist. She might have sighed when they grazed her breasts. His hands were so hot, she could feel them through her slip. Then she could feel them on her skin as he slid one hand under her chemise and rested it on her heart.

The room spun faster, and this time it had nothing to do with golden dust.

The only magic in the room was that of touch and heartbeats and Jacks. And for a moment it was perfect. He felt like hers and she felt as if she was his.

Evangeline didn't want to move. She didn't want to speak for fear of breaking whatever enchantment was on them now. But she also wanted to touch him, she wanted to be closer. If this was all the time she was going to have with him, if in the morning he said goodbye again, she wanted more.

She reached up for his shoulders. "My turn again."

She pressed her hands against him, guiding him to lie down, to let her be the one to touch him as she started with his doublet, which he still hadn't taken off.

She slid her hand under the damp fabric, ready to take it off of him. And that's when she felt it. Her fingers brushed against a slip of paper.

Jacks murmured something that sounded like *don't*.

Or maybe she only heard the word in her head.

His eyes were shut, dusted in a perfect layer of gold. And he was suddenly still, save for the rise and fall of his chest.

He'd finally fallen under the sleeping spell of the gold dust.

Her hand was still inside his doublet touching the edge of the paper. Was this why he'd stopped her before?

She felt a little guilty as she tugged the edge of the page, but not nearly enough to stop her from pulling it out of the doublet. It was miraculously dry, although it looked rather worn, like something he'd folded and unfolded in order to read over and over. And immediately she recognized the faded handwriting.

It was hers.

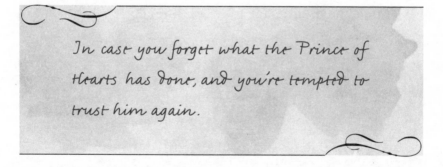

In case you forget what the Prince of Hearts has done, and you're tempted to trust him again.

She quickly reread the words, hoping she might have a memory of writing them. But there was nothing. She opened the note, careful not to tear it, as the paper was so worn and thin.

It must have been important if it was something Jacks carried with him and reread again and again.

The page was covered in more of her handwriting—but it

wasn't a letter to Jacks, it was a letter to *her*. A note she'd written to herself.

Why would Jacks be carrying this around?

Like the outside of the note, the writing was so faded, she almost couldn't make it all out.

Dear Evangeline,

Eventually you will see him again, and when you do, do not be fooled by him. Do not be tricked by his charming dimples, his unearthly blue eyes, or the way your stomach might tumble when he calls you Little Fox—it's not a term of endearment, it's another form of manipulation.

Jacks's heart might beat, but it does not feel. If you are tempted to trust him again, remember all that he's done.

Remember that he was the one to poison Apollo so that he could frame you for murder in order to make a long-lost prophecy come true—one that would turn you into a key capable of opening the Valory Arch. That is all that he wants, to open the Valory Arch. He will probably be kind to you at some point in the future, to try and influence you into unlocking the arch. Do not do it.

Remember what he told you that day in the carriage—that he is a Fate and you are nothing but a tool to him. Do not let yourself forget what Jacks is or feel sympathy for him again.

If you need someone to trust, trust Apollo when he wakes. Because he will awake. You will find a way to cure him, and when you do, trust that the two of you will find your happily ever after and that Jacks will get what he deserves.

Good luck,
Evangeline

It might have been the magic of the letter, of past Evangeline telling herself to *remember* over and over, as if she'd known that someday she'd forget.

Or it might have been another type of magic that arose inside Evangeline as she wondered why Jacks would have carried around this letter. It wasn't a letter of love. In fact, it was quite the opposite. And yet he'd read it again and again. He'd carried it with him, close to his heart. Her words—or rather, the words of the girl she'd been. And she wanted to be that girl again. She wanted to remember!

And at long last . . . she did.

She remembered.

30

Evangeline

The memories started out like rainfall, slowly falling over Evangeline and blurring everything else as she remembered writing the letter to herself in the first place. She'd been sitting in her royal suite on the verge of angry tears, but she'd also been heartbroken. She hadn't recognized the emotion at the time, but present-day Evangeline immediately knew the feeling.

It was the same ache she'd felt in her heart ever since she'd lost her memories. She'd thought it would go away when they eventually resurfaced, but the hurt seemed to grow as her recollections turned from a misty trickle into a steady downpour.

She remembered Jacks again. She remembered visiting his church and meeting him for the first time, thinking he was horrible. Then realizing who he was—that he was actually the Fated Prince of Hearts, and then still thinking he was awful.

Every time she met Jacks, Evangeline thought he was a little worse. He was always eating apples and taunting her, and even when he was rescuing her, he was wretched. She remembered the night she'd been poisoned by LaLa's tears. He'd held her like a grudge. His body had been rigid and tense, as if he really didn't want her there, and yet his arms were tight around her waist as though he had no intention of ever letting her go.

She'd still thought he was awful then, but as Evangeline relived that night, something inside her shifted. It happened again when she relived spending the following night with him in the crypt.

Suddenly she understood why thinking of Jacks made her think of biting.

There were other memories of biting as well—of wanting to sink her teeth into him when she'd been infected with vampire venom, and then actually biting down on his shoulder when she'd been in excruciating pain—the night that she'd killed Petra.

Evangeline remembered it all in a backward rush. How she and Petra were both prophesized keys capable of opening the Valory Arch. Evangeline had been trying to find all four of the arch stones to do so, and Petra had tried to murder her in order to stop her.

Evangeline had killed Petra in self-defense. Jacks had found her afterward, covered in blood. Then he'd taken Evangeline to the Hollow, and she'd finally admitted to herself that she was hopelessly in love with him.

She'd been in love with him for quite some time. Evangeline wasn't sure if that part was a memory or just a thought she was presently having.

Her memories didn't feel so much like her past as they felt like their story. The story of Evangeline and Jacks. And it was a beautiful story, her new favorite story. She hated that she'd forgotten it. That it had been lost and Apollo had tried to rewrite it, to tell her that Jacks was the villain.

Although, to be fair, from Apollo's standpoint he was: Jacks had put a love spell on him; then he'd put Apollo in a state of enchanted sleep. Jacks hadn't put the mirror curse or the Archer's curse on Apollo, but Evangeline wondered if Apollo knew that.

Even though her memories were returning, there were still a number of things she didn't know. She still didn't know what all was locked up inside the Valory.

No one had been able to tell her because of the story curse. But she had found she had stopped caring about the Valory's contents as soon as she learned that Jacks didn't actually want to open it; he had just wanted to use the Valory Arch stones to turn back time, in order to be with the girl who'd made his heart beat again. *Donatella.*

Remembering this part felt like reliving it again.

Evangeline's heart shattered as she remembered Jacks saying, *I want to erase every moment you and I have spent together, every word you've said to me, and every time I've touched you, because if I don't, I'll kill you, just like I killed the Fox.*

She'd tried to argue with him. *I'm not that fox!*

But Jacks had been resolute in his belief that there was no happy ending for the two of them. He'd told her he was the Archer.

And she knew, suddenly, that this was the reason her heart had broken when Madame Voss had first mentioned *The Ballad of the Archer and the Fox.* Not because of the name Archer, but because it was Jacks's story and Evangeline knew how it ended. She knew that Jacks had killed the Fox and that he believed that he would someday kill Evangeline as well.

He'd believed this with so much unwavering conviction, he planned to turn back time to pursue a girl he didn't love and make it so that he and Evangeline had never met, effectively erasing her memories and their story.

She remembered being hurt and furious and fighting with him about it after she'd opened the Valory Arch. She'd begged him to go with her, but he'd chosen to let her go instead. He'd told her, *I just want you to leave.*

And she had done just that. She had left.

But it was a complicated sort of leaving. Deep down she knew Jacks cared for her. She believed he wanted her. But she also knew that he was so afraid of killing her, he was never going to choose her. He believed he'd already found his true love and it wasn't Evangeline.

But Evangeline had also never told him she'd loved him.

He'd been scared, but she had been, too. She had said that she wished their story could have had a different ending, but she should have told him how she loved him. Love was the world's most powerful magic.

But love had failed her that night. It hadn't been enough.

She was still in love with Jacks, and yet both past and present Evangeline felt as if they'd lost him.

Past Evangeline felt so naive to present-day Evangeline as she remembered rushing to find Jacks, believing that if she could just tell him that she loved him, it would fix everything.

Clearly it hadn't.

And yet, a part of present-day Evangeline envied her former self's effortless belief in hope and the magic of love.

Evangeline could still hope, but it hadn't felt quite the same since that night. She wondered now if it was because that was the night she'd lost Jacks, despite believing and hoping and chasing.

When she'd raced back to the room with the Valory Arch, to tell him that she loved him, Jacks hadn't been there.

She didn't think he'd turned back time, because she could still remember him. She could also see all four of the magical Valory Arch stones.

But there was no Jacks, only his blood staining the wings of the stone angels who guarded the Valory Arch.

Then Apollo was there. She'd thought he'd let her leave. All she'd done was cause him pain. He was better off without her, but he wouldn't let her go.

Evangeline had actually never been one to believe in fate, but for a second it was hard to believe in love as she finally remembered Apollo ripping away her memories.

He'd stroked her hair as he stole each memory one by one. Evangeline had tried to stop him. She had struggled and begged and cried.

But he had just kept calmly saying, "It will be better soon."

"You bastard!" Evangeline had wanted to hit him, hurt him, but all she managed to hit was the mattress as she finally woke from the dreamlike state her memories had plunged her into.

She found herself returned to the present. To the forest-green bed that Jacks had laid her down upon last night.

Only now there was no Jacks.

Evangeline could feel his absence the way she used to feel his presence before she'd lost her memories. It was a prickling chill all over her skin that left her cold and afraid.

She told herself not to panic.

But she was still reeling from the merging of her past and her present. She couldn't just remember Apollo stealing her memories, she could feel it. Now she understood why her heart had beat out *danger, danger, danger,* that first night with Apollo on that rooftop. But she hadn't listened to her heart; instead she had kissed him.

Was this why Jacks had left her? Did he think she was in love with Apollo?

The idea made her so sick, it was difficult to push herself out of the bed. But Evangeline needed to find Jacks. She needed to explain that she had remembered. And she had to tell him that she loved him.

When she looked at Jacks's actions, most of them seemed to say he loved her, too. He kept coming back, kept protecting her. But he also kept leaving her.

Nervously, she reached for her discarded dress. That was when she saw it on her arm.

There was a wide glass cuff encircling her right wrist. It was cool to the touch and crystal clear, and when Evangeline tugged, it wouldn't come off.

There didn't appear to be any type of clasp, and it was too narrow for her to slip over her hand. Someone must have welded it on somehow.

What had Jacks done?

Because she knew it was Jacks. It had to be Jacks. He'd planned to bring her here and put her to sleep with the gold dust. It must have been so that he could put this cuff on her. But why?

Evangeline studied the uncanny glass object. It had appeared at first glance to be plain, but now she could see that it was etched with delicate cherry blossoms that curled around the cuff as if they were flowers stretching out from a tree.

She tried to remember if she'd ever heard a story about a bracelet like this, but she couldn't recall anything. And cuff or no cuff, she needed to leave. She had to find Jacks before Apollo found her.

By now Apollo no doubt knew she was missing and had probably sent half the army to search for her.

Evangeline wriggled into her dress. Then she grabbed her cloak, threw it around her shoulders, covered her hair with her hood, and started for the door. She hadn't really paid much attention to it upon entry, as she'd been more wrapped up in the fact that she'd been wrapped up in Jacks's arms.

Now she noticed that it was a prettyish door. Instead of a simple rectangle, the door came to a dramatic point at its top. It was a slightly faded green with a lovely gold patina. The doorknob might have been a little bit lovely as well, but Evangeline couldn't properly see the handle beyond the splashes of blood. Deep red blood sparkling with flecks of gold covered the entire doorknob.

She flashed back to the night she'd opened the Valory Arch, when she'd found Jacks's blood all over the stones.

"No, no, no . . . this can't be happening again."

It was almost worse that Evangeline could remember everything so clearly now. That she knew this had happened before. That Jacks had chosen to push her away, and then he'd disappeared and she had never managed to tell him that she loved him, and love had lost instead of won.

Evangeline's hands shook as they turned the bloody knob. And then they shook even harder. There was more blood outside the room, staining the floor in the hall.

"Jacks!" she cried desperately. "Jacks—"

She broke off as she remembered that Jacks was a fugitive. She wanted to find him urgently, but she didn't want to alert anyone else that he might be near.

Without another word, she raced down the stairs. Now that she'd stopped shouting, she could hear rain pounding on the walls outside, but everything else was eerily quiet for an inn with a tavern. Wrong quiet. Too quiet.

Her final step down the stairs sounded like a clap of thunder. She knew something had happened even before she found the bodies.

There were three of them. Three lifeless, unmoving forms. Evangeline saw that much before her vision tunneled, going black around the edges and filling with dancing spots in the center.

She grabbed the banister for support, legs buckling. Something inaudible escaped from her throat. A scream—a curse. She didn't know what words came out of her mouth or how long she stood there.

Numbly Evangeline forced herself to check for any life. The barkeeper, whom Evangeline approached first, was lying so close to the door, it looked as if she'd been trying to flee before her throat had been ripped out. The other two bodies were by the fire, and Evangeline imagined they'd been caught unawares.

It looked as if a wild animal had attacked them, but Evangeline knew better now that she had her memories all back.

A vampire had done this.

She must have been spared because of Jacks—but then,

where was he? Why was his blood in her room? His body wasn't among the others, but her mind spun with a million questions as she stumbled out of the tavern. Was he injured? Dead? Had he been bitten?

Evangeline vowed she'd return to cover the bodies with sheets and cloths, but first she desperately needed to find Jacks.

Outside, the rain was still falling in unrelenting sheets. She couldn't see more than a few feet down the path, but she thought she could hear someone coming.

A familiar bird cawed, and Evangeline immediately froze.

A second later, a figure moved toward her through the rain. A figure who was definitely not Jacks.

Garrick of the Guild of Heroes was mostly obscured by his cloak and hood. But she recognized him from the awful bird perched on his shoulder.

She started to back away, toward the inn. But the path was slick. Her foot slipped.

"It's all right, Princess. I'm not here to hurt you." Garrick grabbed her arm, as if to steady her. "I'm here to rescue you."

"I don't need to be rescued." Evangeline tried to shake free of him. But Garrick held her fiercely, like he didn't care if he hurt her, fingers bruising in their grip. "Sir, let me go."

"You're soaking wet," he grunted. "You need to get back inside."

Evangeline took one step, but then she remembered she wasn't just Evangeline Fox, she was Princess Evangeline Fox. "You need to let me go now," she demanded. "I order you to release me."

The hero cursed under his breath and added something that

sounded like *useless royalty*. "Sorry, *Princess*, but you're coming with me and my men."

He snapped his fingers twice and more figures strode forward through the steady fall of rain. There were at least half a dozen men, all concealed by cloaks like Garrick's, yet Evangeline could easily tell that all of them were larger than her.

She could not fight her way out of this. But maybe she could reason with them to let her go.

"You don't understand." She dug her heels into the muddy ground. "It's not safe inside that inn. Go and see for yourself. But please don't take me with you. I can't go back in there."

"Don't worry," Garrick said, "there's no safer place than with us."

"Then why do I feel like your captive?" she protested.

Garrick sighed behind his hood. "Fine, you're a captive. But that doesn't mean I won't keep you safe."

Evangeline continued to argue, but Garrick easily ushered her inside, followed by his gang of *heroes*.

The air smell fetid, metallic with blood and thick with death.

The barkeeper lay frozen on the ground in the same awful position Evangeline had found her.

Garrick's fingers dug into Evangeline's arm a little harder. It was the only indication that he might have been affected by the bodies.

He lowered his hood. It was the first time she'd seen him without a mask. He had a ruggedly handsome face entirely devoid of emotion.

But then he was barking out commands. "Leif, Raven, Thomas—you three go up and check the rooms. See how many others are dead."

The men quickly marched up the stairs, making the wood shake as Garrick turned back to Evangeline. "Did you see who did this, Highness?"

"If you want me to answer your questions, unhand me."

"We don't need her. It must have been Lord Jacks," said one of Garrick's remaining men.

"No," Evangeline said immediately, shooting the man a glare. "This wasn't Jacks."

"My wife is clearly stunned," said a voice that immediately made Evangeline's skin crawl.

Apollo was there. She could hear him, striding up beside her. Then she felt the brush of his hand on the small of her back.

Evangeline spun to the side and slapped him hard across the face. The sound of her hand hitting his cheek echoed through the inn, loud, cracking, and satisfying.

You loathsome, conceited, cowardly worm of a prince, she thought as she watched his skin turn an inflamed shade of red.

She didn't tell him she knew everything that he'd done. She didn't tell him that she knew what he really was and that she would never be his. She wanted to. But she wasn't that foolish. Not when Apollo was surrounded by guards and heroes who could effortlessly subdue her if she picked a proper fight with the prince.

"Oh, Apollo!" she exclaimed instead. "You startled me."

The prince rubbed his cheek. "I didn't know you could hit so hard, my sweet." The words were teasing, but she swore his eyes narrowed. Evangeline told herself that he couldn't have known that she'd regained her memories.

And she realized then that he could never find out.

She needed to keep pretending, and not just because his guards and heroes for hire were there. If Apollo knew her memories were back, he might simply take them away again. Now she understood why he'd had physicians check on her every day. To ensure that if any part of her past started coming back, he could just erase it.

He was horrible. Evangeline knew he was horrible, but the depths of his deception hit her harder and harder. She wanted to slap him again, to yell and scream and rage, rage, rage, but she had to be more careful.

And she had to do it now.

She tried to make herself smaller. Garrick had finally released her after Apollo had appeared. She hugged both her arms to her chest and tucked her head, as if she were shaken up and frightened, which she should have been, but it was so hard to feel it through all the anger pulsing through her.

It was even harder to make her voice tiny as she said, "I didn't realize I could hit so hard, either. It's just all been so upsetting. The bodies, the blood. And did you know that Lord Belleflower killed Hale and tried to murder me?"

"I heard about that."

Apollo wrapped his arms around her, but his hug felt too tight. Suffocatingly tight. "It's all right, I'm here now."

Evangeline told herself, *Keep pretending*. Just keep pretending. She needed to hug him back and act relieved, but she wasn't sure she could. It was hard enough just to breathe regularly with his body pressed so close to hers.

Finally Apollo pulled away, but he continued to touch her. He draped a heavy arm around her shoulders, keeping her close. She wondered if he could sense that she wanted to escape. She tried to relax, but the next words he said made it impossible.

"I'm going get Evangeline out of here," Apollo said to Garrick. "You need to find Jacks before he murders again."

"Jacks didn't do this," Evangeline protested.

Apollo tensed as soon as she said *Jacks*. She could feel his arm go taut around her.

But she refused to take the words back. She could pretend she'd lost her memories and she could endure a hug, but she wasn't going to let Apollo blame Jacks for murders he did not commit. Not again. And not when there was another killer out there. "This was the work of a vampire."

Apollo gave Evangeline a brief, unsettling look that seemed to ask, *What do you know about vampires?* Then he laughed. It was a soft chuckle, but it was enough to make her cheeks blaze with heat as he said, "My wife is clearly addled after all that she's been through."

"My head is perfectly clear," Evangeline protested calmly. "I saw a vampire in the Cursed Forest."

Which was true. She hadn't realized it at the time. But now

that she had her memories again, even more things clicked together. The Handsome Stranger in the Cursed Forest was Chaos. He'd told her as much when they'd met, but Evangeline hadn't remembered who he was, so she hadn't pieced together that he was a vampire and until recently he'd worn a helm that prevented him from feeding.

Now she understood why Jacks had been so quick to incapacitate him. Jacks had been protecting her. He was always protecting her.

And she needed to protect him.

"I know I sound mad," Evangeline said. "But I am certain of what I saw. I saw a vampire and he looked nothing like Lord Jacks."

She added the final Jacks just to watch Apollo flinch. But this time, he didn't. His lips slowly moved into a smile that made Evangeline think of putting on a mask. "All right, my sweet, I believe you."

"You do?"

"Of course. I was merely surprised. It's not often anyone speaks of vampires, so forgive me for my initial skepticism."

Apollo rubbed her shoulder as he looked back toward Garrick. "Lord Jacks is still your priority. But tell your men to search for Lucien, the impostor heir to the throne as well. Warn them that he's a vampire and he has gone on a killing spree."

Evangeline fought the urge to react. She tried to keep her face carefully blank, innocent, however she was supposed to look. She needed to look like a girl without her memories and not like a girl who'd just heard her lying, deceptive husband accuse her first love of murder.

"This heir," Evangeline said softly, hoping she sounded merely curious. "What did he look like? I heard he was young and extremely handsome."

Apollo scowled at the word *handsome,* but Evangeline went on as if oblivious. "My maids all talked about how devastatingly attractive he was. But the vampire who did this—the one I saw in the forest"—she shuddered—"he was old and monstrous." She felt a pang of guilt for this lie. But Evangeline knew if she tried to describe Chaos, Apollo would probably twist it around so that it still sounded like Luc, as both vampires were young, dark-haired, and handsome.

"Evangeline, darling," said Apollo. "Vampires look different when they feed. I know you think the vampire who did this was an old monster, but vampires are quite rare. I'm sure if you truly saw a vampire, then it was the impostor heir. Unless you're not certain it was a vampire?"

Bastard. Murderer. Monster.

I hate you, Evangeline wanted to say. But telling Apollo how she felt right now wouldn't help either Luc or Jacks. Instead she said the only thing she could bring herself to say: "I'm certain it was a vampire." And she desperately hoped that Luc was somewhere safe and far away.

31

Evangeline

Evangeline just had to survive the carriage ride.

It was only one carriage ride.

The last carriage ride.

Once she arrived at Wolf Hall, she would escape using the secret passages that Apollo had told her about before they'd married. With her memories returned, she remembered the passages now. She just had to wait until dark, when the castle was asleep. Then Evangeline would leave to try to find Jacks.

No, she corrected herself, not try. She *would* find Jacks. It didn't matter that she had no idea where he'd gone, why he'd left her, or why he'd put the glass cuff on her wrist.

Evangeline wanted to study the cuff once more. Jacks had taken pains to put it on her, so it must have been important.

Likely magical. But thus far, the cuff hadn't done anything spectacular—or indeed, anything at all.

She kept the cuff concealed under her cloak as the carriage rumbled toward Wolf Hall. Except now it seemed to be going in the wrong direction.

Evangeline didn't know much about Northern geography. But she did know that Wolf Hall was to the south, and she could tell from the direction of the sun shining over all the greenery of the North that their carriage was now rolling toward the west, toward somewhere she didn't know.

All she saw was fields of green and trees budding with new leaves.

She found herself gripping the red velvet cushions beneath her as she waited for the road to curve back toward the south, but the path remained straight as a stalk of wheat.

Until then, Evangeline had been trying to look out the window instead of at Apollo. She didn't know if she could look at him for long without giving her true feelings away. She also didn't want to see him. It was painful enough just sitting so close to the man who'd ripped away her memories and rewritten her history. She didn't want to look at his face. But finally she turned.

He was sitting directly across from her. His hands were steepled, resting under his chin as he stared at her with the same intensity that she'd employed in avoiding him.

A chill tripped down her spine as she wondered if he'd been watching her like this the entire time. As if he knew she had a secret.

"Is everything all right, darling? You look a little nervous."

"I was merely wondering where we're going. I thought Wolf Hall was to the south?"

"It is. We'll be staying elsewhere for a while."

A while could have been *an eternity* from the way hearing it made her feel. Evangeline knew how to escape from Wolf Hall, but it could be much more difficult to flee from somewhere else.

"Where is this elsewhere?" she asked.

"Right here." Apollo waved a regal hand toward the window as the carriage rolled by an overly friendly sign, wrapped in a jolly green ribbon, which read:

WELCOME TO MERRYWOOD VILLAGE!
WHERE EVERYONE IS WELCOME

As soon as she saw it, Evangeline's memories collided with her reality. She remembered riding through this town and its neighboring forest with Jacks. It had been the definition of desolate, hopeless and lifeless and colorless. But now it was teeming with life.

Evangeline could see the main square from the carriage. It was full of glassblowers and metalsmiths, men with axes, and women with hammers all working under colorful strings of bunting and lanterns and streamers that hung from the shops in the midst of repair.

Even with the carriage door closed, she could hear a melody of chirping birds, laughing children, and people hard at work.

"Now that the Hunt is over," said Apollo, "the Vales are having their festival to encourage people to help them rebuild Merrywood Manor and the neighboring village. This was the event they were talking about the other night at dinner. They've promised land and homes and jobs to anyone who helps. It's an old tradition that the other Great Houses support by putting up booths and sponsoring dinners and dances every night."

As Apollo spoke, the carriage veered away from the square, and they quickly came upon a circle of royal tents the color of deep red wine. The atmosphere here was not quite so cheerful as the village. There was a lot less bunting and a lot more soldiers.

Evangeline tensed at the sight of them all. There were too many to count; it was like ants crawling all over a picnic. As she'd feared, it would be much harder to sneak out unnoticed. But she would find a way to manage it.

Guards parted, allowing the carriage to ride toward the center of the royal tents, where soldiers sparred and meat was being cooked over pits of fire.

"It looks as if your guards are preparing for battle rather than a festival," said Evangeline.

"That's what soldiers do," replied Apollo coolly.

The carriage halted, stopping before the tent equivalent of a castle. It was lined in gold with two tented towers on the side, both of which bore flags with Apollo's royal crest.

The guards all bowed as Apollo stepped out, followed by

Evangeline. Immediately, the prince laced his fingers through hers, but she swore his grip was tighter than usual.

She took a shallow breath and reminded herself she just needed to play her part, pretend nothing had changed. As long as Apollo wasn't suspicious that her memories had returned, she would be able to escape.

"Princess Evangeline!" exclaimed a musical voice, and seconds later, Aurora Vale appeared, stepping elegantly through the line of guards. She wore a flower crown on her violet hair. It was made of rosebuds and ranunculus and white starmires that dripped flower petals behind her as she walked.

Evangeline swore that more birds appeared then, just so they could chirp a melody for her.

"I'm so glad you're safe! I've been so worried for the past two days," Aurora said sweetly. "But I knew your prince would bring you back, and I even made you this for when the occasion occurred."

She presented Evangeline with a flower crown that matched the one in her hair.

"Thank you," Evangeline said, although she still didn't trust Aurora.

She quickly searched her newly regained memories, to see if maybe she knew Aurora from the past. But all she found was another memory from the Hollow. Her first morning there, right next to the meal clock, carved into the wood, she'd found two names:

AURORA + JACKS

Was that why Evangeline didn't like Aurora Vale, because she shared the name of a long-dead girl who'd once had feelings for Jacks?

"All the festivities begin tomorrow," Aurora continued to chatter cheerfully. "And it will be such fun to have you here for them. There will be all sorts of booths and treats and pretty things. You're planning on going to the festival, aren't you? My siblings all want to work, but I'm rubbish at building."

"I actually think it would be quite fun to build," said Evangeline.

Apollo laughed.

The sound of it made Evangeline's skin prickle. She told herself not to pick a fight with him, not to do anything that would make him suspicious of her. But she couldn't resist turning toward him to say, "Do you not think I could help build?"

"I merely think there are better uses for you, my sweet."

"Like what?" Aurora chimed in. "I think building sounds ghastly, but isn't that what we're all here to do? Do you fear your wife is so fragile she might hurt herself if she swings a hammer?"

Apollo clenched his jaw. "I did not say my wife was fragile."

"Then perhaps you shouldn't treat her that way or laugh at her wishes," said Aurora.

Something dark flashed in Apollo's eyes.

Around them, all the guards went very still. Even the birds stopped chirping.

Evangeline opened her mouth to say something—anything. Aurora had no idea how vicious Apollo could be, and after the way she'd just stood up for Evangeline, she wanted to protect her. But then to her surprise, Apollo vanquished the look from his eyes and bowed his head. "You are correct, Miss Vale. I should not have laughed at my wife."

"No, you shouldn't have," Aurora scolded.

And it was the strangest thing. Seconds ago, Evangeline had been frightened for her, but now she sensed the power balance had changed.

Apollo looked as if he feared Aurora.

Evangeline might have thought it was only in her mind. But when Aurora finally left, after declaring she'd build with Evangeline tomorrow, Evangeline swore that she saw the girl slide Apollo a note.

It happened when Apollo had kissed Aurora's hand in farewell. Evangeline glimpsed the rolled-up page for only a second. Then she imagined that Apollo must have slid it up his sleeve, for when she looked again, the tiny scroll had vanished.

32

Apollo

The first time Apollo met Aurora Valor, he had thought she was an angel. She was beautiful and he felt more like a ghost than a prince.

Earlier that night, he'd been caged on top of a bed in a vampire's underground lair. Evangeline had locked him in after he'd kissed her and then lost control, nearly killing her.

Once she'd left him trapped in the cage, Apollo had thought the vampires were going to kill him, and he'd almost wanted to die. He was cursed, truly cursed—not the way people said they were cursed when they merely had bad luck.

One curse, and Apollo might actually have been glad of it. A prince who'd been cursed once could go on to become a legend, but Apollo had been cursed three times, and nearly killed just as many times—once by his own brother.

He was ready to let the vampires drain him of blood as long as it was quick. But then a woman had entered the room. He hadn't known her name, not then anyway. He'd just closed his eyes and waited for her to bite. But this woman hadn't been a vampire. This woman had been Honora Valor, and somehow she cured him from the Archer's curse and the mirror curse. But it was one of those situations in which the remedy initially felt nearly as bad as the afflictions.

The cures left Apollo suddenly untethered. His connection to Evangeline had been severed and he wanted it back. He didn't want to be cursed, but he wanted her; the wanting didn't end just because the curses had.

If anything, he wanted her even more. Now that he didn't feel compelled to hurt her, to hunt her, he could finally make her his.

But he knew it wasn't that simple. It wasn't simple at all.

For most of his life, Apollo had always been given what he wanted. As a prince, he was not used to wishing for anything. He was used to taking and getting. But for the first time, Apollo feared he might not get what he wanted.

He'd tried to kill Evangeline. He'd shot and strangled her. The bruises were probably still on her neck from where his hands had squeezed.

He hoped she'd forgive him. He'd been cursed. Unable to

help it. Surely she'd understand. But what if Evangeline never forgot what he had done?

What if, whenever he tried to kiss her, it made her flash back to when he'd also tried to kill her?

Then there was Lord Jacks. Apollo's former friend.

Apollo had never been in competition with another man. Who could compete with a prince who would be king? But when Apollo had tried to kill Evangeline, he had seen the way that she had looked at Jacks after he'd stormed into the room to rescue her. As if Jacks was her savior, her hero.

Something had changed between them.

And Apollo didn't know what to do about it.

Before Honora had left him, she'd lifted the bars of the cage. He'd been free to go. But Apollo hadn't been able to move. He had been too nervous and afraid to leave the room.

Then Aurora had appeared in the doorway like an angel.

She wasn't just beautiful, she was ethereal, with a sweet voice that said all the words he wanted to hear. "Someone as handsome as you shouldn't ever look so sad," she'd told him. And she'd known things, and not just that he was a prince—which everyone was aware of. She knew about the Archer's curse that had forced him to hunt down his wife.

"I could help you fix it all," she said. Then she had offered him an elixir. "Drink this, and for a short while you will have the power to erase it all from her memories. You can start afresh. You can remove whatever memories from her that you wish and rewrite a new story."

Apollo should have asked more questions.

But he hadn't wanted to know the answers. He'd drunk the elixir and regretted it right away.

How could he even consider erasing Evangeline's memories? He wouldn't do it. He'd let the power wear off. Even in his fractured state, Apollo knew it would have been an unforgivable violation.

But then he'd left the cell and found Evangeline, and she'd looked at him as if she was letting him go. She'd said that she wished Jacks didn't have such a hold on her, and then she told Apollo she was sorry.

She was choosing Jacks.

She was choosing wrong.

She was deceived just like Apollo had been when he'd thought Jacks was his friend.

Apollo had to stop her. He had to save her.

He didn't want to hurt Evangeline. He tried to make it painless for her. He'd held her as she cried and promised, silently, that together they would make new memories. Beautiful, extraordinary memories. And he would never do anything like this to her again.

He also didn't think he'd see the angel again, or that she'd turn out to be Aurora Valor.

Like everyone else in the North, Apollo had thought the Valors were dead. When Honora Valor had first healed him, he hadn't known who she was.

It wasn't until later, until after Apollo had taken Evangeline's memories and then fled into the Valory, that he'd seen the entire Valor family and began to understand the full scope of what had happened.

The Valors had not been beheaded, as the stories had always claimed. The family was alive and had been in a state of suspended sleep for hundreds of years. They were the true treasure hidden behind the Valory Arch.

Wolfric and Honora had assured Apollo they weren't there to steal his kingdom or his crown. But all Apollo could really hear was the blood rushing to his ears as he saw their daughter Aurora.

She'd winked as if it was all a great game and Apollo had just stood there, like a child.

"All we want now is a place to live quietly," said Wolfric. "No one need know we've returned."

If Apollo had possessed more of his senses, he might immediately have said something like, "I couldn't agree more," and then sent them off to the far, far edges of the North where no one would ever see them again.

But these were the Valors, he was stunned to see them alive, and their daughter knew his most terrible secret.

Her beautiful eyes had been on him as she'd said, "What if you just made us a Great House instead? We could go by another name, like Vale."

Apollo had waited for Wolfric to object. Great Houses were not quiet. But it seemed Wolfric did not truly want to live a quiet life, after all.

"I think that could work. What say you, my love?" he asked with a look to his wife, who agreed.

"Just as long as we keep our true identities a secret," Honora said. "I don't feel like repeating the past."

Next to her, Aurora smiled as if it was all done. Then the rest of the Valors' impressive children were nodding and smiling.

How could Apollo refuse?

He'd heard himself say, "Excellent. There are lands I can give you. A manor, a village, a forest—they need to be rebuilt, but once I make you a Great House, people will come together to help you. I just need a little time."

"Don't take too long," Aurora chimed sweetly.

And when she winked again, Apollo knew he'd made a deal with a devil, not an angel.

Now Apollo's heart pounded as he felt the note that Aurora had slipped him. He'd tucked it up his sleeve quickly, but just knowing it was there made him sick.

Aurora's most recent request had been an introduction to Evangeline. "Don't look so worried, Your Highness," she'd said sweetly. "I just wish to be friends. I've been locked away for a long time, and all of mine are dead."

Apollo hadn't quite believed her about just wanting to be friends, but he knew he couldn't object. Just as he knew he wouldn't be able to object to whatever she asked for today. But perhaps he could ignore her message for a while.

He needed some time alone with his wife.

Apollo watched her carefully as they stepped into the tent.

Embroidered gold and burgundy carpets had been laid across the ground, beeswax candles had been lit beside the cushions and furs they'd be using for the bed. Next to that was a low table piled with fruit and cheese and goblets of wine.

And yet Evangeline stood just past the threshold. She didn't take any food from the table, she didn't throw herself on the cushions, and she didn't even attempt to remove her sodden cloak.

"Where will you be staying?" she asked.

"We'll be sharing," Apollo said softly as he moved behind her. "This way I can protect you." He wrapped his arms around Evangeline's waist.

She stiffened under his hands.

It was only for a second. Evangeline tensed, and then she seemed to melt in his arms.

He brushed her hair to the side and kissed her neck.

Once again, she tensed. This time she didn't relax.

He needed to let her go. She was scared again. He'd sensed something similar at the inn where he'd found her, but he hadn't been sure until now. His mouth lingered on her neck, close enough to feel her pulse, rushing under his lips. Then he heard her suck in a sharp breath.

Again, he knew he should release her, but he couldn't let her go. The pounding of her pulse triggered something inside him, an urge to keep her in his grasp. To hold her until she no longer wanted to escape.

"I thought we were over this nonsense about your not acting like my wife." His arms tightened around her and—

It hurt! The pain was sudden and intense and so strong he couldn't hold on to her. He doubled over. His vision went black and spotty.

It felt as if a burning knife had been plunged into his ribs, then twisted. But just as quickly as he felt the sharp stab of pain, it was gone.

When he could see again, Evangeline was watching him with a new kind of horror.

"Apollo, are you all right? What happened?" she asked, clutching both hands to her chest.

It was then that he noticed the cuff on her wrist. It was made of glass. That must have been how he had overlooked it before. He might not even have noticed it were it not faintly glowing, lit up with words in a language he could not read, although he feared that he knew what the words meant. What the cuff really was.

He wanted to ask where she found it, how it had become hers, why she wore it, if she knew what it did. But he assumed Evangeline had no idea what it was, and he didn't want to draw attention to it. He also hoped that he was wrong.

Because if Apollo was right—if this was Vengeance Slaughterwood's missing cuff of protection—then that meant Apollo had been about to hurt her.

He had to get control of himself.

"I'm fine," he said, slowly backing away. "I just remembered something important I need to take care of."

"What is it?" asked Evangeline.

"Boring, princely business. Don't worry, I'll be back shortly." He might have tried to give her a goodbye kiss, but he didn't trust himself. And he did have business to take care of.

As soon as he left the tent, Apollo pulled the note from Aurora Valor out of his sleeve.

> *Meet me at the border of the Merrywood and the road that leads to the Cursed Forest.*
> *Be there at sunset.*
> *Come alone, and I suggest you tell no one.*

Instead of her name, she'd drawn a wolf wearing a flower crown.

He burned the note as he passed the closest fire.

Apollo arrived at the crossroads early. He wanted to get this business with Aurora done as quickly as possible.

He'd ridden here on horseback, surprised at how much Merrywood Forest had already changed. Moss covered the rocks. New leaves grew on trees. Apollo could even hear sounds of life—deer and birds and crickets.

The Merrywood Forest had been reborn since the Valors had

returned. It no longer felt like the haunted place he'd feared as a boy—and yet Apollo had never seen his horse so agitated. After he tied it to a tree that bordered the Merrywood Forest and the wet road to the Cursed Forest, the animal stomped and whinnied. When Apollo tried to feed it an apple, the horse knocked it from his hand.

He wondered if the beast was upset by how close they were to the enchanted road to the Cursed Forest, or if it was perhaps because of the arrival of Aurora Valor.

Aurora, of course, still looked like an angel as she rode toward Apollo on a horse that appeared to glow silver underneath the moonlight.

"Don't look so sullen. It's unattractive," she scolded before hopping off her horse. "And believe it or not, Prince, I'm here to help you."

"Like that last time you helped me?"

"Evangeline is yours, isn't she?"

"For now," Apollo grumbled. "I'm starting to fear that some of her memories might be creeping back."

Aurora finished tying her horse to a tree. Unlike Apollo's, her animal seemed perfectly content. "Why do you say that?"

"She's acting strange. Do you have any more of that memory elixir?" he asked. And he hated himself for asking.

Aurora scoffed as she strode closer, her long silver skirts sweeping the forest floor. "You think that was an easy potion to come by?"

"You're a Valor."

"Yes. But our magic is not limitless. Do you imagine I just carry around bottles of magic with me?"

"You did that day."

Aurora briefly pursed her lips shut. "Do you want to keep asking silly questions, Prince? Or would you like to become the sort of man your wife will never dare to think about leaving?"

33

Evangeline

After Apollo left Evangeline in the tent alone, she studied the glass cuff that wrapped around her wrist. It was magical. She'd assumed as much, but she hadn't known what it did until she'd seen Apollo double over in pain.

She held the glass closer to the candlelight. She had seen it light up with curious writing when Apollo had been clutching his stomach. She couldn't make the letters appear again now; all she could see were the little cherry blossom flowers etched into the glass.

She wondered if it had been specifically enchanted against Apollo—if that's why the strange words had appeared minutes ago when he'd touched her and she hadn't wanted him to. It seemed like just the sort of enchantment Jacks would place on an object.

What she didn't understand was *why*. If Jacks didn't want Evangeline with Apollo, then why did he leave her with him? *Why didn't Jacks take me with him?* she wondered. But she already knew the answer to that.

You and I aren't meant to be.

Sorry to break your fairytale, Little Fox, but ballads don't end happily, and neither do the two of us.

Every girl I've kissed has died, except for one. And you are not that girl.

I want to erase every moment you and I have spent together . . . because if I don't, I'll kill you, just like I killed the Fox.

Jacks had already given her all his reasons for leaving.

Although the last reason she recalled gave Evangeline pause. Jacks had wanted her to find all the Valory Arch stones, not so that he could open the Valory, but so that he could use them to turn back time and be with Donatella, the one girl he'd kissed who he hadn't killed. But Jacks hadn't done that. If he had, she wouldn't have ever met him, and he'd be with Donatella in Valenda right now.

What *had* happened, then? There were four arch stones. Each one had a different magical power, but when all four stones were combined, they had the power to turn back time. But they could be used for this purpose only one time.

Had Jacks changed his mind about turning back time? Was he waiting to use the stones? Or had they already been used?

Before she'd gotten her memories back, Chaos had told her: *I'm here because a friend of ours needs help—your help. He's about to make a horrible decision and you need to change his mind before it's too late to save him.*

Clearly he'd been speaking about Jacks. But what was the horrible decision?

Evangeline had been heartbroken and terrified when she'd learned that Jacks wanted to go back in time and change the past so that she and he had never met. But this didn't sound as if he was going to do that—this sounded like something else. Something possibly worse.

Evangeline needed to get out of this tent and find him.

She considered setting the tent on fire and then escaping in the melee. But fires could too easily get out of control, and she didn't want to hurt anyone.

Unless it was Apollo. She did want to hurt him.

"I hope you appreciate just how much trouble I've gone to in order to break into this tent," said a wonderfully familiar voice as Evangeline's tent flapped closed.

She hadn't even heard it open, but it must have. A girl dressed like a guard stood in the center of the tent, hands on her hips as she scanned the lavish space with a shrewd twist of her lips, which were painted with a sparkling gloss.

"LaLa!" Evangeline exclaimed, too loud. But she could not contain her excitement at the sight of her friend. "What are you doing dressed like a guard?"

"I kept trying to visit, but they wouldn't let me. Some nonsense about how you were too overwrought to see *friends*. So I had to fashion a costume."

LaLa twirled around, and as she did, her three-quarter-length skirt lifted just enough to reveal that underneath the plain burgundy fabric was a shimmery sequin petticoat that sparkled like firelight. She'd also added little puffed sleeves to her bronze jacket, and a matching belt that tied into a bow in the back.

LaLa was a number of things. First and foremost, Evangeline thought of her as a friend, so sometimes it was easy to forget that she was also an immortal Fate, like Jacks.

She was the Unwed Bride.

She'd once confessed to Evangeline that the Fates were always fighting the urge to be that which they were made to be. LaLa's urge was to find love. She wanted it more than anything, even though she knew that it would never last. Because her love always ended with her alone at an altar, bawling poisoned tears. Because no matter how many loves she found, the love she really wanted was her first love—a dragon shifter who had been locked away in the Valory.

To deal with her urges to find love, she sewed. She sewed a lot. And she was very good at it.

"I know it's not exactly the same uniform," she said with another swish of her skirt, "but I think I've improved upon it."

"I love it," Evangeline said. "And I love seeing you even more."

With her memory back less than a day, Evangeline had not

had time to properly miss her friend. But now that LaLa was here, Evangeline could feel that the missing had been there all along, part of the emptiness inside her that was only now starting to feel as if it was filling up. She hugged her then, so tightly she might have feared hurting her, if LaLa wasn't a Fate.

"Where's your dragon?" Evangeline asked. She realized then that even though she now remembered opening the Valory Arch, she still didn't know exactly what had been inside of it, apart from LaLa's dragon shifter. She also had no idea if LaLa had actually reunited with him.

"Oh, he's around," LaLa said vaguely as she pulled away. "I'm sure you'll meet him soon," she added, but it was a little half-hearted, which wasn't at all like her.

LaLa might have been a Fate, and thus her emotions weren't quite human, but Evangeline knew that LaLa had loved her dragon shifter; she'd loved him so much that she'd actually been the one to put the Archer's curse on Apollo, misguidedly hoping to ensure that Evangeline opened the Valory Arch.

Evangeline had been quite hurt at the time, but like LaLa, she had also made terrible decisions because of love.

"Is everything all right?" Evangeline reached out again and took her friend's hand. "Do you need to talk?"

"It's fine, really. It's just . . ." LaLa paused to exhale. "The world has changed *a lot* since Dane was locked away, and apparently so have I. But it's fine. Truly. What's that saying about love? You know the one that mentions the sugar, the fire, and cost of desire?"

Evangeline shook her head. "I'm not sure I've heard that one."

"Well, perhaps it's not that much of a saying. Now, don't get me wrong, my friend, I'm thrilled you're asking about all of this. But I'm perplexed. I thought you had lost all of your memories?"

"I did," Evangeline said softly. "I only just got them back."

She then quickly filled LaLa in on how it was Apollo who'd stolen them. How he'd tried to convince her that Jacks was the villain, and he might have succeeded if Jacks hadn't kept returning to save her life. She told LaLa of every time he had visited and how her heart remembered him even when her head did not. Until at last she found the letter she'd written that Jacks had been carrying around next to his heart.

"That's surprisingly sweet," LaLa said.

"I thought so, too. As soon as I read it, I finally was able to will myself to remember. That was last night—or maybe it was early this morning. I'm a little mixed up on timing."

She smiled, but it was wobbly. She was so relieved to see her friend. She just wanted to flop down on some of the cushions in the tent and talk about nothing and everything. But there wasn't time for that.

Not if she wanted to find Jacks and try and stop him from doing whatever it was that Chaos had warned her about.

"I didn't want to come back here with Apollo, but when I woke, Jacks had left me, and then Apollo was there with his heroes and his guards and his lies."

"Bastard," LaLa muttered. "I know princes are the worst, but I wanted to hope being cursed might do him a little good."

"I do wonder if in his own way he thinks he's doing good."

"But you still hate him, right?"

"Of course—I loathe him. I can't stand the sight of him or the sound of his voice, and I want to get out of here before he returns so I never have to see him again."

"Let's do that then. Although I would love to wait until he returns so that I can stab him in the heart and then cook it over a fire. But I suppose I can do that another day," LaLa mused. "So, what is our escape plan?" Her eyes gleamed as she clapped her hands together. "It's been a while since I've been in a sword fight. That could be a fun route."

"Tragically, I can't wield a sword," said Evangeline.

"What about those self-defense lessons you told me about? Did Jacks teach you anything, or was it just an excuse to put his hands around you?" LaLa waggled her brows.

Evangeline's cheeks turned very warm. "He taught me a few things . . . but mostly it was a lot of his arms around me."

"That's what I thought." LaLa smiled, but Evangeline could tell it was one of those trying-to-be-happy-for-a-friend smiles.

Only since LaLa was a Fate, it looked just a little more dangerous. It was a smile that also said: *If he hurts you, you let me know and I will happily hurt him even more.*

It reminded Evangeline of the last conversation she'd had with LaLa. Before Evangeline had lost her memories, LaLa had come to warn her about Jacks. *As long as you are with Jacks, you're not safe,* she'd said.

"Do you still think Jacks is going to hurt me?" asked Evangeline.

LaLa's forced smile faded. "Jacks hurts everyone. He hasn't been the same since the day my brother died, and Castor died, and everything in the North went to hell."

For a flash of a second, LaLa didn't look like a Fate. She didn't look vicious or powerful, or like she might kill someone just for making her friend cry. LaLa simply looked like a girl who needed a friend just as much as Evangeline did.

In addition to being a Fate, LaLa was also one of the original Merrywoods. Her brother had been Lyric Merrywood, who had been one of Jacks's closest friends, along with Prince Castor Valor. They'd died on the same day, and even though it hadn't been Jacks's fault, Evangeline knew Jacks blamed himself for being unable to save Castor.

"If anything could spark a change in Jacks, I think it could be his feelings for you," said LaLa eventually. "But you still need to be careful. Because even his feelings are dangerous."

"I know."

"Do you?" LaLa looked at her seriously, her vivid eyes narrowed with concern.

There were three rules about Fates that Evangeline had been taught as a child. The most important of those rules was to never ever fall in love with a Fate.

Evangeline knew this rule, but she hadn't thought about it for a while, and she wasn't sure she'd properly understood it before.

But now it was making a new kind of sense. Earlier, when Evangeline had regained her memories but once again lost Jacks, she'd started to fear that maybe he was right and that they weren't meant to be.

If they were truly meant for each other, shouldn't it have been easier? Shouldn't there have been less bloodshed and heartbreak and people trying to tear them apart? Shouldn't love have *won* already?

But maybe the reason for the warning about falling in love with Fates wasn't because loving a Fate could never work, but because it was so much harder. Nearly impossible.

All LaLa wanted was love, yet she was the one who kept leaving her grooms at the altar. Even now, after finally being reunited with her dragon shifter, LaLa didn't seem to be sure that she wanted to be with him anymore.

Evangeline had once heard that Fates were not capable of love in the same way as humans. She'd taken it to mean they couldn't feel the emotion. But she wondered if this also meant that Fates didn't believe in love in the same way. Maybe they believed love with humans was doomed, and then acted in ways that brought that doom about.

"I'm not giving up on Jacks," Evangeline said.

LaLa briefly pursed her lips. "That's a very human thing to say."

"I can't tell if that's a compliment or an insult."

"I think it's a bit of both." LaLa gave her another half hearted smile. "I know you like to do the right thing, but the right thing doesn't always win with our kind. I think that was part of the reason Jacks became a Fate. He'd always tried to do the right thing as a human, but it didn't seem to matter, and the people he loved the most kept dying."

LaLa paused to frown. "I want to be supportive. I really do love lost causes and terrible ideas. But I fear that if you try to save Jacks, you will die, too. I know you have your memories back, but just in case you need a reminder, Jacks is a supernatural being who will kill you if you ever kiss him."

"Or," Evangeline offered, "I could kiss Jacks, and he could finally see that he is *not* going to kill me."

"No, no, no!" LaLa said furiously. "This is the world's worst plan."

"But what if it's not? I know what the stories say about Jacks's kiss being fatal to all except for his one true love—and I know he's supposedly already kissed that one girl. But I also know the stories here lie and twist the truth, so that could be a lie. *I* am Jacks's true love. I believe it with the same confidence that I believe that water fills the oceans and morning follows the night. I believe it with all my heart and soul. And there has to be some sort of magic in that."

"I don't think that's how magic works." LaLa looked at her sadly. "Believing something doesn't make it true."

"But what if the reason I believe this is because it *is* true? I know the stories all say otherwise, but my heart keeps telling me that Jacks's story isn't finished."

LaLa continued to frown as she toyed with one of the buttons of her coat. "His story might not be over yet, but that doesn't mean it's going to end happily. I've known Jacks forever. He is excellent at getting what he wants. But I don't think Jacks wants a happily ever after. If he wanted that, he could have it. But there's a reason he doesn't."

"Well then, it's a good thing he has me."

LaLa looked as if she wanted to argue.

"I know I seem naive," Evangeline pressed on. "I know my faith in love might appear foolish. I also know it might not be enough. But I'm not doing this because I believe I'll win. I'm actually a little afraid I'm going to lose. I no longer think love is a guarantee of victory or of happily ever after. But I think it's a reason to fight for those things. I know my attempt to save Jacks could end in a fiery explosion, but I'd rather go up in flames with him than watch while he burns."

At this, LaLa finally smiled. "This is perhaps the worst declaration of love I've ever heard, but I do believe your passion deserves a toast." She picked up two goblets of wine from the table and handed one to Evangeline. "To foolish hearts and fire! May you and Jacks only ever burn with passion and desire."

34

Evangeline

After toasting, Evangeline and LaLa drank a little more wine than they probably should have.

Evangeline didn't usually drink, but despite all the bold words she had said to LaLa, Evangeline was quite terrified that she might tell Jacks that she loved him, and then he still might leave her.

She had been turned to stone, poisoned, shot with arrows, flayed by a magical curse, and nearly killed over half a dozen times. But all those things didn't scare her as much as the idea of Jacks deciding that he didn't want to love her back.

Evangeline knew that LaLa was right, Jacks was excellent at getting what he wanted. When Jacks made up his mind, there was no changing it. The only thing that could make Jacks stay was Jacks.

"Having second thoughts?" asked LaLa.

"No," Evangeline said. "In fact, I have an escape plan."

Earlier, as LaLa had toyed with the buttons of her coat, an idea had come to Evangeline that didn't involve swords or fire or anything related to fighting.

"That could work." LaLa tapped her chin thoughtfully upon hearing Evangeline's proposed plan. "You could leave right before the changing of your guard, when these guards are tired. I could escape right after the new guards arrive. They'll have no idea that I hadn't been properly let in. And they'll be too dazzled by my beauty to question it."

Evangeline's head was spinning a bit now. She'd definitely had too much wine. It was all a bit of a blur as she put on LaLa's clothes and LaLa raided Evangeline's trunks until she found a shimmering off-the-shoulder gown that definitely looked dazzling.

After that, LaLa took pains to tuck Evangeline's hair under a cap. Then she darkened the roots with some of the table wine, just enough to change her appearance at a glance.

"If the guards look too long, they'll recognize you," warned LaLa. "So try to be quick—but not suspicious quick."

"I don't think I could be suspicious quick right now if I wanted to," said Evangeline. But she also couldn't dally much longer. The guards would be changing soon. If she wanted to leave, this was her window.

"I'll be close behind you," LaLa said. "And don't forget this." She handed Evangeline a map that she'd drawn of Merrywood

Forest—it was mostly just a bunch of triangles for trees with a line cutting through them that led to a circle labeled *the glowing spring.* The plan was for them to reunite there, and then together they would search for Jacks.

"Thank you for doing this," Evangeline said.

"What is the point of having friends if they're not there to support your bad decisions?" LaLa gave her a final hug just as the bell tolled. "You should go now."

Evangeline darted outside right on time for the changing of the guards. One appeared to glance her way, but the evening sky must have helped to cloak her. The torches everywhere filled the night sky with plumes of smoke that gave everything a slightly ethereal look. It made Evangeline feel as if she was skirting the burnt pages of a storybook. A story she was eager to leave.

The dinner hour was winding down as she wove her way through the royal encampment. The atmosphere was slightly drunken, celebratory, and flirty. Some of the merriment from the Merrywood rebuilding festival had finally infiltrated the royal encampment.

From a glance, it seemed that men and women from other camps had come to mingle with the royal guards, which was good for Evangeline. Yet she still held her breath until she reached the edge of the tents.

Her insides felt warm from the wine, but she was growing nervous again as she slipped behind a pile of lumber just off the path, to avoid the soldiers who watched the entrance to the camp.

She was careful to be quiet, although the night was full of songs and laughter and crackling fires. The noise died down as she entered Merrywood Forest, and soon there was only the crunch of her footsteps, the low croaks of frogs, and the occasional howl of a wolf, which set off a chorus of even more howls in the distance.

Evangeline held out her lantern to check the map that LaLa had drawn to the glowing spring.

She had thought the path on the map was an actual road. But Evangeline didn't see any road in the forest. Either she'd missed it or LaLa's path was just the route she was supposed to follow, not an actual road.

As Evangeline tried to memorize the path on the map, the forest grew very quiet—eerily quiet. The rustle of squirrels was gone, as were the sounds of the deer and the baby dragons. She couldn't hear a thing save for the very loud crack of a twig.

She jumped.

And then Jacks was there.

He was alive.

He wasn't injured.

She couldn't see so much as a scratch on his beautiful face. Evangeline felt as if she could breathe again. Until that moment, she hadn't realized just how worried she'd actually been.

"Did I scare you, pet?"

"No—I mean, yes—not really," she said, flustered, although she couldn't have said why. She was going to go out searching for him and now here he was. Being very Jacks-like.

He tossed a pale white apple as he moved through the forest, the way a shadow might move at sunset. Slow and quick, all at once. He'd been several feet away, but now he was in front of her, looking down on her with clear blue eyes that shone in the dark.

"I remember," she breathed.

"Do you now?" He smiled, and just like everything else, it was a very Jacks-like smile. Sharper at one corner, giving the impression of being both cruel and playful all at once. It reminded her vaguely of the first time they'd met, when she'd thought he looked like a half-bored young noble, half-wicked demigod.

"Tell me, pet, just how much do you remember?" The tips of his cool fingers found the base of her neck.

Her pulse spiked. Just a little, and yet it was enough to erase some of the warmth inside of her as Jacks slid his fingers from the hollow of her throat up to the line of her jaw.

This, too, felt like Jacks.

And yet . . . her heart was beating *wrong, wrong, wrong,* and she was now thinking about how he'd called her pet twice. Not Little Fox, not Evangeline.

But the problem with wanting something you can't have, or shouldn't have, is that the second it seems possible, all reason flees. Reason and wanting go well together only when the reason encourages a person to get what they want. Any reason opposed to this want becomes the enemy. A distant part of Evangeline told her that Jacks was acting strange, and that she didn't like it when he called her pet. But the part of Evangeline that wanted Jacks to love her tried to ignore this instinct.

"I remember all of it," she said. "I remember everything from the moment we met in your church to the night at the Valory Arch. I'm sorry it took me so long."

"It doesn't matter," Jacks said flippantly, still smiling crookedly as he dropped the apple in his hand. It fell to the ground with a heavy thud.

"Evangeline. Back away from him," called a smoky voice through the trees. It was vaguely familiar, but she couldn't place it until Chaos carefully stepped closer. "He's not safe right now."

"I'm never safe," Jacks said. Then with a smirk toward his old friend, he added, "Playing the hero doesn't suit you, Castor."

"At least I don't give up just because I fail."

"I'm not giving up," Jacks drawled. "I'm giving the girl what she wants." His fingers moved down her jaw to Evangeline's chin. For a second, time seemed to slow as he carefully lifted her chin in a way that made her think of only one thing: *kissing*.

Evangeline felt suddenly sober.

"Isn't this what you want?" Jacks whispered.

Yes, she wanted to say. But again, she could hear that small, reasonable voice telling her that this was wrong. Jacks was supposed to tease her, taunt her, touch her, but never try to kiss her. He didn't believe they could kiss. He believed in doomed love and unhappily ever after.

And Evangeline still wanted to prove him wrong.

She might have felt suddenly terrified as he leaned in closer.

Yet she couldn't make herself pull away as Jacks brought his lips to—

He immediately doubled over in pain and cursed loudly, saying words Evangeline had never heard anyone utter. His face contorted, turning bone white as he clutched his ribs before dropping to his knees with a groan.

"What's happening?"

She bent down to help him. And that's when she noticed the words on the cuff around her wrist had started glowing again.

"Sorry about this." Chaos's hot arms went around her, nearly scorching her as he picked her up. "We need to leave before Jacks tries to kill you again."

35

Apollo

Aurora dropped flower petals on the path as she walked. She tossed them out before her like some fairy goddess of the forest. And the path to the Cursed Forest treated her as such.

It always rained on the roads to the Cursed Forest—except where Aurora Valor walked. As soon as she tossed her petals and took a step, the rain fell no more. All Apollo felt was a subtle breeze as he walked in step beside her on a path paved in shoes and lined in overturned carriages, some of which still had wheels spinning.

"You haven't told me what this will cost," said Apollo, "or where we are going."

"I'm taking you to the Tree of Souls."

"Your father—"

"Is very stubborn," Aurora interrupted. "He knows a great many things, but he does not know everything."

Something twisted inside Apollo—a feeling that told him either he'd eaten some bad mutton earlier or this was a very poor idea. He knew better than to trust Aurora. She was not half as sweet as she looked as she continued to pull flower petals from her silver cloak and toss them onto the path.

Yet, how could he walk away from this? A chance to be immortal.

"There's just one small thing I ask in return," Aurora said, so softly he almost missed it.

Apollo immediately tensed. "What do you want?"

She slowly turned toward him, and for once there was nothing sweet in her expression. She looked wolfish in the moonlight, white teeth gleaming as she said, "I want you stop this nonsense about trying to kill Jacks. After tonight, you will clear his name of crimes and he will no longer be wanted or hunted."

"I can't do that."

"Then I cannot show you the Tree of Souls." Aurora stopped walking as the path ended and they reached the misty in-between that led to the Cursed Forest. "Either you can have immortality or you can choose to hunt Jacks, who I actually doubt you'll ever be able to kill—not as long as you're human. You've sent a whole kingdom after him, and what have you come up with? Perhaps once you're immortal, you'll have a fighting chance. But I don't want you to take that chance, which is why right now, you'll swear in blood on your life never to harm Jacks."

Apollo's shoulders tensed. "Why do you want to save Jacks?"

"That's none of your business."

"It is if you're asking me not to kill him." Apollo glared. "Did he bewitch you, too?"

Aurora bristled. "No one bewitches me. I'm a Valor." She looked at him with all the haughtiness of a princess.

And this was exactly why Apollo had never liked princesses. Like Aurora, they often looked good on the outside, but so many of them were rotten at the core.

"If you're worried about Jacks winning back Evangeline or taking her away from you, you don't have to," Aurora said. "I've already taken care of it."

"How?"

"You don't need to fret about that. I keep my secrets, just as I'll keep everything between us secret. Now what will it be, Prince?"

Apollo knew he couldn't walk away from this. His father had always told him to be more, and there was nothing *more* than immortal. He imagined that he could probably keep fighting Aurora about Jacks, but he doubted he'd win. Despite what Aurora had said, clearly Jacks had bewitched this girl, just as he had bewitched Evangeline. "After you take me to the tree, then I'll swear in blood. But not before then."

Aurora narrowed her eyes.

"You have my word," Apollo said. "If I'm lying, you can tell the entire kingdom I took the memories of my wife."

"Very well," said Aurora. Then she was tossing petals again as she led Apollo deeper into the in-between.

"Why are you still doing that? It's not raining here."

"I do it because the forest likes it," Aurora said. She tossed out several more petals, and as she did so, the ground beneath them glowed, lighting up more of the in-between.

"Is that where we're going? Into the Cursed Forest?"

"Not if it can be avoided. You can reach the Tree of Souls by venturing to the other side of the forest. But there should be an old arch around here that can take us to the Tree of Souls quicker." A crease formed between Aurora's brows as she scanned the misty stretch of land. Finally she squeaked, "Found it!"

Apollo didn't see anything except a patch of mist that looked darker than the rest.

Then Aurora tossed out more of her petals. This time she threw them high into the air, and as they hit the mist, they clung to it. Briefly the petals formed the outline of an arch, and then they seemed to melt and spread until the arch wasn't just an outline but an actual structure made of glowing white marble.

Apollo had heard stories growing up that there were hidden arches in the North, but this was the first time he'd seen one of them.

He almost asked how Aurora knew it was here. But then he remembered that the Valors had built all the arches in the first place.

As the North's ruling monarch, Apollo had a couple of arches of his own. One he'd used to dazzle the guests who'd attended Nocte Neverending. The other protected a very old phoenix tree. That one actually looked a little like this arch, as both were covered in curious magical symbols.

Aurora bit her lip as she looked over the symbols. Then she took one of her fingernails and jabbed it into her palm until it bled. She smeared the blood on the side of the arch.

"Good arch, please open and let us through to the Tree of Souls," she said.

A second later, a door appeared, the same glowing white as the arch. The door opened to what looked like a tunnel, although it was too dark to properly see.

Aurora pulled out a match from within her cloak and struck it against the wall before dropping it to the ground. As soon as it fell, a row of fire spread along one wall in a fiery streak. She repeated the process with the other side until the cavern was lit bright as day by two outstretched lines of fire.

Aurora entered gracefully, humming as she strolled between the rows of flames. The air was hot and grew even warmer as they continued down the path, until the tunnel expanded into an enormous cavern formed of sparkling white granite ringed in the same fire as the tunnel.

Apollo could not see the sky, yet the cavern must have opened up to it, for ahead of them a perfect beam of moonlight illuminated the most colossal tree that Apollo had ever seen.

Although *tree* didn't feel like quite the right word. Trees weren't supposed to have heartbeats.

The bloodred trunk of this tree appeared to be pulsing. Beating. Apollo swore he could hear it as he drew closer. *Thump* . . . *Thump* . . . *Thump* . . .

And were those human faces carved into the trunk?

He thought he saw terrified eyes and twisted mouths frozen in the wood, as if people were trapped inside the tree, but it was a little difficult to be certain it wasn't a trick of the flickering firelight.

The Tree of Souls was dotted with spiky burnished red leaves and full of branches the same bloodred color as the trunk. Some of the untamed branches crawled up toward the sky, while others grew outward and downward toward the ground.

When Apollo had first read about this tree in the scroll from Lord Slaughterwood, he'd thought it would be similar to his phoenix tree. Something enchanting and magical. He'd imagined a perfect place to pose for portraits—not that Apollo did that sort of thing anymore.

"It's ugly," he muttered.

Aurora shot him a scolding look. "Be careful what you say."

"It's just a tree," Apollo said. But then he heard its heartbeat again. *Thump. Thump. Thump.*

It was beating faster now, eagerly, hungrily, bringing to mind Wolfric's warning: *I was also a fool to plant it in the first place. The Tree of Souls is evil.*

It certainly didn't feel good to Apollo.

"Don't tell me you're scared now," said Aurora mockingly.

But Apollo noticed that although she had drawn close to the tree, she didn't dare touch it.

"Do you plan on drinking from it as well?" he asked.

According to the scroll from Lord Slaughterwood, all Apollo had to do was pierce a branch and blood from the tree would pour forth. He then had to drink the blood straight from the tree, and immortality would be his.

He would no longer get sick or age; he would stay young and strong and healthy forever. He could still die if someone tried to kill him, but he would not perish of natural causes, and according to the scroll, the same magic that kept him youthful would also make it harder for him to be killed.

He might have thought it was too easy, but the scroll had also laid out that growing one of these trees was not a simple task. After Wolfric Valor had been given the very rare seed to plant this tree, he then had to feed the tree with his blood— every morning and every night for a full year. Miss one feeding and the tree would wither and die.

"I'm waiting a few more years," said Aurora. "It's hard enough being female. I don't wish to be a young female forever."

"At least you have some sense, although not enough for me to feel like calling you *daughter* right now," bellowed a loud voice from the tunnel behind them.

Seconds later Wolfric Valor marched into the cavern, flanked by what looked like two of his sons. Like all the Valors, his sons seemed a little more than human.

Aurora flinched ever so slightly at their entrance. "You're looking surly as ever, Father."

Wolfric gave her a scathing look before turning to his sons and commanding, "Take her back to the camp. Her mother and I will deal with her there."

Before they had even gone, Wolfric prowled toward Apollo.

Apollo reached for his weapon.

"Don't bother," Wolfric said. "I'm not here to kill you, boy. You have been good to my family, so I will give you one more warning about this tree. The only reason this tree is still here is because I cannot cut it down. If this tree dies, then I die. And before you get any ideas, I'm the only one who can cut it down."

"I would never—"

"Don't lie," Wolfric cut in. "The fact that you're here says you would do a lot. But do you know what you're doing? Or did you simply just follow my cloud-headed daughter?"

Apollo thought about telling Wolfric that his daughter was more like a mastermind who had been blackmailing him, but he doubted that would help the situation.

"Do you want to know why I told you no when you asked me about this tree?" Wolfric continued. "Do you want to know what it costs to drink from the Tree of Souls? There is always a price to magic, and to gain eternal life, another life must be sacrificed. In this case, you would lose the life of the one you love the most. That's the reason I was given the seed to plant this tree."

Wolfric craned his neck to give the tree a bitterly appraising look. "When I was younger, I was a bit of a fool, like you. Once when visiting a neighboring kingdom, I saved the life of their princess. Her name was Serenity. She was pretty and I was a little friendlier than I should have been. Before leaving the kingdom, Serenity gave me the seed to plant this tree. She told me it was a thank-you for saving her life and I believed her. I thought myself deserving of immortality and didn't think to ask any of my trusted advisors as to what this tree truly was before I fed it my blood every day.

"It was only after the tree was full-grown, just before I was about to finally drink its blood, that I learned Princess Serenity actually gave me the seed to this tree in hopes that I would plant it and that my wife would die as soon as I drank from its branches.

"After I'd saved her life, Serenity fancied herself in love with me. But she knew that I would never be with her unless Honora was dead. But I would rather die than hurt my wife."

"So would I," said Apollo. Everything he'd been doing had been to protect her.

"I hope you mean that," said Wolfric gravely. "Do not come near this tree again or it will be the last thing you do."

36

Evangeline

What—no—how? No!" Evangeline panted, unable to properly string together words. She wanted to say that Jacks couldn't have tried to kill her and that he would never hurt her. But she feared those words might not be true, and that if she said them aloud, it would make them even less true.

If Jacks truly never would have hurt her, it shouldn't have been something that she needed to say at all.

Evangeline pressed her hands to her eyes, hoping to stop the tears that threatened to fall.

Chaos made a strained sound somewhere between a grunt and a clearing of his throat. She wondered if the vampire was trying to think of a way to comfort her or an excuse to leave, now that he had spirited her away from Jacks.

When she brought her hands down from her eyes, Chaos looked exquisitely uncomfortable. The vampire, clad in a black cape and smoke-gray leathers, leaned stiffly against a tree on the other side of the glowing spring.

Evangeline didn't remember telling him to bring her to the glowing spring, but she must have. The place she found herself now was secluded and pretty, with illuminated waters that made the circle of trees around them shine with hues of greens and blues, while the rocks that surrounded the pool glittered in the bewitching light.

Everything looked touched by an ethereal breed of magic, except for Chaos. The magic touching him appeared to be a different sort.

The light of the water was bright enough that she could see the tips of his fangs were peeking out, growing longer and glowing brighter than the water as the moonlight hit their sharp points.

"Are you planning on biting me?" she asked.

"I just saved your life," he said, but the words came out with a bit of a growl. "I'm not going to hurt you."

"I feel as if that's what people always say just before they hurt you."

"Then you should feel lucky that I'm not technically a person." His mouth moved up slightly at the corners.

Evangeline imagined he was trying to smile, but it looked more hungry than reassuring.

"What happened to Jacks?" she asked.

"I think you already know." Chaos inclined his head in the direction of the glass cuff that wrapped around her wrist.

It wasn't glowing now, but it had been when Jacks had tried to kiss her minutes ago, just as it had lit up when Apollo had been hurting her.

A buzzing started in Evangeline's head, or maybe it had been there all along. Maybe the buzzing was there to keep her from thinking too much about what had just happened with Jacks and how he might have tried to kill her.

"That cuff is very old magic," Chaos explained. "It was supposed to be a wedding gift from Vengeance Slaughterwood to my twin sister."

"I didn't know you had a sister."

"I do. I believe the two of you are actually friends. Although I doubt you'll still be friends after I finish this story. You know my sister as Aurora Vale, but originally her name was Aurora Valor."

The mossy grounds around the spring felt suddenly unsteady under Evangeline's feet. "Did you just say Valor?"

Chaos nodded while Evangeline's thoughts raced to catch up. Within the last day, she'd remembered so much and been through so much, it was difficult to sort it all out. But she knew about the Valors. She'd studied them as she'd searched for the Valory Arch stones. But she'd never realized Chaos was one of them.

She felt instantly foolish. Minutes ago, Jacks had called him Castor, and Castor Valor had been Jacks's close friend. He was supposed to be dead, just like all the other Valors—but clearly that wasn't the case.

And if Aurora was Castor's sister, then her parents must have been Wolfric and Honora Valor. Evangeline didn't know how she would have figured out that they were in reality the first king and queen of the North returned from the dead after hundreds of years. Yet she felt as if she should have been able to piece it together somehow. She had always distrusted Aurora, but she'd just thought Aurora had the same first name as Aurora Valor. She'd never imagined the two were one and the same.

"I can see you have lots of questions," Chaos said.

"I have nothing but questions," Evangeline said. "Did your family come back from the dead? Or were they simply pretending to be dead? Where have they been all of these years? Why return now?"

"I know this will be hard, but I suggest you hold on to any questions until I finish this story, in case Jacks returns." Chaos didn't give her time to object before saying, "I think Jacks already told you that my sister was engaged to Vengeance Slaughterwood."

Evangeline nodded and Chaos continued.

"Vengeance thought Aurora was nothing more than a pretty princess who wasn't capable of taking care of herself. He had a protection cuff made for her—one that would thwart anyone who intended to harm her.

"There was just one catch to the cuff: once it is on, it can't be taken off. Knowing this, my sister refused to put it on. She also didn't need any amulet for protection, or so she thought. She held on to the cuff instead. I don't know what she planned to do with it, but while she was locked away in the Valory, the cuff turned into a legend."

"Hold on," Evangeline interrupted. "Your sister was inside the Valory?"

"My whole family was in the Valory trapped in a state of suspended sleep. Why do you think I wanted to open it so badly?"

"I thought it was because of your helm," Evangeline said. Before she had opened the Valory, Chaos wore a cursed helm that prevented him from feeding. But now that she thought back on it, it made perfect sense that Chaos also had a deeper motivation for opening the arch. He must have been the monster that some believed to be inside the Valory, but instead his family had been locked away.

"After the night that you opened the Valory Arch, Jacks was half-mad. He kept raving about you dying. About how he had to save you. I didn't take him seriously." Chaos paused to run a hand through his hair as he mumbled, "I might have bitten him, by accident, and I thought it was just the blood loss talking. Then, a couple of days later, I found out about how he'd made a bargain with my sister for the cuff. He wanted it for you, so that no one could ever hurt you again."

"He's been obsessed with that," Evangeline said. She remembered him being protective of her before, but it seemed he was fixated now. Or he had been. Obviously, something had changed between tonight and when she had last seen Jacks at the inn. Chaos had said the protection cuff worked based on a person's intent, and it had stopped Jacks just as he'd intended to kiss her.

"What did Jacks trade this cuff for?" Evangeline asked.

"I tried to stop him," Chaos said. "I told him not to do it, but he wouldn't listen."

"What did he trade the cuff for?" she asked more forcefully this time.

Chaos looked at her but wouldn't meet her eyes.

Evangeline reminded herself that you weren't supposed to meet a vampire's eyes because vampires took it as an invitation to bite, but in this instance, it felt different. Chaos didn't look hungry now so much as he looked sad.

"Jacks traded the cuff for his heart."

"His heart?" Evangeline repeated. "What kind of heart? Is this some sort of magical object? A trinket? Surely not his actual heart."

"Everyone has two different hearts," Chaos said. "There is the heart that beats and keeps you alive. Then there is the other heart, the second heart, the one that breaks instead of beats, the one that loves so that there is a point to all this living. This is the heart that my sister wanted."

"Why would Aurora want that?" Evangeline asked, although she feared she already knew the answer and that it had something to do with two names she'd once seen carved into the walls of the Hollow.

AURORA + JACKS

The names had been carved into the wall hundreds of years ago, but for Aurora it must have felt like a few years, maybe just months, since she'd been trapped in a suspended state in the Valory all this time.

"She loves Jacks, doesn't she," Evangeline said.

"That's what I've always suspected," Chaos replied. "Aurora has never confessed it, but I imagine that's only because Jacks has never shown any interest in her. Lyric Merrywood was the one who loved her, but I always thought my sister was with him just as a pretext to be near Jacks, who never even looked her way.

"If Aurora had really wanted to call off her engagement to Vengeance in order to marry Lyric, our father would have been upset, but he would have let her do it. He isn't a tyrant. But Aurora enjoyed being the object of desire. She liked having both Lyric's and Vengeance's attentions, and I think she kept hoping it would make Jacks jealous.

"Of course it all went wrong. I don't think it ever occurred to Aurora that after she left Vengeance he'd come after Lyric and raze the entirety of the Merrywood lands. But that's the problem with my sister. She never thinks things through, and I know she's not thinking now."

"Do you know what she plans to do with Jacks's heart? Is she going to put a love spell on it?" Evangeline guessed aloud. Although she knew from experience that a person didn't need someone's heart for that. Love spells could also be broken.

"I have a feeling she plans to do something more permanent," Chaos said darkly.

"Like what? Give him an entirely new heart?"

"I don't know. But I imagine when she's done, Jacks will finally be hers."

Evangeline wanted to throw up and pace, or maybe pace and throw up. She couldn't stomach the idea of Jacks with Aurora—and she couldn't imagine that Jacks would want that either.

How could he have done this? How could he give away his heart? How could he give up on her like this? Although she very much doubted he saw it this way. Jacks probably told himself he was doing something right, something noble by sacrificing his heart to protect her.

Unfortunately, that wasn't what he'd really done. Jacks might have told himself he'd given up his heart to save her, but Evangeline feared he'd also done it to make it easier for him to let her go.

There had to be a way to change this. To fix this. To stop Aurora from forever changing Jacks's heart or giving him another heart entirely. Who would Jacks even be if that happened?

"How do we get his heart back?" Evangeline said.

"Not we, just you. I'm afraid I can't help you."

"Why not?"

"I would, but I believe my sister has hidden the heart in the one place I can't go. I think it's somewhere in the Hollow."

"Evangeline!" LaLa's singsong voice trilled through the surrounding trees. "I hope you weren't waiting too—" LaLa's voice cut off abruptly as she stepped out of the wood and caught sight of Chaos on the other side of the glowing spring.

"What are you doing here?" Her lips twisted with displeasure.

"I just saved your friend's life," Chaos replied sharply.

And was it just Evangeline's imagination, or did he puff out his chest? Until that moment, she'd still been thinking of him as Chaos. But now as he sat up taller, with his cape rakishly tossed over one shoulder, she could see him as Castor Valor, the cocky young prince of the Magnificent North.

"Well, I'm here now, so—" LaLa waved a hand toward the forest.

"Did you just dismiss me?" Castor asked.

"I tried," LaLa said. She was the smallest in stature of the three, and yet there was something about the way she glared at Castor that gave the impression of her looking down upon him. "Don't you have virgin blood to drink or something?"

"Virgin blood?" Castor smiled one of those devastating vampire smiles as he shoved a hand through his hair in very devil-may-care fashion. "What kind of stories have you been reading about me?"

"I don't read any stories about you," LaLa huffed, but Evangeline swore there was a deeper color on her cheeks.

"So it's just a coincidence that you're quoting one of them?"

"I know you drink blood," she said.

Castor's gaze turned heated. *I'd like to drink your blood,* it seemed to say.

And suddenly everything felt a little hotter than it should have been. LaLa did not seem to like Castor, but Evangeline surmised that the vampire felt quite differently about her.

"I think we're getting off topic," Evangeline interjected before the vampire took a bite out of LaLa. "Jacks is in trouble."

LaLa immediately looked away from Castor.

Evangeline quickly explained to LaLa what the vampire had told her about Aurora and Jacks's heart.

"I can't believe I used to think Jacks was the smart one." Once again, LaLa glared at Castor. "Why didn't you stop him?"

"I tried."

"*Pfft,*" LaLa said. "Clearly you didn't try hard enough."

"This isn't Castor's fault," Evangeline said, but neither of them was paying attention to her.

"Have you ever successfully stopped Jacks?" asked Castor.

LaLa raised her chin imperiously. "I once stabbed him with a butter knife."

"I remember that butter knife fiasco," Evangeline said. "It caused a great mess. Speaking of messes—what are we going to do about Jacks's heart?"

"I say we kidnap Aurora and torture her until she tells us where it is," said LaLa.

"I'm not letting you torture my sister," Castor interrupted.

"Your sister is a monster!"

Castor's nostrils flared. "We are all monsters." With a growl, he shoved away from the tree he'd been leaning against.

For a second, Evangeline thought he might cross the spring as well and finally sink his teeth into LaLa. The tension had returned, tightening his jaw and his shoulders. Then slowly he took a step back.

"I'm not asking you to forgive her for what she caused to happen to your family," Castor said quietly. "But you don't need to hurt her. She was locked in the Valory for hundreds of years; she's already suffered enough for her crime. If you want to hurt her for this, just find the heart and return it to Jacks. That will be torture enough for her."

Castor turned to leave.

"Where are you going?" LaLa called.

"The sun is going to rise soon. I need to leave, but I've already told Evangeline where she has to go."

And with that, Chaos vanished into the night.

37

Apollo

The tent was empty.

Evangeline was gone.

At a glance, it looked as if there'd been a struggle. Everything was a mess—trunks of clothes were toppled. Pillows were slashed. The table lay tipped over in a riot of spilled wine and spattered food. Berries had been stomped into the ground next to meat now smeared with dirt.

"Guards!" Apollo bellowed, calling forth two soldiers who had been outside.

It was clear from the moment they looked into the tent that they hadn't heard any commotion. There'd been no battle, no kidnapping—just as Apollo had feared.

Evangeline had left willingly—and left this scene to throw him off the trail.

Which could mean only one thing.

She remembered.

"I want my wife found," Apollo said. "Bring her back to me, by whatever means necessary."

38

Evangeline

I would still prefer to personally torture Aurora," said LaLa as she walked beside Evangeline on the path that would take them to the Hollow. The sun was slowly starting to rise, casting warm morning light on all the droplets of dew clinging to the grass that lined their path.

"I think I'd like to torture her as well," said Evangeline. But it was mostly because saying something—anything—took her mind off the fact that Jacks was without a heart, and when he got it back, it might not be the same heart.

LaLa was a good distraction, suggesting setting Aurora's hair on fire, pulling out her fingernails, and other things Evangeline couldn't even bring herself to repeat.

"I just want to kiss him," Evangeline said softly. "And . . . I don't want to die."

Before last night, she had never truly believed Jacks would kill her. The night they'd spent together at the crypt—she'd been afraid he would bite her and turn into a vampire, but she'd never been afraid she would die by his lips.

Until now.

LaLa turned to her then, with a particularly gentle smile. "I hope that someday you do get to kiss Jacks in front of Aurora. That would be the best sort of torture."

"But I thought you believed Jacks's kiss would kill me?"

LaLa shrugged. "What can I say? Revenge makes me hopeful."

A few feet later they reached the sign that read: *Welcome to the Hollow!*

A little dragon dozed atop it, snoring tiny adorable sparks.

With a pang, Evangeline thought about the night that she and Jacks had spent here together.

Then she thought about how the Cursed Forest had brought Jacks back to the Hollow.

Could it be that the best day of Jacks's life had been the one he'd spent with Evangeline there? It felt like an awful lot to hope for, yet just the idea reignited some of the light in Evangeline. Maybe Jacks didn't want a happily ever after, but she still refused to believe he didn't want her. Although who knew what he would want once Aurora changed his heart?

"We should be close," LaLa said. "If I remember correctly, Aurora had an evil lair hidden at the base of a tree. Her family always vacationed at the Hollow. I remember trying to play with her the first few years, but she always wanted to chase the boys."

LaLa directed Evangeline off the path through a forest full of trees and velvet-capped mushrooms that went all the way up to their knees and thighs. There were more sleeping dragons atop them, filling the air with sparks of golden light. Then the mushrooms stopped and for several feet the ground was bare—no mushrooms, no grasses, not even a broken twig. There was just a large circle of untouched dirt, surrounding a tree with a carving in the center of a wolf wearing a flower crown.

"I should have brought an ax," LaLa said as she stopped in front of the tree.

"I can probably just use my blood to open it."

"Yes, but it would be much more fun to take an ax to that sigil of hers."

"We can come back after we find Jacks's heart."

Evangeline pulled out the dagger Jacks had given her, and for a second she felt a pang of something like regret. She knew it wasn't her fault she had lost her memories. But she wished she had been able to get them back sooner. She wished that when Jacks had tossed her this knife she had remembered him.

Looking back now, it clearly hurt him that she had forgotten. If she had remembered sooner, maybe then she could have stopped all of this.

She cut her finger with the dagger and then pressed several

drops of blood to the tree, willing it to open. After several long moments a door appeared in the wood. There were stairs on the other side. White, and covered in carved flowers. They must have been magical, for when Evangeline set foot on them, they started to glow.

"Where did Aurora get the magic to do all of this?" she asked.

"I have no idea," LaLa said. "It's believed that all the Valor children had magic, but no one ever knew what Aurora's magic actually was."

Evangeline counted twenty steps before she and LaLa reached the bottom. Like the stairs, the floors in this room glowed, lighting up walls entirely covered in shelves. On one side, there appeared to be mostly books—pretty books in pastel colors like violet, pink, gold, and cream, all tied with neat little bows.

Evangeline hardly spared them a glance before turning to the other side, which was filled with jars and bottles. Some were bulbous and others were slim, sealed with melted wax or sparkling glass stoppers. And they had all manner of things inside them. Evangeline spied dried flowers, dead spiders, fingers—*blech*—gem-bright potions, a bottle that glittered like starlight. But there was nothing that looked like a heart, beating or otherwise.

Her eyes scanned the array of jars until they landed on a bottle full of a wine-red liquid that shimmered when she looked at it. She picked it up. Attached to the glass stopper was a ribbon with a small handwritten label that read: *Dragon blood.*

Evangeline cringed. She didn't like the idea of bottled blood at all, but it seemed particularly cruel to drain it from little dragons.

Evangeline set the blood down and picked up a pretty jar full of sliver sparkles. The sparkles flinched as soon as she touched the glass. Then they all fell to the bottom of the jar in an ashen heap. This container didn't have a label, but Evangeline didn't think it contained Jacks's second heart.

She would recognize Jacks's heart—she *knew* Jacks's heart. His heart was wounded like hers, but it was strong, it wouldn't flinch or shy away from her. It would beat faster, harder, in concert with hers.

Evangeline closed her eyes and reached out a hand toward the shelves, letting her fingers graze the smooth glass bottles.

Please beat. Please beat, she quietly repeated, touching jar after jar after jar.

Nothing. Nothing. Nothing. Just cool glass and more cool glass and—

Her fingers touched something that was not a jar or a glass. It felt like leather against her skin. Evangeline opened her eyes to find a white leather book with gold embossing on the spine.

"I wonder," she mused. "Could it be possible that Aurora cut out the center of one of these books and put the heart inside?"

"I suppose anything is possible," said LaLa, who went to work yanking books from shelves. She untied their ribbons, shook them, and turned them upside down to see if anything fell out—Evangeline heard a few keys clatter to the ground.

Then she watched a long brown wig fall from one volume before LaLa recklessly tossed it to the floor. "It's not the same as taking an ax to the door, but it feels rather good," LaLa said, throwing another book over her shoulder.

Evangeline was more careful as she took the white leather volume from the shelf. The cover had no words, just another image of a wolf's head wearing a crown.

Evangeline didn't know if Jacks's heart was hidden in this volume, but there was clearly something inside it. She could sense an otherness as she tried to open the book, but it refused to budge. *Magic.*

Evangeline quickly pricked her finger and drew her blood along the pages of the book as she said, "Please open."

The book immediately obeyed.

The words *Aurora's Book of Spells* were written carefully on the first page.

"What do you have there?" asked LaLa, just before she tossed another book on the floor.

"It's Aurora's spell book." Evangeline turned the page, hoping to find a table of contents. But this book appeared to be more of a journal.

The first entry had a date, followed by a line that said: *I attempted my first spell today.*

"I don't think you're going to find Jacks's heart in there," said LaLa.

"I know, but perhaps I'll find the spell Aurora plans to use to change Jacks's heart or give him another one."

"Or maybe we could find a spell to use on her," LaLa suggested brightly.

Evangeline kept turning pages. The paper was old and brittle underneath her fingers as she carefully looked at entry after entry.

Aurora was determined, Evangeline had to give her that. Most of her early spells had failed, but that hadn't seemed to stop her. She resolutely continued trying spells until at last she began to succeed.

> *I changed the color of my hair today! It is now a glorious shimmering violet. Although Jacks didn't seem to notice.*

"Of course he didn't," LaLa grumbled, reading over Evangeline's shoulder.

Evangeline felt a brief flutter of something like happiness, but it quickly faded a few entries later.

> *My sister, Vesper, finally had a vision of Jacks's future. "He'll fall in love with a Fox," she said.*
> *"What do you mean, a fox?" I asked.*

But of course Vesper didn't know. She's still trying to master her visions. Right now they don't always make sense. But I think I've brilliantly figured it out.

My brother, Castor, has been building a network of spies to keep the North safe—as if our father needs any help with that! Fortunately for me, Castor's spies are very handy. One of them fancies me, of course. The other day, as he was undoubtedly trying to impress me, he told me of a peasant girl he'd met who could turn into a fox. He planned to tell my brother, thinking this girl would make an excellent spy.

I persuaded him otherwise.

This girl has to be the "fox" that Jacks will love. Not that I'm letting that happen.

In fact, I may have already done something that I shouldn't have done to prevent it. But it's too late to change it now.

"It's not too late to torture her," said LaLa.

"I never trusted her," Evangeline muttered. "But it's still hard to believe that she could be this terrible."

Although Aurora hadn't written what she'd done, Evangeline imagined she knew.

Jacks had once told Evangeline the story of how he'd become the Archer from *The Ballad of the Archer and the Fox*. How he'd been hired to hunt a fox, but then he'd found out the fox was actually a girl—a girl he'd started to fall in love with. He'd told the men who'd hired him, certain they'd made a mistake in asking him to hunt a girl, but instead of freeing Jacks from his contract, a spell was placed on him that forced him to not only hunt but to kill the fox girl. Jacks fought against the spell and didn't shoot the girl—but then he kissed her and she died.

"Do you think this means Aurora put both curses on Jacks—the Archer's curse, and the curse that made his kiss fatal?"

"I wouldn't put it past her," said LaLa. "Aurora took Jacks's heart. I think that falls under the rule of *If I can't have him, then no one else can.*"

39

Evangeline

More festival bunting seemed to have sprouted overnight. Merry little triangle flags in all sorts of fabrics and colors covered the entirety of the bustling Merrywood Village—striped peach, mint green, speckled robin's-egg blue, sunset pink, and polka-dot purple all waving happily in the gentle breeze.

The brilliant yellow sun was beating down, unobstructed by clouds, although there was a dampness in the air that made Evangeline feel as if it might rain, even without the clouds. She pictured the sky cracking open as if cut by a knife.

Discreetly she adjusted the wig she'd taken from Aurora's lair, the brown one that had fallen out of one of the books. Evangeline hoped it would help her blend in and avoid any guards as she and LaLa searched for Aurora. The plan was to find the former princess among the festivalgoers, then follow her in the hopes she would lead them to wherever she was actually keeping Jacks's heart.

Yesterday Aurora had mentioned her interest in all the Merrywood festival booths and treats and pretty things. Thinking back now, Evangeline remembered how happy Aurora had seemed, how she'd worn a flower crown and a buoyant smile. In hindsight, Evangeline wondered if that joy had in fact been because she finally had taken Jacks's heart.

Evangeline scanned the crowd for Aurora, looking past the vendors of saws and hammers, berries and beer, and endless baubles. Around them, children giggled and squealed as they ran with spinning paper pinwheels. Happiness swirled through the air like pollen. It was everywhere, touching everything except for Evangeline. All she could feel was a tightness around her chest, a sense that time was closing in on her.

It had already been a day since Aurora had taken Jacks's heart.

What if Evangeline was too late? What if the reason she couldn't see Aurora was because she was off somewhere with Jacks and his heart had already been changed? What if—

"Do you see the evil princess anywhere?" asked LaLa.

Evangeline shook her head. She saw people bartering, chattering, and helping to rebuild. But she did not see a girl with violet hair.

"Dragon-roasted apples, get your dragon-roasted apples!"

cried a vendor wheeling a sweet red cart. It appeared to have been carefully painted. The words *Dragon-Roasted Apples* were written in an elaborate curling script, and around them were delicate paintings of little apples and outlines of adorable dragons.

He slowed the cart to a stop in front of LaLa.

"We're not interested, thank you," said LaLa.

"But someone has already bought something for the young miss." The vendor, a young man with a friendly, open face, smiled. But it was a little off, a little wrong, like a grin that a child might have added to a master's painting.

The vendor's fingers trembled as he handed Evangeline a small scroll tied up with a crisp white ribbon. "I was asked to give you this first."

Nervously she unrolled the scroll.

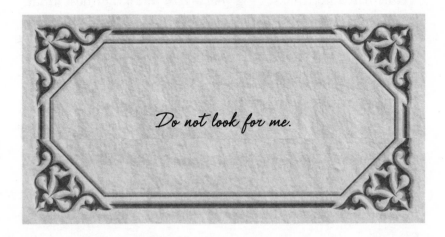

Do not look for me.

There was no name, no initial, but Evangeline instantly knew who it was from. *Jacks.*

She turned back to the apple roaster. If Jacks was telling her not to look for him, then he was thinking about her. There was still hope.

"When was this given to you?" she asked.

But the young man didn't answer. He didn't even look at her. The vendor appeared to be in some sort of trance as he poured a sack of sugar over the top of his precious apple cart and then turned to his little dragons. There were three of them. One was brown, one was green, one was peach.

"It's time," the young man said quietly.

The dragons whimpered.

"Just do as I say," he muttered, still ignoring Evangeline.

He must have been under Jacks's influence, Evangeline realized with a start. She'd seen Jacks do this before, control other people, but in the past, it had always been to protect her.

She had a horrible feeling that was not the case now as she watched the vendor swipe a tear from his eyes right as the dragons breathed out sparks of fire, igniting the sugar. In seconds, the entire cart was blazing, covered in white and orange flames. The vendor stood motionless beside it, as though pinned to the spot.

"We need to get some water!" Evangeline called to LaLa, turning toward the well in the center of the square.

"No!" LaLa grabbed her arm. "We need to go." She dragged Evangeline away from the vendor and the square, just as the royal guards appeared to catch sight of the burning cart and festivalgoers began rushing over with buckets of water.

The young man was now crying. The little dragons were crying.

The fire was already out. But the cart was destroyed, reduced to just smoldering pieces of ashen wood.

"I can't believe Jacks would do this," Evangeline murmured as LaLa urged her farther away from the crowd. "That just seems unnecessarily cruel."

"Jacks *is* unnecessarily cruel," said LaLa. "He used to do things like this all the time. You don't know this Jacks because he's always been different with you." Her voice softened and although she didn't say it aloud, Evangeline sensed that LaLa was thinking that version of Jacks was gone now.

"Do you think that Aurora has already changed his heart or given him another one?"

LaLa bit her lip but didn't answer, which seemed like a yes to Evangeline.

The sun beat down hard on Evangeline's face as she and LaLa reached the edge of the village.

It was the time of day where there were no shadows. Everything was bright and light. A girl like Aurora should have been easy to spot in a crowd like this, where most people wore homespun clothes and had plain-colored hair.

"I don't see her," Evangeline said. A part of her worried that she was too late. That Aurora had already changed Jacks's heart or given him another one. But Evangeline couldn't give up on him and she knew that if he was still *her Jacks*, he wouldn't give up on her if Evangeline lost her heart.

"I think I may have found her." LaLa pointed away from

the village to a trail of pale pink flower petals that led into Merrywood Forest. Then she rolled her eyes. "When Aurora was younger, she wanted people to think that she left a trail of flowers wherever she went, so she would often carry baskets of petals and toss them when she walked. I bet if we follow that trail, we find Jacks's heart."

The trail of pink flower petals dotted stones and grass and even a few sleeping dragons, taking LaLa and Evangeline on a circuitous path that led into the shadows of Merrywood Forest. Following the petals reminded Evangeline of a story that she couldn't quite remember, but she was fairly certain it didn't end well.

Evangeline wanted to hope her tale would be different. She believed that every story had the possibility for infinite endings, and she tried hard to hold that belief in every breath she took and every step she made.

Until at last the trail of petals came to an end.

It stopped at the base of a tree. There was a fox there. It was reddish brown and white, with a gorgeous bushy tail. But the tail wasn't moving and neither was the fox; it was lying at the base of the tree, a golden arrow shot straight through its heart.

"Oh no!" Evangeline dropped to her knees and checked for the fox's heartbeat. But all she found was a note attached to the arrow.

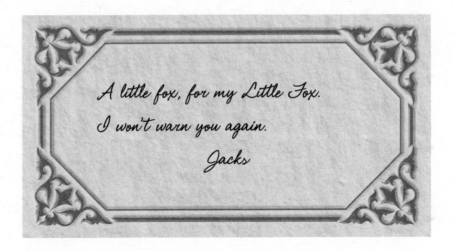

A little fox, for my Little Fox.
I won't warn you again.
Jacks

"I hate him a little right now," Evangeline said.

"At least it's not a person," said LaLa.

"But it will be soon. That's what this note is really saying."

First he'd destroyed the cart. Then he'd killed this fox. Next it would be a human.

"Does this mean you want to give up?" asked LaLa.

"No. I'm going to save him."

"There is no saving him now," droned a voice from the tree. A second later, the wood creaked, a hidden door cracked open, and Aurora Valor stumbled through.

Her violet hair was disheveled, her face was pale, and there was a great bruise forming at her temple. "If you're here for Jacks's heart, you're not going to find it. You're already too late."

Evangeline

Aurora Valor's iridescent skirts fanned out around her in a perfect circle as she slumped to the ground in an elegant mess. Strands of violet hair fell across a forehead without so much as a thin worry line. Her expression seemed almost serene. Aurora reminded Evangeline of a damsel in distress, patiently waiting for her prince to come.

But when Evangeline looked more closely, Aurora's countenance seemed more of a veneer than an actual reflection of how she was feeling.

Her pretty eyes hardened and her musical voice struck a bitter chord as she looked up at Evangeline and asked, "What did you do? Why did Jacks fall for *you*?"

"Well, she's not a raging bitch like you," said LaLa.

Aurora flinched. Another piece of her veneer cracked as her mouth pinched into an ugly frown.

"Where is Jacks?" Evangeline demanded. "And what have you done to his heart?"

Aurora laughed. "You think I'm the reason he did this?" She picked up the dead fox's tail and swatted it carelessly back and forth while the poor fox lay there, its eyes vacant. "As much as I appreciate the symbolism, I had nothing to do with it."

"I don't believe you. I know you cursed him," Evangeline said. "I found your old spell book. You're the reason he killed the first girl he loved, the one who turned into a fox."

"Yes, but I'm not the reason for *this*." Aurora dropped the dead fox's tail. "Jacks did this on his own, for you." Her voice turned sour with something like jealousy, as if she wished for Jacks's torment the same way she'd wished for his love.

"You're the one who took his heart," said Evangeline.

"I didn't take it! He gave it to me willingly. But I don't have it anymore."

"How do you not have it?" asked LaLa skeptically.

Aurora threw her head back against the tree in another dramatic pose. "Jacks came to see me earlier. He demanded the heart. When I wouldn't give it to him, he knocked me out." She pointed to the growing bruise on her temple. "Once I woke up, Jacks was gone. So was the heart."

"That doesn't make sense," Evangeline said. "If Jacks took his heart back earlier, then why would he do all this?" She motioned her hand toward the dead fox.

Aurora laughed. "You think Jacks took his heart because he wanted it back?" She laughed again, happier and harder.

"I think we should get out of here," murmured LaLa.

"You should," said Aurora, still laughing. "Once Jacks finishes destroying his heart, he'll be back and he'll kill more than just a wild fox."

Aurora started playing with the fox's tail again. She swished it back and forth, back and forth as the blood rushed hotter and faster between Evangeline's ears.

LaLa might have said something, but Evangeline couldn't quite hear it over the words repeating in her head: *Once Jacks finishes destroying his heart.*

She wanted to believe Aurora was just being awful. That she was trying to torment her. She wanted to say that Jacks wouldn't destroy his heart, but she'd also never thought that Jacks would trade his heart, either. One of the things Evangeline loved about Jacks was his determination, his drive, his intractable pursuit of the things that he wanted most. But she didn't want to believe that what he wanted now was to feel nothing. That he could disdain his heart so much. That he could give up on love, on everything, entirely.

Evangeline wanted to scream and curse. And a part of her also just wanted to drop down to her knees and cry.

Jacks was the Prince of Hearts—he'd been searching almost all his entire life for love. And now here she was—and he was giving up?

"Where has he gone?" she asked Aurora. "And how do I stop him?"

"You don't." Aurora sighed and wearily tilted her head to the side, as if she was the one who'd been the most inconvenienced by all of this. "I told you, you're too late."

"Then just tell me where he's gone!"

Aurora rolled her eyes. "He didn't exactly tell me his plans before he clocked me on the head."

"I know where he's gone," murmured LaLa. "There's only one way to destroy a person's second heart."

"How?" Evangeline asked.

LaLa swallowed thickly and looked at her guiltily. "I'm sorry, Evangeline."

"Why are you sorry?"

"Because if it wasn't for me, there would be nowhere for Jacks to go. The heart that a person uses to feel is a powerful thing and it can only be destroyed by fire. But not just any ordinary fire."

"How do you know this?" asked Evangeline.

LaLa continued to look pained. "After Dane was locked up in the Valory, I wanted to destroy my heart."

"You wanted to destroy your heart because of *Dane*?" Aurora snickered.

LaLa glared at her. For a second, Evangeline could see she was reconsidering the idea of torture.

"You can hurt her after you tell me how you think Jacks is going to destroy his heart," said Evangeline.

"The only way to destroy a second heart is with the fire of a royal phoenix tree."

"You planted a phoenix tree? Are you an idiot?" Aurora shoved up to her feet, and suddenly she looked genuinely frightened. Her cheeks were high with angry color. She must not have truly believed that Jacks was actually going to succeed at destroying his heart; she had been toying with Evangeline, taunting her for fun.

"Where did you plant the tree?" Aurora asked.

"As if I would tell you," LaLa said.

Aurora turned to Evangeline. "Do you know where it is?"

Evangeline had a feeling she did, but she wasn't about to tell Aurora. She'd seen the tree her very first night in the Magnificent North.

It was the night before Nocte Neverending; Apollo had been lounging across the branches of the phoenix tree, posing for a portrait. Although she'd actually noticed the spectacular tree before she'd noticed the prince.

Her mother had told her the myth of the phoenix tree, as had her former tutor, Madame Voss. It took the leaves of a phoenix tree over a thousand years to slowly turn to gold—real gold—but if a person plucked one before all the leaves changed, then the entire tree would go up in flames.

That must have been what Jacks planned to do. Pick a golden leaf, turn the tree to fire, and then toss his heart in the flames. And she had no doubt he would do it. Unless she stopped him.

"I don't want Jacks to actually destroy his heart," said Aurora. "If you tell me where you planted the tree, I can show Evangeline how to get there using an arch."

"I don't want your help," said Evangeline. "And I wouldn't trust it." Thankfully, she also hoped that she didn't need it. She was fairly certain she knew where LaLa had planted the phoenix tree—she just needed to get there before Jacks did.

"LaLa, where is the closest arch?" she asked.

If LaLa could tell her where the arch was, Evangeline was certain she could coax the arch to take her to the clearing with the tree. Her blood opened any door, and arches in particular always responded to her.

"I'll go with you," LaLa said.

"Thank you," Evangeline said. "But I think I need to go alone this time. If I'm going to save Jacks, it's not going to be through force."

"Then how are you going to save him?" asked Aurora.

"With love."

Aurora laughed again. The sound of it was getting uglier.

Evangeline's cheeks heated, but she refused to be embarrassed. "Love is nothing to laugh at."

"It is today. Because you see, Evangeline, even if you save Jacks's heart, it's not going to be enough to save you. If you ever kiss him, you will die. It doesn't matter if your love is the truest love that the world has ever seen."

Evangeline reminded herself Aurora was a liar; until moments ago, this whole scene had a been a charade. But she didn't look as if she was acting now. Aurora looked disturbingly triumphant.

"When I realized Jacks was never going to kill the fox girl, I put another spell on him," Aurora said. "But the story curse twisted the truth of it. It's not Jacks's true love who will be immune to his kiss and make his heart beat again. Only a girl who will *never* love Jacks can survive the kiss. Maybe your love can save his heart, but if you decide to kiss him, you'll just be one more fox that Jacks has murdered."

41

Evangeline

Finding the arch was easy.

It seemed to take only minutes.

Evangeline imagined the actual journey from Aurora to a hidden arch on the edge of the Cursed Forest couldn't have been that quick. It had probably taken her and LaLa closer to an hour to find it. But time felt as if it was speeding by. Evangeline's blood still pumped impossibly fast. Even standing still, she found herself woefully short of breath.

She felt one relief as she entered the clearing: Jacks wasn't there yet.

It was just Evangeline, the phoenix tree, and the slowly setting sun.

Her first time in this clearing, there had been lively musicians playing harps and lutes, courtiers bedecked in all their finery, a banquet table piled high with food, and promises of wishes come true in the air.

Tonight there was just the nervous rustle of leaves as Evangeline drew closer to the shimmering tree. She could hear the leaves quiver and shake against each other, as if they somehow sensed that their time was almost up.

The last time she'd been here, all the unchanged leaves had been red and orange and bronze, but tonight they were green as emeralds and dewy grass.

She saw the veins of a shaking leaf rapidly turn from green to gold. Then she watched as the gold began to spread across the surface of the entire leaf, as if it could outrace what it feared might be coming. And yet, unless the other leaves changed as well, this leaf's transformation would not be enough to protect it from what Jacks would soon do.

Evangeline took a deep calming breath, both for herself and for the fearful tree.

She was afraid as well. She felt as if she shouldn't have been. She felt as if her faith in love was supposed to be unflinching.

But Evangeline was flinching a lot.

Every light sigh of the breeze made her shoulders tense. The quietest shift of the leaves made her gasp.

On the night she'd opened the Valory Arch, there had been a sense of something inevitable. She'd known that opening that arch was exactly what she'd been born to do. She'd felt that every event in her life had led her to that moment.

Now she was living in the moments after the inevitable, and she felt that, too. Instead of being carved in stone, this moment felt like a fragile sort of tapestry that could unravel with one tug on a thread—or one pull of a leaf.

The clearing brimmed with anticipation; it burst against her skin like sparks from a match, making her feel as if anything could happen. She'd always loved that feeling before, but now it made her as nervous as that little leaf that had just changed from green to gold.

Evangeline had changed as well since the first time she had entered this clearing on her first night in the Magnificent North, when she had believed that marrying a prince could make all her dreams come true. Looking back, her dreams had felt impossible and she had felt so courageous for believing in them. But now she realized those were never her dreams, not really. They had been dreams borrowed from stories, dreams she had clung to because she had yet to imagine her own dreams.

That first night in the North, she would have never dreamed of a future with Jacks. She might have been attracted to him, but he wasn't what she was supposed to want.

Jacks wasn't safe. He came with no promises of a happily ever after. If anything, he guaranteed the opposite. He didn't believe that heroes got happy endings. Loving Jacks felt doomed from the start. But Evangeline had learned that love was more than a feeling. And it didn't have to be the safe choice, because love was also more powerful than fear. It was the ultimate form of hope. It was stronger than curses.

And yet . . .

She worried that her love might not be enough.

Aurora's last words still haunted her.

It doesn't matter if your love is the truest love that the world has ever seen. The story curse twisted the truth. It's not Jacks's true love who will be immune to his kiss. Only a girl who will never *love Jacks can survive the kiss.*

Evangeline didn't like to think about Jacks with other girls. She didn't like to imagine him caring for them or kissing them or killing them. When she'd first met Jacks, she had imagined that he didn't really think about them, either. The careless, disrespectful version of Jacks she'd met in his church hadn't seemed capable of caring for anyone.

But now, when she pictured Jacks on the first day she had met him, she didn't think about their first awful conversation. She saw him sitting in the back of his church, roughly ripping his clothes and bowing his head as if in mourning or performing some act of penance.

He'd been brokenhearted. Not in the same sense that most people thought of, as if one person had broken his heart. Jacks's heart had been broken over and over again until it was no longer capable of hope and care and love.

The stories always made it sound as if the girls that Jacks had kissed before had not really loved him. They'd just been girls he'd tried on and then discarded like clothes that didn't fit.

But now Evangeline wondered if Jacks hadn't been quite so callous with his kisses at first, if perhaps he had cared for some of the girls before he'd kissed them. Then she wondered if some of the girls had truly loved him. If there had been ones who had believed, just like she did, that their love could be enough to save him, to break the curse. But it never was.

No wonder Jacks thought her feelings weren't enough. And maybe they weren't. But that didn't mean he was beyond saving. Maybe it wasn't *her* love alone that would save him. Maybe it had to be *his* love, too.

Evangeline looked up at the newly changed gold leaf, and watched it sway against another green leaf as if begging it to change as well. Because unless the entire tree was gold, it would all go up in flames. Just like she and Jacks would, if she was the only one who believed in the power of love.

The air crackled with something that made Evangeline think of little sparks. Then she felt a tingling on her wrist in the shape of her broken heart scar.

Jacks had arrived.

She turned. And it was almost like the first time she'd seen him in this clearing.

He'd been so sharp that night, so cold that the fog had still clung to his boots as he walked.

She remembered telling herself that night not to turn around. Not to look. And when she had looked at him, she'd tried to glance for only a second.

But it had been impossible. Jacks had been the moon and she'd been the tide, controlled by his impossible force. That much had not changed.

Heart or no heart, she still wanted Jacks to be hers.

But this Jacks wasn't hers.

There was something in his pale hands, a jar he was tossing as if it were one of his apples. Only it wasn't an apple. It was his heart.

Evangeline's own heart broke a little at the sight of him, tossing his heart so carelessly as if it were a bit of fruit that he'd dispose of, instead of something unspeakably precious and beautiful.

The heart looked like rays of sunlight before they melted into the horizon. The jar was full of so many colors, mostly gold, but there were sparks of iridescent light that burst against the jar, making the gold look as if it were pounding.

Meanwhile, Jacks looked completely unmoved. "You shouldn't be here."

"Neither should you!" Evangeline shouted.

She hadn't meant to shout. Her plan hadn't been to yell at him, her plan had been to finally tell him how much she loved him. But seeing him, treating his heart so recklessly and negligently, made her scream, "What are you doing?"

"I think you already know the answer, pet. You just don't like it much." Jacks tossed the jar higher up in the air.

Evangeline didn't think—she just leaped forward with outstretched arms, reaching for the heart. Her fingers touched the jar, but Jacks caught her first.

He put his hand at the base of her throat. His grip was strong enough to hold her at bay, to keep her away from grabbing the heart in the jar. Yet he wasn't hurting her. His fingers were not bruising in their grip.

Either he was trying to be careful because of the protection cuff on her wrist. Or . . . he didn't want to hurt her because the nearness of his heart was giving him some feeling.

The light inside the jar pounded harder, as if it were fighting to break free. And Jacks no longer looked entirely unmoved. His blue eyes were almost feral in their brightness, as if he were trying to fight off the feelings that were creeping back in.

"You should go," he ground out.

"Why? Because you're going to burn your heart, and once you do that, you think you'll hurt me? You're already hurting me, Jacks."

She reached out—not for the jar, but for him.

His jaw felt like a rock, hard and implacable beneath her fingers. He clenched it even tighter and shook her hand away.

"If I try to hurt you, the cuff will stop me," he said roughly.

"I'm not talking about physically."

My heart, it hurts.

And it did. Evangeline had never felt so close and so far away from someone all at once. His cold, hard hand was still on her throat, his eyes were locked on hers. But it was a look that said this was the last time he'd be touching her, the final time.

This was all there was for them.

He wasn't giving up. He'd already given up.

"How can I make you understand," he growled, "you and I together don't end well. We just *end.*"

"How can you know that if you haven't even tried?"

"Try?" Jacks laughed and the sound was awful. "This isn't something you try at, Evangeline."

The laughter died on his lips, and the fire in his eyes went out. For a second, Jacks didn't look like a Fate or a human, he looked like a ghost, a shell that had been emptied out and tossed in the waves too many times. And once again, Evangeline thought about how his heart had been broken over and over, so many times that it couldn't hope, it could only fear.

"This is something that gets one chance to be right or wrong, and if you're wrong, there's no trying again. There is nothing."

Silence filled the space between them. Not even a leaf on the tree dared to rustle.

Then so softly she almost didn't hear it, Jacks said, "You were there, you saw what the cuff did to me when I tried to kiss you."

Something like shame filled his eyes and Evangeline didn't know how it was possible, but he looked even more fragile than before. As if it would take less than a touch to break him, as if the wrong word might shatter him into a thousand pieces.

"This is as close as we get," Jacks said.

He stroked her throat, and she knew that in a second, he was going to let her go. He was going to release her, pluck a leaf, and set his heart on fire.

Evangeline felt terrified to move, petrified of speaking for fear of saying the wrong thing. Her hands were shaking and her chest felt hollow, as if there was a hole and the hope was draining out of her as well, disappearing into the same place that had stolen all of his hope.

But she knew where that place led and she refused to go there.

"I love you, Jacks."

He closed his eyes as she said the word *love*.

She hoped a little harder. She wanted to ask him to look at her, but all that mattered was that he didn't let her go.

"I used to wonder if fate was real," she said gently. "I used to fear it meant that I had no real choices. Then I secretly hoped fate was real and that you and I were fated, that by some miraculous chance I was your true love. But now I don't care if fate is real—because I don't need it to decide for me. I don't need it to make this choice. I've made my decision, Jacks. It's you. It will always be you, until the end of time. And I'll fight fate or anyone else who tries to tear us apart—including *you*. You are my choice. You are my love. You are mine. And you are not going to be the end of me, Jacks."

"I think I already am." He opened his eyes and they dripped red tears. "Let me go, Evangeline."

"Tell me you won't set fire to your heart, and I will let you go."

"Don't ask me to do that."

"Then don't ask me to let you go!"

His eyes bled more tears, but his hand held tight to the jar. "I'm broken. I like to break things. Sometimes I want to break you."

"Then break me, Jacks."

His fingers tensed against her neck. "For once I want to do the right thing. I can't do this. I can't watch you die again."

The word *again* scraped against her like a thorn. "What do you mean, *again?*"

"You died, Evangeline." Jacks pulled her closer until she could feel the ragged rise and fall of his chest as he rasped, "I held you in my arms as it happened."

"Jacks . . . I don't know what you're talking about. I never died."

"Yes, you did. The night you opened the Valory. The first time you did it, I didn't go with you." He went silent for a moment and then she heard him think, *I couldn't say goodbye.*

"It was only you and Chaos," he whispered. "As soon as his helm was off, he killed you. I tried to stop him—I tried to save you—but—"

Jacks opened and shut his mouth as if he could barely get the words out. "I couldn't. When I got there, he had already bitten you—and he'd already taken too much blood. You died as soon as you were in my arms. The only thing I could do was use the stones to turn back time. I was warned that it would cost me something. But I thought it would cost *me*. I didn't imagine it would take from *you*."

I'm sorry, he thought.

"You don't need to be sorry, Jacks."

"It's my fault," he gritted out.

"No it's not. I didn't lose my memories because you turned back time. I lost them because Apollo took them from me."

Jacks looked murderous for a second. Then just as quickly, he shook off her words. "It doesn't matter. What matters is that you died. And if you die again, I cannot bring you back."

"So you'd rather live without me?"

"I'd rather you live."

"I am living, Jacks, and I am not going to die anytime soon." Evangeline closed her eyes and then she kissed him.

It was a kiss like a prayer, quiet, almost pleading, made of tremulous lips and nervous fingers. It felt like reaching out in the dark, hoping to find a light.

Jacks's lips were slightly sweet and metallic, like apples and bloody tears as he whispered against her mouth, "You shouldn't have done that, Little Fox."

"It's too late now." She wrapped her hands around his neck, drawing him closer as she parted her lips. Slowly the tip of Jacks's tongue slipped inside.

It was a gentler kiss than she would have imagined. Less of a fever dream and more of a secret, a whispered dangerous thing that might escape if he was too reckless. His hands were careful as they moved to her jacket. One by one, with gentle flicks of his fingers, Jacks undid the buttons.

Evangeline's legs forgot how to work and her lungs forgot how to breathe as he slid off the jacket and let it fall to the ground.

She'd been wrong before. Her life hadn't been full of moments leading to the Valory Arch. Every moment of everything had brought her to this place. It had taken all the heartbreak, all the almost love and the wrong love, to know that this love was true love.

Glass shattered. He'd dropped the jar—and as soon as he did, the kiss took on new life. It felt like stars colliding and worlds ending. Everything was dizzying and spinning. He kissed her harder. She held him tighter, fingers bruising on the back of his neck before slipping into his soft hair.

Evangeline never wanted to pull away. But she was starting to feel light-headed. Her eyes were closed. But she could see stars.

"Little Fox—" Jacks's panicked voice broke the kiss.

I'm all right, she said, or she tried to say. Evangeline couldn't quite get out the words. Her head was spinning too fast. The stars were spinning, too. Little constellations behind her eyes.

Her legs gave out.

"No!" Jacks cried.

Then Evangeline felt his arms catching her as she fell. She tried to stand, tried to move, but her head would not stop spinning.

"No!" Jacks screamed. "Not again!"

He dropped to the ground with Evangeline in his lap. She could feel his chest shaking as he held her.

Jacks—she thought his name. She couldn't speak quite yet, but she could open her eyes again. The stars had left them and now the world was slowly coming back to focus. First the sky, all indigo and violet. Next, she saw the tree, all glowing and gold.

Then there was Jacks.

He looked angelic and anguished. His beautiful face was

drained of color. Tracks of blood fell from his eyes down his pale cheeks.

"Don't cry, my love." She carefully wiped his tears with her fingers. "I'm all right."

She gave him a wobbly smile.

His eyes went wide and as blue as a clear sky after a storm.

"How is this . . ." he trailed off.

It was a little endearing to watch. His sulky mouth gently parted as he seemed to forget how to speak.

"I already told you. You are the love of my life. You are mine, Jacks of the Hollow. And you're not going to be the end of me."

"But you were dying."

"No," she said, a little embarrassed. "I just forgot to breathe."

42

Once upon a time, there was nothing but kissing, and everything was perfect. And then there was even more kissing.

43

Evangeline

All the heartbreak and the pain and the fear and the terror almost felt worth it, just to see the way Jacks looked at Evangeline when their first kiss ended.

She thought she knew all his looks. She'd seen his taunting, his teasing, his anger, his fear. But she'd never seen him with so much wonder in his blue eyes. They glittered as the leaves of the phoenix tree rustled with a sound that made her think of a slow exhale.

At some point, they'd moved closer to the tree. Now Jacks's back was resting against the trunk as she rested against him. The sky had turned to dusk, but there was illumination from the tree's glowing golden leaves. She didn't remember the leaves glowing before, but there was enough light to see a wave of golden hair fall across Jacks's forehead as his mouth twisted darkly and he held her a little tighter on his lap.

"You look as if you're contemplating something I'm not going to like," she said.

Jacks idly stroked her jaw with his fingers. "I love you," he said simply. Then his face went abruptly serious. "I'm never going to let you out of my sight."

"You say that as if it should be a threat."

He continued to look at her solemnly. "This isn't just for now, it's for always, Little Fox."

"I like the sound of *always*." She smiled against his fingers, and then she reached up to touch his cheek, because now he was smiling, too.

And he loved her.

He loved her.

He loved her.

He loved her.

He loved her so much he'd rewritten history. He'd given up what he had believed was his only chance at love. And now he had finally broken the spell that he never thought he'd escape.

Evangeline wanted to spin in circles around the clearing and sing it all out loud for the whole world to hear, but she wasn't ready to leave his arms. Not yet. Maybe never.

She traced one of his dimples with his fingers. "You know," she confessed, "I've always loved your dimples."

"I know." He smirked. "You were so obvious with your love at first sight."

"It was not love at first sight." She huffed. "I only said I liked your dimples at the start." She dropped her hand from his cheek. "I didn't even like you. I thought you were terrible."

"And yet." He grabbed her hand again and wrapped it around his neck. "You kept staring."

"Well . . ." She wrapped her other hand around his neck before sliding her fingers back into his hair. She really loved his hair. "I might not have liked you, but you were always ridiculously handsome."

She gently tugged on his neck until he lowered his head and brought his lips down to hers.

For a moment, everything was perfect again.

Jacks had his heart. She had Jacks. They were in love. This was everything she wanted. This was happily ever after.

But the problem with happily ever after is that it's more of an idea than a reality. A dream that lives on after a storyteller is finished. But real stories never finish. And it seemed that Evangeline and Jacks's story wasn't over yet.

The green and gold leaves on the phoenix tree had started rustling again. Moving frantically, louder than when Evangeline had first stepped into the clearing, as if the entire tree was quaking. Shaking. Frightened.

Then she heard the applause.

Three loud slaps, followed by a bitter voice. "That was a rousing show!"

Evangeline pulled away from Jacks's lips to see Apollo standing just a few feet away, his stance wide, his head tipped high.

He smiled broadly as he finished clapping. "You two know how to put on quite a performance. That was romantic and self-destructive. The only thing it's missing is the grand finale." Apollo's grin widened. It was a smile that would forever make Evangeline dread princely smiles. "But I think I can help with that."

He reached up toward the phoenix tree and plucked a golden leaf.

There was a crackle.

A spark.

"Evangeline, run!" Jacks pushed her from his lap just as the tree burst into flames. It was blinding light. White and bright. It consumed the beautiful tree in seconds. The trunk, the branches, the leaves, all of them were burning.

Evangeline ran hard and fast.

She told herself not to turn around.

But where was Jacks? Why wasn't he following her?

The smoke was growing thicker, the flames were burning hotter. She paused just for a second. She turned to look.

"Jacks!" There was so much smoke. *Jacks!* She started to run back.

"Oh no you don't!" Apollo's arms wrapped around her from behind, quick and far too strong.

"No!" Evangeline cried. She tried to break free, but Apollo was so much bigger than she was. "Jacks—"

"Stop trying to fight me." Apollo picked her up roughly and tossed her over his shoulder, pinning her legs in place with one large arm as her head and arms hung upside down. "I'm trying to save you, Evangeline!"

"No! *You* did this!" She beat Apollo's back with her fists, she kicked his chest with her legs.

"Jacks!" she screamed again.

Briefly she paused her fighting to lift her head, to see if he'd come through the fire, if he'd come for her.

But all she saw was smoke and flames.

44

Apollo

Evangeline continued to scream and hit Apollo with her fists, hard enough that she might even leave bruises. Yet he barely felt the blows.

She'd chosen Jacks, again.

She'd chosen wrong, again.

Apollo had tried to save her. He'd tried to protect her, but he hadn't been enough. He could see that now. The spell Jacks had cast on her wasn't going to be broken by anyone who was merely human. It was just too bad that Apollo couldn't be human and still save her.

It didn't take long for him to make his way back to the arch that had brought him to the clearing with the phoenix tree. He hadn't seen Jacks coming after them through the flames, but he wasn't feeling optimistic enough to hope that meant Jacks was dead.

But it didn't really matter if he was alive. Apollo didn't think Jacks would be able to use the arch on his own. He wouldn't be able to take Evangeline away from him, not this time.

Pain sliced through Apollo at the thought.

He wished he could rip the damn protection cuff off her.

But he had expected the pain this time. And he was used to pain; he'd felt it constantly under the Archer's curse. But this pain was much worse.

He stumbled and nearly dropped Evangeline as he went through the arch.

"Let me go!" she screamed. "Please! Please, I have to go back—" She continued to cry. "If you care for me at all, let me go!"

Apollo finally dropped her on the ground. She tried to crawl away. But he was larger and stronger. He grabbed her by the ankle and yanked hard enough that she landed on her stomach. The pain that lashed through him this time was nearly blinding. But it took only one pull to make her fall. Then he used his body to keep her immobile as he reached for the shackles he'd attached to his belt.

"No!"

"Calm down, darling." He shackled her arms first, behind her back.

"Don't do this!" she screamed and thrashed, kicking both legs wildly.

She got him in the shoulder once. But then he managed to grab her and bind both legs at the ankles.

He immediately stumbled away once it was done. The pain was nearly unbearable now. Apollo doubled over and retched at the side of the tunnel where he'd brought her.

He thought about leaving her there. He wasn't sure how much more pain he could handle. And he wasn't even certain he needed her there with him.

But he still loved her. He looked at her, bound on the ground, pink hair clinging to her cheeks as she cried. She'd betrayed him and broken his heart, but if she had only a few minutes left on this earth, he wanted them to be together.

"Don't worry, my sweet, soon enough this will all be over," he whispered. Then he picked her up once again and carried her in his arms.

45

Jacks

All Jacks could see was smoke. Thick and gray, it burned his eyes and his throat. But he needed to find her.

"Jacks! Help me! Jacks!" He could hear her voice. It was tiny and terrified. He'd never heard her sound so small before.

It didn't even sound like her after the initial few cries.

At first her voice had been like the smoke—he'd heard it everywhere. Screaming his name, calling for him. But then no matter where he went, Evangeline sounded farther away.

"Jacks!"

"I'm coming, Little Fox!"

Sweat dripped down his neck as he ran through the smoke.

"Jacks—over here—" She broke off with a hacking cough.

But she sounded closer now.

He chased the sound of her cough, farther away from the burning tree, away from the smoke.

The air was still thick with dirty soot. But he could see again through all the grimness, through the ash. He could make out a tree in the clearing that hadn't caught fire. An ordinary oak tree with a violet-haired girl leaning against the bark, hand on one hip of her iridescent dress as she brought the other hand to her lips and feigned another cough.

Aurora.

Not Evangeline.

"I'm guessing I'm not who you expected," Aurora said sweetly.

He hated the sound of her voice. He had never liked it before, but now he wished that he could grab hold of the voice and toss it into the flames of the burning phoenix tree behind him.

"Where is she?" Jacks snarled.

Aurora pouted. "Why do you think I would know?"

He slowly clenched and then unclenched his fists. He was trying to be nice because this was Castor's twin sister. But how many times had he done that? Made excuses for Aurora because of who she was? Told himself she wasn't dangerous because she had something he wanted? He knew she wasn't the one who'd set fire to the phoenix tree, but she'd just lured him away from Evangeline. And whether she knew where Evangeline was or not, he wanted to hurt her—badly.

"I'm going to give you one more chance." Jacks reached out and took Aurora by the throat. "Where is Evangeline?"

Aurora pursed her lips.

"Do you want to die?" Jacks squeezed lightly. "Is that what you want, Aurora? Because I'm this close."

"You won't kill me," she said. "From what I hear, strangulation isn't really your style. You'd have to kiss me, and I don't think your precious Evangeline would like that very much."

"I could always make an exception." Jacks put a little more pressure on her throat. "Just tell me where she is."

Aurora sniffed. There were tears in her eyes now, though Jacks imagined they were about as real as her cough.

"Tell me why you picked her," she said. "I've been trying to figure it out, but for the life of me I don't understand the fascination. Is she prettier than me? Is that it?"

"Are you really this petty?"

"Yes."

"And you wonder why I don't love you."

Aurora flinched at this, and when a tear fell, this time it looked real. "You're never going to save her, Jacks of the Hollow. Apollo has taken her to the Tree of Souls."

46

Evangeline

Evangeline fought with everything she had against the metal that Apollo had bound her with. She tried to rub her skin until it bled. If she could just manage one drop of blood, she could get the bonds to open. She could get back to Jacks.

Although Evangeline was fearful that Jacks was not the only one she needed to worry about.

Apollo had used an arch to transport her somewhere she'd never been before. An enormous cavern lit with lines of red-orange fire on the ground that made her think of a vampire lair, full of blood and cruel, punishing magic.

Apollo had carried her in his arms for a few minutes, but

when she had continued struggling he had tossed her over his shoulder again, carrying her like a sack of food and making it difficult to get the best view.

Evangeline could see there was some sort of tree. The largest tree she'd ever seen, an enormous, horrid-looking thing with feral branches and distorted faces carved into the trunk, and—was that a heartbeat she could feel?

Thump. Thump. Thump.

It was definitely a heartbeat. Evangeline felt it pulsing through the ground as Apollo laid her down like a sacrifice in front of the dreadful tree.

"Apollo, please don't do this!" She fought wildly against the cuffs binding her wrists. "Please, let me go!" she begged. "I—"

She tried to say she was sorry. She knew it would have been the smart thing to say just then. But she couldn't bring herself to apologize for kissing Jacks.

Instead she gritted her teeth and glared at Apollo. "Is your pride really so wounded that you would kill me over a kiss?"

"That's not what I'm doing." He worked his jaw as sweat dripped down his forehead. "I wanted us to be together forever, I wanted my legacy to be yours as well. I was going to make you a queen."

"And now you're not, so you're going to kill me?"

"It's not like that—I don't want to kill you. If there was another way, I wouldn't do this, but there's not. I can't keep you safe as a mere human, but I can't have you and be more." He dropped to his knees and stroked her cheek with his fingers. "This is the hardest choice I've ever had to make. You're the love of my life, Evangeline, and I will miss you desperately."

He leaned in closer and he kissed her lips.

47

Jacks

Jacks thought he could not witness anything worse than Evangeline dying in his arms. But this was close. She was on the ground, bound up in front of a tree, and the bastard who stole her memories was leaning in to kiss her. "Get your hands off her, you son of a bitch!"

Jacks ran across the cavern and punched Apollo in the face. Then he punched him again and again. He punched until he stopped feeling his fist, breaking Apollo's bones. When blood spewed from the prince's nose, Jacks felt it spray his cheek.

It would have been easier just to stab the bastard in the throat. But Jacks needed to hurt him first.

"I will kill you for this!" Jacks rained down more punches on Apollo's face.

"Stop him!" someone screamed. Footfalls rushed across the cavern.

Then Jacks was being grabbed. He felt large gloved hands on his arms. He tried to shake them off, tried to use his powers to make them stop. But either he was entirely drained or these guards were somehow more than human.

"Let me go!" Jacks thrashed as the guards firmly took hold of his arms and began to drag him away.

Only these weren't guards. He knew these men. They looked liked Dane and Lysander Valor, Castor's older brothers. "Let me go! This isn't your fight."

Dane, the most hard-headed of Castor's brothers, might have muttered something, but Jacks couldn't hear it over the rushing blood in his ears or the cries of Evangeline, who was still tied up on the ground.

"Why aren't you helping her instead of restraining me?" Jacks yelled.

And that's when he saw Wolfric.

It was the first time Jacks had seen him since that night in the Valory. Tonight he looked dressed for battle, knives strapped to his arms, swords strapped to his sides, another weapon across his back.

He was talking to Apollo. Jacks waited for Wolfric to run the blackguard through with one of his knives and then pick up Evangeline. But everyone in this cavern seemed to have lost his mind. Instead of stabbing him, Wolfric clapped the prince on his shoulder and handed him a handkerchief. Then he marched toward Jacks and his sons without so much as a glance at Evangeline.

"What's wrong with you?" Jacks bellowed.

Wolfric looked at him grimly and ran a hand over his beard. "I'm sorry, son. But I can't let you go to her."

"You can't stop me," Jacks roared. He tried to throw Dane and Lysander off his arms, but all the Valors were so much stronger than they should have been.

"She's his wife," Wolfric said, as if that somehow made this all right.

"He's going to sacrifice her to a tree!" Jacks screamed.

Apollo looked half dead. His face was bloody and almost unrecognizable from the beating Jacks had given him. But he was still standing, and now he was holding out his sword.

And Wolfric was still doing nothing. Jacks hadn't always liked Wolfric Valor, but he'd respected him. He knew Wolfric believed in honor and justice and all the things he spouted about during toasts.

"Is this because I'm a fugitive?" Jacks shouted at Wolfric. "Those stories about me aren't true. I never erased her memories—Apollo did!"

"I don't care about any of that," Wolfric grunted. "I'm doing this because it's the right thing to do."

"It's not and you know that," cried Jacks.

On the ground, Evangeline was still struggling and crying. Her cheeks were stained with tears as she lifted her head from the ground to meet Jacks's gaze. Her eyes were shining. Even now, she looked so sweet. She didn't speak, but he heard her think, *It's going to be all right.*

But it wasn't all right.

Nothing was going to be all right ever again if Jacks lost her now.

48

Evangeline

Evangeline continued to struggle against the shackles binding her wrists. All she needed was one drop of blood. She had to save herself and Jacks—if she didn't make it out of this, she didn't want to think about what would happen to him.

This couldn't be how their story ended.

Evangeline knew that Jacks had told her heroes didn't get happy endings. But that didn't mean they were supposed to give them to the villains.

Apollo looked as if he could barely stand after Jacks's beating. The prince's nose was broken and bleeding. One of his eyes was swollen shut. But he still managed to hold his sword high above his head.

The blade glinted in the moonlight.

The ground pulsed faster. Tiny pebbles bounced from the ground and hit Evangeline's cheeks as the tree's disturbing heartbeat pounded harder than before. *Thumpthumpthump.*

She held her breath. If Apollo stabbed her and didn't kill her, she could use the blood to finally get free of the cuffs.

"Little Fox!" Jacks lashed his arms against his captors as he screamed and cursed everyone in the cavern. "Little Fox, I'm sorry." His tortured voice echoed toward the sky.

The broken sound of it would have made Evangeline cry if she wasn't already. She wanted to tell him not to be sorry, she wanted to tell him again that it would be all right—but just in case it wasn't, she called, "I love you!"

"Shut up," Apollo screamed and then swung his sword. The blade whooshed through the air.

But he didn't cut her. Apollo sliced through one of the crimson branches of the tree. Blood gushed from the wood.

Evangeline had never seen anything quite so ghastly. She half expected the tree to cry out, but if anything, it seemed to come alive even more as the blood poured forth. Its trunk grew redder, as if its skin was flushed, and stretched wider, as if it was ready for something.

"Farewell, my love," Apollo said. And then he brought his mouth to the bleeding branch.

It was awful to watch. The blood stained Apollo's lips and his chin as he drank and drank. He choked a little and sputtered, but then he finished with a scarlet smile made of red teeth and bloody lips.

Other than that, he was perfect.

He should have looked awful. But he had changed. Apollo was glowing the way that Jacks did sometimes. His nose was no longer broken. His eyes were no longer swollen. Apollo's gaze was golden, as brilliant as the stars above.

"I feel like a god," he said with a laugh.

The ground pulsed faster and harder. The force of it shook Evangeline. Dirt clung to her cheeks as she rolled several feet away from the tree.

When she looked up again, Apollo stumbled. He righted himself quickly, but then he stumbled again as he tried to walk away from the tree. Evangeline watched his glowing skin go gray and his handsome face contort as he attempted to take another step.

"What's happening?" Apollo grimaced in pain and looked at Wolfric accusingly.

"I warned you," Wolfric said. "I told you before, if you valued your life, you would forget all about this tree."

Apollo suddenly dropped to his knees and clutched the ground with one hand as if trying to find purchase. "You told me it would take the life of the person I love the most."

"It is," Wolfric replied. "It's taking you."

The ground thumped harder. More rocks and dirt sprayed into the air as long fingerlike roots sprung up from the ground and reached for the prince.

"Stop!" Apollo screamed. Branches from the tree dropped down like bars on a cage.

"No! This is wrong—you're not supposed to take me."

Evangeline watched him slash wildly with his sword. Tears ran down Apollo's cheeks as he swung again and a branch caught his weapon in its bark. The tree immediately flung the sword away. It landed with a clang next to Evangeline.

The faces trapped in tree's trunk twisted. Their lips curled. Their eyes widened as the tree's branches closed tighter around Apollo and started dragging him toward the trunk.

Apollo's hands clawed at the bark as he screamed, "You're supposed to take her, not me!"

Evangeline had never witnessed anything so awful. She watched the trunk split open like a mouth, ready to consume the prince.

Apollo made a terrified sound somewhere between a child's wail and an animal's cry.

Evangeline closed her eyes, but she couldn't stop the screams.

"No!" Apollo yelled. "Please, don't—"

His last words broke off.

Silence.

Everywhere.

Perfect quiet filled the cavern the same way Apollo's screams had.

There were no screeches.

No cries.

No stretching branches.

No thumping heartbeats.

Cautiously, Evangeline opened her eyes. The Tree of Souls was exactly as it had been before. Only now there was a new horrified face trapped inside the trunk.

49

Evangeline

The story could have ended there, with the villain defeated and the happy couple about to go off to some ambiguous happily ever after.

Unfortunately, the fight did not simply cease because Apollo was now trapped inside of a tree for eternity. Jacks was still furious. And so when Wolfric Valor's sons finally released him, more punches were thrown and violent curses were loosed. The words echoed across the moonlit cavern as fists hit faces and clothes were ripped.

Evangeline cried out, "Stop!" after the first punch. But it quickly became apparent that no one was listening to her and the fight would soon escalate if she didn't find a way to stop it.

Apollo's discarded sword wasn't too far away. After scooting across the rocky ground toward it, she managed to slice her finger on the blade and then use the blood to free herself from the shackles.

"Enough!" she yelled as she ran toward the melee.

The two Valor sons were both now battling Jacks, noses bloody and making an awful mess. Wolfric was the only one who'd stepped out of the fray. It looked as if he was inspecting the tree—or perhaps talking to the tree. Evangeline merely glanced at him before jumping in between the three fighters and yelling, "Stop all of this nonsense, right now!"

Jacks was the first to freeze, followed by one of the Valor sons. The other Valor son, the broader of the two, punched Jacks in the stomach one final time—as if he couldn't stop himself. But Evangeline had the feeling that he was just the sort who needed to get the last punch in.

Jacks doubled over with a grunt.

Evangeline rushed to his side. "Are you all right?"

"I'm fine." He put a protective arm around her shoulder as he straightened up once again. "I'll kill them later."

"Good luck with that," said the broader Valor, the one who'd punched Jacks last. He took off his dark gray shirt to mop up his nose.

"That's Dane," Jacks grunted.

It took Evangeline a second to place the name. *Dane.* LaLa had said it a couple of times. Dane was her dragon shifter. Evangeline had never actually tried to picture him before, but she wasn't sure she would have imagined this brute who'd just gotten the final punch in.

His brother, who was very tan and golden and even glowed a touch, seemed a little nicer. "It was nothing personal, Jacks. We were just doing what our father asked."

Jacks tightened his arm around Evangeline as he shot a glare at Wolfric, who had just rejoined the group. "Couldn't you have found an easier way to get rid of the prince?" Jacks asked. "Like maybe just shoving a sword through his stomach or chopping off his head?"

All three Valors flinched at the mention of chopping off heads.

Jacks grinned.

The Valors' heads had not actually been chopped off, of course, but they must have been familiar with the story by now, and they'd possibly seen their headless statues in the Valorfell Harbor.

"I'm sorry about putting you in that position," Wolfric said to Evangeline. He looked contrite, but there was something about his words, about the way he'd added *putting you in that position*, that made her think he wasn't really sorry.

Evangeline had the impression that Wolfric believed he'd done the right thing and that his action was more important than whatever hurt or terror it had caused her. He then explained the history of the awful tree, how he'd planted it not knowing what it was and how Apollo had found out about it and asked him how to use it. Wolfric told Evangeline and Jacks he'd warned the prince two times. Evangeline believed this, but she didn't believe that Wolfric Valor was regretful in the least that the prince hadn't listened to his warnings.

"Do you plan on taking back the kingdom now?" asked Jacks.

Wolfric laughed. "There's no taking back—the North has always been mine." He started whistling as he walked toward the mouth of the cavern. "Let's go, sons," he called over his shoulder. "We need to find your sister."

The brothers shot looks at each other that made Evangeline think they were reluctant to follow their father on another quest. Not that she could blame them, as she wouldn't have been eager to find Aurora, either.

"What do you think they'll do to her?" Evangeline asked once they were gone.

"I don't think they'll ever find her," Jacks said. "Those boys don't want to hunt their sister. They'll give up after two days. And Wolfric's too proud to let anyone outside of the family know that his daughter is a monster."

Just like Castor, Evangeline thought. But she didn't want to say it aloud; she actually liked Castor quite a bit. And she didn't want to talk about the Valors anymore, even though she was sure this wouldn't be the last of them. With Apollo now gone, Evangeline imagined her title of princess didn't mean much anymore. But if Wolfric Valor wanted the kingdom, he could have it. Just as long as she could have Jacks.

Jacks laughed softly beside her, and Evangeline had the impression he'd heard what she was thinking.

She turned to him. A purple-and-blue bruise was growing beneath his left eye, a split cut through his lip. His clothes were torn. The buttons on his shirt were gone; his left sleeve was ripped at the shoulder and hanging at an angle.

And he still looked as beautiful as ever.

He actually reminded her of the first time they'd met in his church, when he'd been sitting in the back, tearing at his clothes. Only he was smiling now. She watched his lips curve into a cocky grin as they started to walk out of the cavern.

"Where are we going?" she asked.

A dimple appeared just below a cut on his cheek. "We can go wherever you want, Little Fox."

Epilogue

The Magnificent North's infamous story curse watched the star-crossed lovers, who were star-crossed no more, walk out of the ancient cavern.

The curse was relieved they were finally leaving. It had always disliked this cavern—it made for such a dreary setting—and it absolutely loathed the wretched tree that lived here. The curse set fire to any stories that mentioned the accursed tree in an attempt to warn away mortals, but humans could be such foolish creatures.

The curse was glad to see this human girl and her not-quite-human boy were smart enough to walk away from the tree.

The curse supposed the pair would now be on their way to

some sort of happily ever after. Usually, the curse would have stopped watching at this point.

Happily ever afters were notoriously boring. They did not make for very good stories, which gave the story curse little to do unless it felt like upending the blissful endings. It didn't want to do that now. But it did want to find out the answer to one particular question that still remained.

And so the story curse watched as the wounded not-quite-human-boy kept his arm around the shoulder of the girl he had once brought back from the dead.

The curse really did hope the two of them would find happily ever after. It wasn't entirely sure if the not-quite-human-boy deserved it, but the girl with the rose-gold hair definitely did.

She looked up at her not-quite-human-boy adoringly, despite the bruises, cuts, and blood spattered on his person.

"I still have one question," she said.

If the story curse had been capable of breathing, it might have held its breath just then.

It watched as the not-quite-human-boy raised an offended brow. "You only have one?"

"No—I actually have far more." She worried her lip between her white teeth.

Something shifted in the not-quite-human's eyes; he looked as if he wanted to take her lip between his teeth as well. "You can ask me whatever you want, Little Fox."

"Splendid!" Her mouth turned up into a sweet smile. "Tell me about the apples."

"Next question."

"You said I could ask whatever I wanted."

The not-quite-human-boy's eyes turned teasing, sparking with little flecks of silver. "I didn't say that I would answer."

The girl's mouth fell into a pout.

The not-quite-human reached out with one finger and traced her lower lip. "It doesn't matter," he said softly. "I don't need them anymore."

The girl's lashes fluttered with surprise.

The not-quite-human-boy leaned in closer . . .

And the story curse decided to stop watching. It was time to leave these two alone and let them have their ever after.

Other stories were brewing in the Magnificent North.

Acknowledgments

I always feel nervous as I write acknowledgments. I'm afraid that I won't be able to capture how grateful I am to all of the amazing people in my life. This book was especially difficult for me to write, and I truly would not have been able to do this on my own.

First, I want to thank God because I feel as if it was honestly a miracle that I finished writing this book.

Sarah Barley, you are part of the miracle that helped me finish this book—and you are just wonderful. Thank you so much for all the phone calls, the edits, and the much-needed encouragement. I could not have survived this book without you.

I am so thankful that my books have an incredible US home at Macmillan, and I am endlessly grateful for all the fantastic people who work there and for the incredible team at Flatiron Books. Thank you, Bob Miller, Megan Lynch, Malati Chavali, Nancy Trypuc, Maris Tasaka, Cat Kenney, Marlena Bitter, Sydney Jeon, Donna Noetzel, Frances Sayers, Emily Walters, Keith Hayes, Kelly Gatesman, Louis Grilli, Erin Gordon, and the entire teams at Macmillan Audio, Macmillan Library, and Macmillan Sales.

I feel so blessed to also have a wonderful UK home at Hodder & Stoughton. Kimberley Atkins, you are a dream to work with—thank you for coming in and reading when it was so desperately needed, and for all of your brilliant edits.

These books wouldn't be quite the same without some of the incredible artists who've worked on covers and maps and alternate covers, not just for this book but for the entire series. Thank you so much, Lydia Blagden, Erin Fitzsimmons, Virginia Allyn, and Sally Pham.

Thank you, Rebecca Solar, for bringing these characters to life in such an extraordinary way with your spectacular audiobook narration.

This book would have been a train wreck without my friends—I am so grateful for your encouragement, your love, your questions, and for letting me know whenever I made a bad decision with this story. Thank you, Stacey Lee, Kristin Dwyer, Isabel Ibañez, Anissa de Gomery, Jenny Lundquist, Kristen Williams, Brandy Ruscica, J. Elle, and Kerri Maniscalco. And a huge special thanks to Mary E. Pearson for being the first reader of this book—I am especially grateful for the advice you gave me.

Huge thanks to my wonderful agent, Jenny Bent, and to everyone at the Bent Agency. I am so grateful for all the work that all of you have tirelessly done on my behalf.

I'm tearing up now as I'm thinking about how I can say thank you to my family. This last year was so incredibly hard and I cannot thank my family enough for their love and their help and for just being so wonderful. Thank you, Mom and Dad and Allison and Matt—I love you all more than words can say.

Finally, thank you, readers. This last year, I have just been overwhelmed by the love this series has received. I am so grateful for your pictures and your videos and all of the kind words. So often, I receive messages that start with *I doubt you'll ever see this*—but I do see them! I'm not able to respond to everyone individually, but I want you all to know that I see you and I am so grateful for all of you!

About the Author

Stephanie Garber is the #1 *New York Times* and internationally bestselling author of *Once Upon a Broken Heart*, *The Ballad of Never After*, and the Caraval trilogy. Her books have been translated into thirty languages.